The Dragon's Bite and other Flights of Fantasy Imaginings from Near and Far

Matias F. Travieso-Diaz

The Dragon's Bite
and other Flights of Fantasy
by Matias F. Travieso-Diaz

All rights reserved. No part of this book may be reproduced or transmitted in any form or by any means, electronic or mechanical, including photocopying or recording or by any information storage and retrieval systems, without expressed written consent of the author and/or artists.

The Dragon's Bite is a work of fiction. Names, characters, places, and incidents are products of the author's imagination. Any resemblance to actual events or persons, living or dead, is entirely coincidental.

First Printing January 2025

Cover art "Enchanted" by Vonnie Winslow Crist
Cover design by Marcia A. Borell

Hiraeth Publishing
P.O. Box 1248
Tularosa, NM 88352
e-mail: hiraethsubs@yahoo.com

Visit www.hiraethsffh.com for online science fiction, fantasy, horror, scifaiku, and more. Stop by our online bookstore for novels, magazines, anthologies, and collections. **Support the small, independent press...and your First Amendment rights.**

The Dragon's Bite and other Flights of Fantasy
Imaginings from Near and Far

By Matias F. Travieso-Diaz

Over the last seven years, I have written many short stories in a variety of genres, covering multiple subjects, set in a wide range of times and places. Following are thirty-five of my numerous short stories, collected under the name "The Dragon's Bite and Other Flights of Dark Fantasy" (84,000 words), all of the speculative fantasy genre. (I also have other published and unpublished short stories that can be added, or substituted for, those in the collection.) A collection of some of my speculative short stories of the horror genre, *"The Satchel and other Terrors,"* was published in February 2023 and is available through Amazon and other retailers: https://www.amazon.com/Satchel-Other-Terrors-Matias-Travieso-Diaz/dp/1951716337/ref=sr_1_1?crid=3PB84I2J28PMJ&keywords=The+Satchel+and+other+terrors&qid=1676328685&s=books&sprefix=the+satchel+and+other+terrors%2Cstripbooks%2C121&sr=1-1.

Other collections of my short stories are in the process of publication and will be available to the public in the next few months.

With one exception, all the stories in the proposed collection have been published or accepted for publication as of the present time.

I, the author of the collection, was born in Cuba and migrated to the United States as a young man for political reasons. I became an engineer and lawyer and practiced for nearly fifty years. I then retired and turned my attention to creative writing. My stories have been published or accepted for publication in over one hundred and sixty short story anthologies, magazines, audio books and podcasts in the United States and abroad.

Matias F. Travieso-Diaz

Table of Contents

- 7   The Dragon's Bite
- 15   The Blue Pearls
- 24   A Viennese Story
- 38   The Hungry Wolf and the Maiden
- 42   The Adoration of the Magi
- 51   The Lunar Moth
- 60   Gwarwyn Goes Fishing
- 68   The Girl, the Wyvern and the Talking Ape
- 77   Whistles in the Forest
- 80   The Mapinguari
- 83   The Tenth Symphony
- 87   Alfhildur and Posthumous
- 94   The Fractious Familiar
- 98   End of Term
- 101 Henrietta: A Fable
- 106 The Ugly Fairy
- 112 The Dopey Lion
- 117 Blame Rupert
- 126 The Yellow Butterfly
- 132 Medusa's Stare
- 139 Killing the Jabberwock
- 146 The Witch and the Crows
- 151 Azathoth is Amused
- 161 The Caged Bird and the Fairy
- 165 A Bad Bargain
- 174 A Mask for Every Mood
- 184 The Hollow Tree
- 188 The Mutants
- 195 On the Path to Nirvana
- 199 The Magic Chrysler
- 213 Hope for the Future
- 223 Figaro on Wheels
- 232 Selling Adama
- 244 Christmas in Ushuaia
- 252 Scheherazade's Last Tale
- 258 *Original Publication Credits*

The Author

This book is dedicated to the three most important women in my life: my late mother, my deceased wife, and my daughter.

The Dragon's Bite

The hunger of a dragon is slow to wake, but hard to sate.
— *Ursula K. Le Guin*

As the rays of the sun pounded on the surface of the dry lake, an egg cracked open, sending leathery shards flying in all directions.

The wyrmling shook himself free of egg remnants and slid onto the hardened muck. He was small, less than three feet from muzzle to tail, and had trouble keeping his eyes open in the blazing afternoon light. His instincts told him that something was wrong. He should have awakened immersed in cool, dark waters replete with swimming food. He was hungry, but nothing edible seemed to lie within the thrust of his tongue. He began to slither towards the shore.

A couple of times along the way he attempted to fly. His wings, however, were still pinned to his flanks and hardly stirred when he made a gesture with his shoulders to unfurl them. He let out an exasperated howl, a ragged cry for help. Where was his mother?

He reached the shore of what once had been a deep body of water. Except for desiccated shrubs covered with dust, there were no signs that life had ever existed in this corner of the world. Yet, he smelled a living being of some kind a little distance away. He moved clumsily at first, digging his clawed feet into the pebbles that covered the ground. As the scent of prey became more pronounced, the wyrmling picked up speed and in a few seconds reached the top of a rise from which he could see the prairie below. A skinny four-legged animal, slightly larger than him, was grazing at a clump of yellowed grass.

The wyrmling's next actions were automatic. He ran towards the animal, inhaling big gulps of air, contorted, and emitted a very thin ray of incandescent gas towards his victim. The animal had already detected peril and started to run away, but the flame caught up to it in a moment and singed its legs, forcing it to the ground. The wyrmling kept spitting fire at the prone animal, and when the two were next to each other, the predator jumped onto his partly carbonized victim, held it between his forelegs, and started taking huge chunks of flesh with his two rows of sharp teeth.

It was all over in a matter of seconds. The wyrmling consumed every bit of his victim down to the fragile bones. He let out a satisfied grunt and lowered himself to the ground to digest his meal and take his first nap since birth.

***

His exploration of the barren land continued when he arose. There was nothing to see for a good distance but, far away to the west, he came upon a clump of timbered structures arranged in a semicircle around a hole in the ground from which rose the remembered smell of water. Thirst more than curiosity drew the wyrmling towards the hole. He was nearly there when he felt motion around him, as creatures that stood on two legs began emerging from the wooden structures. Cries resonated and the air filled with projectiles aimed at him. One of those hit the wyrmling on the back of the head. It did not quite penetrate the hard scales that covered his body, but the projectile exploded on his hide, burning it and causing him to scamper for cover, fleeing to safety among the loud noises emitted by his attackers.

He marked the bipeds as enemies and vowed to come after them as soon as he could.

***

Over the next several moons, the wyrmling managed to survive in the barren land. He preyed on birds by downing them off the air with blasts of fire, swallowed crawling creatures that failed to escape his pursuit, ate carrion left behind by other predators. His keen sense of smell allowed him to find oases and pools that held muddy waters, but both the meager food and the foul waters left him unsatisfied. He felt he had to get more and better sustenance if he was going to grow to his full potential. These needs went largely unmet, but he grew rapidly nonetheless.

In one of his forays, he came across a lone biped accompanied by half a dozen four-legged animals like the one that had served as his first meal. He made a quick calculation: he could down several of the four-legged animals or go after the biped. Resentment dictated his choice, and he charged at the biped and carbonized him with an angry blast. Turning to the four-legged creatures, he managed to roast a couple before the others dispersed.

He turned his attention to the fallen biped. The victim's body was mostly charred but several morsels of intact anatomy remained. The wyrmling bit into those, reveling in anticipation of sweet meat and revenge.

He found the biped's meager flesh disappointing. It was stringy, dry, and almost flavorless. It was also marred by a lingering undertaste of unnatural substances that revolted him. Whatever these bipeds were, their bodies were deeply polluted and unfit for consumption. He would kill them if the occasion presented itself, but would not partake of their flesh again.

***

Half a cycle around the sun after his hatching, the wyrmling – now a dragonet – had grown into a twenty foot of terror capable of swooping out of the sky like a bolt of lightning onto an unsuspecting prey. There were few wild animals left in the empty lands he called home, but he lorded over all of them and had developed a particular predilection for the four-legged beasts tended to by the bipeds. He played a game of hit and run in which he would come close enough to the biped's habitations to taunt them and steal one or two of the animals they kept, and then fly away out of reach of their projectiles. Through repeated contacts, he had learned some of the bipeds' language, who called themselves "humans" and referred to the dragonet as "L'ong." To the humans, L'ong was a deadly threat, to be destroyed if possible but warded against by all possible means.

As he grew to adult size, L'ong developed into a daunting figure. He had a powerful, spiky tail, enormous wings whose span extended twice the length of his red body, a skin reinforced by armored scales containing tiny bones that functioned as a natural chain-mail, razor sharp serrated teeth that measured a couple of inches in length, and a long, forked tongue that he used to detect, smell, and taste those objects that came within its reach. He had loosely articulated jaws that now allowed him to swallow, in a single bite, animals almost the size of humans.

He loathed the midday heat that was always present in this blasted land, so he only hunted at dawn and near sunset, and sometimes at night. His silhouette, appearing like a sudden dark blot in the sky, sent humans into a panic, forcing them to seek refuge in the underground shelters they had to construct once L'ong started to visit their village.

***

Despite their precautions, humans never remained unscathed whenever L'ong paid them a call. The terror the dragon inspired and the bloody toll he exacted forced the inhabitants of the villages to think of ways of setting traps to capture him before he wiped out their entire population. A resident of one of the settlements came up with a plan: "Let's start paying L'ong a tribute. We'll sacrifice animals to him so he will leave the rest of us alone." The plan was not well received at first, until its proponent clarified: "At some point, the sacrificial animal could be poisoned."

Initially the plan was carried without a glitch. L'ong feasted on a pig chosen for its relative plumpness compared to other emaciated domestic animals. He did not return for a week or so, but when he did the humans were ready. They placed in the middle of the village common a calf that had been fed a blend of poisonous herbs and could barely stand. L'ong descended in front of the offering, examined him with his sensitive tongue, issued a harsh cry of disgust, and directed a wall of flame at the calf and the three nearest huts, turning all to cinders.

The humans were discouraged by this setback, but came up with another plan. "We won't feed him poison, but our sacrificial offerings will be the sickest among our cattle. Perhaps he will eat them and fall sick himself."

The modified plan was put into effect shortly thereafter. The next offering was a goat that was near death from affliction with black quarter disease. The goat was breathing with difficulty and exhibiting swelling of the hip, back and shoulder due to the internal accumulation of gas. L'ong landed next to the animal, examined it carefully with his tongue, and took a huge bite of the goat's back. He did not swallow the morsel, however. He spat the flesh and flew away after burning to the ground half a dozen huts.

When it was clear that the dragon was gone for the evening, the village's inhabitants advanced gingerly to the place where the goat lay, writhing in pain. Then they made a startling discovery: the goat was bleeding profusely from the dragon's bite, but the body swelling was disappearing and the animal appeared to breathe more normally, though in fits and starts from the pain.

They picked the goat up and took it back to its pen, keeping it isolated from other animals. Three days later, a scar was forming at the site of the dragon's bite and the animal was back on its feet, bleating as if all was well.

"It's a miracle," said some humans. Others of a more scientific bent hypothesized: "There may be something in L'ong's saliva that cured whatever was causing the disease. We need to investigate this further."

Further modifications were made to the human's plan for dealing with L'ong. The site of the sacrifices was moved to an altar built on a hillock some distance from the village, to try to avoid further dwelling incinerations, and the offerings were made in the evening. Once a week, animals were presented for sacrifice suffering from a variety of cattle diseases: foot and mouth, rinderpest, even a suspected early attack of anthrax. L'ong devoured some of the offerings, flew away with disdain at others, took a bite or two of other victims before going away. In all cases, an animal that was left alive after being bitten by the dragon managed to recover.

"What are we going to do now?" asked a human. "It seems that L'ong's bite will cure some diseases, but we don't know if it will work on all, plus he is still eating our animals and destroying our homes."

A heavy silence followed, broken at last by an old man: "Something is gnawing at my innards, and I feel more exhausted each day. I I don't think I have much left to live. I'll offer myself as a sacrifice to the dragon."

***

They tried hard to dissuade him from his suicidal plan, but at the end they allowed the old man to place himself on the sacrificial altar each night, awaiting L'ong's arrival. On the fourth night the dragon swooped down from the sky, approached the hillock, glanced at the sprawled offering, and veered away. As he parted, L'ong issued three guttural words: "No eat humans."

"Wait!" replied the old man, getting up from the altar. "I don't want you to eat me, just to take a bite!"

L'ong stopped in mid-flight and returned to the ground. "Why?" he asked suspiciously.

"I'm very sick" replied the old man, "and something in your bite may cure me, as it did some of our animals. Please give it a try."

L'ong moved next to the old man. "I do this only once." The dragon bit sharply below the old man's shoulder, almost severing an arm. The man screamed and fainted.

A week later, an old man with a heavy bandage on his shoulder led a discussion of the leaders of his village on how to deal with L'ong. "I declare, other than the wound on my shoulder, I feel as good as I did when I was a youngster." His wife nodded her head, a knowing smile on her lips.

"We are all glad about your recovery, but we can't beg this monster to come bite every sick person in this town. After all, most of us have some form of death working its way inside us."

"Why not?" replied the old man. "The worst that can happen is that he will bite us and the disease will kill us all the same. We have nothing really to lose except for a painful bite by those teeth. I say we find a way to persuade L'ong to work with us on this."

***

One evening later in the week, there were two victims lying on the altar: a young, emaciated woman who hardly moved at all and a lamb that fought energetically to free itself from the ropes that kept it tied to the altar's supports.

"What this?" questioned L'ong as he hovered above the scene.

The old man L'ong had bitten in their previous encounter joined the couple at the altar and replied: "Your bite cured me, and we want you to do the same for many of our kin who suffer from disease. In exchange, we'll give you a healthy animal to enjoy for each human you help."

L'ong lacked the ability to formulate a verbal reply to this offer, but substituted action for words. He approached the young woman and bit her on the neck gently. He then cleansed his mouth by spitting into the ground and yanked the lamb from its bindings, swallowed it whole in a single motion, and took off, a patch of deeper darkness against the night sky.

***

A strange form of commerce then developed between dragon and humans. L'ong's bite cured many, but not all, the humans who presented themselves for treatment. There was no explanation why some "patients" failed to respond to the dragon's ministrations, but their demise was accepted as a limitation in an imperfect medical practice. After all, sometimes not even the potent kiss of a dragon can push death away.

The village started to prosper as its inhabitants regained good health and energy, though the livestock losses were grievous.

Everything seemed fine until one evening in the early spring of the following year. L'ong appeared late, yanked a lamb off the altar, ate it in a single gulp, and prepared to leave, ignoring the trembling man that had been waiting for L'ong's bite.

"Are you leaving without treating me?" asked the man querulously.

L'ong's final words were lost as he rose to the skies: "Need to find mate."

He was not seen again in that village or any other human settlement in the entire area. His story has become another legend among the folks who scratch a living in the inhospitable prairie. "Not even dragons like to live here" is often the melancholy conclusion of L'ong's tale.

But others retort, forgetting L'ong's depredations: "He left in search of a mate, but there are no dragons left on Earth. He is bound to return." For mankind is always capable of finding a bit of hope even in the most dreadful events.

The Blue Pearls

Celia always waited for him, sitting uncomfortably on a chair that barely fit on the tiny wrought iron balcony, one eye affixed to the spyglass that scanned the glassy surface of the sea. A Madame Butterfly brought to life, she knew nothing of the multitude of wives, fiancées, lovers, and mothers that had preceded her and would follow in her steps through the centuries, all with the same yearning for the return of a long-gone man, all blind to the likely futility of their vigils. She would regard, without really seeing, the collapse of each evening as it sunk in violet spasms below the horizon and ushered in another fragrant night, another day of fruitless waiting gone. Her free hand, which she was barely able to see in the deepening dark, caressed the pendant which was the only jewel she allowed herself; the pendant that she had made to house the dusky blue pearl that he had given her as a farewell token. "Wear it always," he had admonished, "because it will bear witness that I am alive and am always thinking of you."

Celia had smiled when Marcos uttered those words, which sounded more like an endearment than a real promise. But he hastened to add: "No, really. It is part of a set that I bought in a fishing village in one of the Greek islands, during the campaign against the Moors." He took out a small pouch he kept over his chest and, opening it, dropped in his hand another blue pearl, identical to the one he was giving her. "They say the blue ones are the rarest of all pearls, and those of a dusky color have mystical powers. If you have two of them as a set, they will forever search each other out and will find a way to reunite no matter the time or distance."

She had smiled again, indulgently, and asked with just a touch of sarcasm: "And where did you get that fine prediction?" If he detected incredulity in her question, he chose to ignore it, and replied in earnest: "There was an elder at the village, a soothsayer consulted by people from all corners of Greece, who told me the story of how Andromache and Ulysses had matching blue pearls just like these, and they were reunited after a decade of separation because of the pull of the pearls." "And you believed him?" "Why not? I had already paid an exorbitant price for the pearls from a local fisherman. The seer had no incentive to tell me a lie. Anyway, whether true prediction or fairy tale, I mean it when I say that I will return to you, unless Death takes me first. I swear it by my faith as a Catholic and my honor as the last member of the noble Bazan family."

For a while after his ship took sail Celia had kept the pearl in the casket where she stored the few trinkets she owned. But one year went by, and then another and, as her anxiety mounted, one day she took the blue pearl out of the casket and had it mounted on a simple silver pendant. Thus, she transferred her hopes to the pearl in the pendant, and silently leveled heathen prayers at the pearl seeking its help in bringing in its sister, and with her the long-departed Marcos.

Celia's prayers remained stubbornly unanswered, and a decade went by without news of her lover. Family and friends had pestered her for years trying to persuade her to forget her probably dead (or if not, deserting) fiancé and seek a new life. She had rejected all pleas and, one by one, the voices that counseled forgetfulness became themselves silent and abandoned her to the fate.

So it was that, in a late summer afternoon in the fourteenth year of her wait, Celia's spyglass scanned the emptiness of the waters as she sighed discontentedly. A heretic thought was forming in her mind, dulled by inactivity and longing. Should she quit this vain search? After all, she was no longer in the budding bloom of her youth, but was more like a withering rose shedding, one by one, every petal of beauty and joie de vivre, leaving only a charmless husk, an old maid fit only to be pitied and ignored. She was starting to course through those dangerous inner waters when she noticed with a start that the waters outside were no longer empty. A ship of a type she remembered well was making a lumbering approach towards the harbor. It was a frigate, a square-rigged warship like the one that had carried her Marcos away.

It was of course too soon to identify the vessel, but just the same Celia hurriedly changed into her best clothes and rushed out towards the harbor, where a crowd had already gathered. As the ship maneuvered towards the pier, Celia's heart began an irregular pounding; it was the Medusa, the frigate in which Marcos had departed towards the North Sea, to make war for the glory of the Crown. The ship had suffered much from war and adverse weather: most of its rigging had been blown away, and only the lower foremast, lower mizzenmast, and bowsprit remained operational. The crew had experienced similar ravages, with many sailors appearing wounded and those that remained intact ambling about lifelessly.

Celia was able to corner a disheveled officer as he set foot on the pier: "Officer, is Don Marcos Bazan part of your crew?" "Err... si, señora," was the polite but evasive sounding answer. "Where is he?" "He is below deck. He was seriously injured in our last engagement with the Brits and has not recovered. But..."

Celia did not wait for him to finish, and ran up the plank before he could stop her. She went the length of the main deck, miraculously avoiding the obstacles on her path, and went down the narrow stairs to the area under the prow that housed the sick bay. The sight she encountered was appalling: the sick or wounded were slung up to the beams in hammocks, subjected to deafening noise, in constant collision with other swinging beds, and exposed to the heat and odors of cooking from the nearby galley. Instead of quietude, ventilation, and natural light, the area beneath the water-line that served as sick bay was close, dark, and dismal. The stench, the noise and the heat were indeed unbearable.

Standing at the edge of the confusion, Celia asked as loudly as she could over the surrounding din: "Does anyone here know where Marcos Bazan is?" There was an abrupt silence, and then out of the middle of the room came a feeble voice: "He is here, next to me."

Celia followed the voice, which kept repeating "Here," until she found herself close to the back wall, near a point where several hammocks coalesced into an uninterrupted mesh of rope. The voice, she now saw, belonged to a dirty looking sailor with a leg on a cast. With great effort, the man half rose on his hammock and pointed to his left: "There is poor Marcos."

The hammock to the left of the sailor was occupied by a dark hulk of humanity that appeared oblivious to the world. Celia approached the body and cried out: "Marcos, my love! It is I, Celia, come to rescue you!"

That bold declaration elicited no response. Celia repeated her cry again, now with a tinge of desperation in her voice. Again, no response. Turning to the sailor in the next hammock, she questioned: "What's wrong with him? Why doesn't he answer?"

The response came from behind her. The officer she had ditched had finally caught up with her and had seized her arm, seeking to lead her away. "He suffered a head wound in our battle with the English privateers. His body seems to be healing, but his mind is gone."

Celia swallowed an anguished cry and, making an effort to regain her composure, asked: "What is the Royal Navy going to do with him?"

"Our ship is badly battered, as you can see. We will have to stay in port for months to get it repaired. He will remain onboard while work on the Medusa is ongoing. If by the time we are ready to depart he has not recovered, we will leave him behind in some institution. I am sure some order of nuns runs a hospice or a hospital for the disabled here."

"Is it possible for him to be released to me now, rather than waiting many months? I am his fiancée and would take care of him better than any institution."

"I will need to speak to the Captain. Bazan was a brave soldier and a fine seaman, not to mention a nobleman who volunteered for service to the King, and we want to make sure that as good a care is taken of him as is possible. His papers do not list any family members or other relations to whom we could transfer his custody. Your suggestion may be well received. Of course, we would need to know more about you…"

"Of course," she replied haughtily. "I am Celia de Roxas, direct descendant of one of the first Spanish governors of this island. Our family is famous for its rectitude and loyalty to La Corona. We are not wealthy –

never were – but our piety and good works are well known throughout the colony. Ask anyone."

"Madame, I meant no offense. It is only that we bear some responsibility to the men under our command...." Celia cut him off. "No offense taken. But please talk to the Captain and let's take care of this matter as soon as possible."

It did, however, take more than a few days for Marcos to be turned over to Celia. The ship doctor had insisted that he should be kept under medical care until his physical wounds were sufficiently healed. The Captain had demanded a stiff bribe to consent to generate the necessary paperwork, and it took Celia a bit of effort to round up the money from her friends and relatives. Finally, one bright but unusually cool late November morning Celia led Marcos down the pier and into a carriage she had hired to bring them home. Marcos walked hesitatingly, like a small child or a drunk unsure of where to set his foot next. His gaze was unfocused and there was a vacuous smile on his lips. His beard, so heavy it obscured most of his features, was speckled with gray.

"Yes, my dear, you are a mess. But I will take care of you" announced Celia brightly. When the carriage deposited them at the door of Celia's home in the old section inside the walls of the city, Celia took him firmly by the hand, made him climb the three stone steps that led to the threshold of their dilapidated mansion, and pushed him indoors as Matilde, the old Indian slave, opened the heavy mahogany doors. As they entered, the bells in the nearby cathedral announced the hour. It was eleven in the morning, and all was well – no pirate ships or English corsairs were in sight.

"First thing we are going to do is give you a bath and get you into new clothes. I will be glad to burn the stinking rags you are wearing." He nodded, but it was not clear whether in agreement or as an automatic response to her commanding voice.

Between Matilde and Celia they disrobed Marcos, sunk him in a huge copper bath that saw use only on Easter and Christmas Day, lathered his body with precious Castile soap, and poured bucket after bucket of hot water to wash away months of grime from his body. Marcos did not protest, even when Matilde accidentally doused one of his eyes with soapy water; he merely rubbed the liquid away with a mechanical grunt. Indeed, he let them scrub and rub and poke at him, until he was as clean as a hairy forty-year-old sailor could ever be. "You have been baptized again" declared Celia with satisfaction. "Now, for the next step, we are going to trim your beard." She took him by the hand and led him into the parlor.

She then produced a large cast iron straight razor that had belonged to her father. It was wide at one end and tapering into the handle, and very heavy. She thought for a moment of sending Matilde out to get a barber but decided she could do this herself, if she was very careful. She soaped Marcos' beard thoroughly and set to work, trying to eliminate as much of the excess hair as possible and still leave a fashionable moustache and pointed goatee, in the style of reigning King Philip IV. However, her skills with the clumsy razor were limited and she failed to achieve an even moustache, or a presentable goatee. So, she ended up giving Marcos a totally clean shave, except for a few cuts here and there for which she stanched the flow of blood the best she could.

Celia then stood back to admire her handiwork and did a double take. The man whose face she had cleaned and shaved was deeply tanned, with wide set eyes and thick black brows that nearly touched and made the face look slightly sinister. Looking at him closely, Celia also noted that his pupils were lighter than Marcos' – amber rather than brown. This man was NOT Marcos!

"Who are you?" she shrieked, and started to shake the man as if trying to dislodge the truth from him. At first, there was no response, but after a short while the man let out a big sigh and replied: "No, I am not Marcos, but he was my friend."

"What do you mean he was your friend? Where is he?"

"He is dead. He was killed in 1624 during the siege of Breda in the Netherlands. I was by his side when he fell."

"How did he die?"

"We were in the Royal Navy together and were sent as reinforcements to the army laying siege to the city. At first our army, composed largely of pikemen, was unaccustomed to facing the large numbers of musketeers fighting for the Dutch. As a result, we took many casualties at the start of the siege, and Marcos was one of them. He was hit in the chest by a musket shot and perished."

"But why did you steal his name?"

"He was a nobleman and I am a nobody, son of a slattern from the back alleys of Burgos. I was a deckhand on the Medusa, he a gunner. Despite the differences in class, we had become very close friends. I realized that he no longer had need for his name or rank, and I could make more of myself by becoming respected Marcos Bazan instead of low-class Ramon Garcia. I took the personal papers he had on his person, deserted, hid in the countryside for a few days, and finally returned to the Medusa impersonating him. I got some strange looks at the beginning but I had grown a full beard, was of similar size, and knew him so well that I was able to fool everyone. Luckily, my skills as a gunner were never really tested until we ran into the Brits."

"And you thought you could fool me too?" asked Celia angrily. "Did you think you could continue to pretend to be an imbecile, and I would never know any better?"

"No" he replied, lowering his head in shame. "I was in fact suffering from some mental disorder on that day you met me, but later recovered but kept the pretense since I knew you were taking steps to free me from my indenture on that hateful ship. I was hoping to keep you in the dark for a while, before revealing myself. It was not meant to be," he finished ruefully.

"And, apart from getting me to rescue you, did you have any other purposes in mind? Maybe you intended to murder me or steal the little I own?"

"Well, I did have another purpose. See, he had told me all about himself and you. When he was shot and lay dying, he asked me to find you and tell you that he had loved you to the very end and only Death had kept the two of you apart. Also, he had something for me to give you... But where is my scapular?"

"Do you mean the brown scapular of Our Lady of Mt. Carmel?"

"Yes."

"We took it out to bathe you. It is in the kitchen, on the table next to where we put the copper bath tub."

"Can I have it back, please?"

Celia was incensed at Garcia's deception, but she went back to the kitchen and brought back the scapular -- two wool squares of cloth, connected by woolen strings. One square contained a leather-bound image of the Lady of Mt. Carmel, the other showed a picture of the Holy Heart of Jesus. She handed the scapular to the man, who carefully pulled apart the square containing the picture of Jesus, tilted and shook a hidden receptacle, and drew out an iridescent, dusky blue pearl. "He asked me to give it to you to always remember him by."

Celia's eyes clouded with tears. She exclaimed sadly: "Yes, one blue pearl will always find her sister. But not carried by the same man." And, more acidly: "Not even similar. You are only a common thief. I shall denounce you for impersonating a member of the Spanish nobility."

"You certainly could. But please consider this: turning me over to the King's justice will not bring Marcos back, and you will die as you currently are, bitter and alone. Let me stay with you as your servant and, if nothing else, your companion. I promise to be your friend as I was the friend of Marcos. He trusted in me, why will you not give me a chance to prove my worth?"

Celia was indignant at Garcia's request. "You are vile and brazen and I will see you punished as you deserve." She turned her back on the man, started to walk away, and called her slave out: "Matilde! Please come here at once!"

Garcia begged again with mounting agitation: "My lady! Please give me a week to prove myself. If you are dissatisfied with me in any manner, I will walk over to the mayor's office and ask to be placed in chains. In the meantime, let me honor the memory of the man we both loved. Let me serve you. Please!"

Celia stopped. If Marcos had trusted this man with a priceless pearl and he had delivered it, perhaps he deserved a chance, maybe as a servant in her staff. She turned to him: "I can't pay you and have only menial tasks for you to perform. If those conditions suit you, I will not turn you in, at least for a week. But be aware that you are on trial, starting now."

"Thank you, my lady. I don't need money. I will get my pending wages ... er, Marcos,' from the ship's paymaster. I will pull my own weight, and contribute to this household's expenses."

At that point, Matilde entered the parlor. "Did you call, Miss Celia?"

"Yes. I heard the bell in the cathedral strike three. Can we have dinner now?"

"Yes, Miss Celia."

"Then, let us have a little celebration to toast and give thanks for this reunion," she said ironically.

And so it was that Ramon Garcia came to stay in the old house of Celia de Roxas and, as time went by, proved satisfactory in every way. Later, Celia would re-introduce him to her family and friends as Don Marcos Bazan, returned after many years of pilgrimage. And, one day, they married and went to live in Marcos' manor house in Navarra, where they lived happily ever after. And each of them kept a perfect dusky blue pearl as a token of their undying love.

A Viennese Story

To win applause one must write stuff so simple that a coachman might sing it.
Wolfgang Amadeus Mozart

Being slight of build and juvenile looking was a mixed blessing for Alicia. On the one hand, people tended to be cloyingly condescending towards her – as if she were nine years old instead of seventeen. On the other, her apparent young age allowed her to get away with much that would be criticized in a teenager, particularly in a backwater country like Ruritania. Also, she was able to maintain her child prodigy status far longer than her age warranted. So, on balance, being small and child-like was helpful though often an annoyance.

Her breakout moment came in the spring of 2038, when her piano piece *"Nostalgia,"* which she had entered in her Senior High School talent competition, was a surprise winner. As luck would have it, when she played it in the awards program, the music critic of the local paper (who had attended the show because his niece was a violin player) had raved about the piece, and written a column that compared *"Nostalgia"* to Sibelius' *Valse Triste* in its wistfulness and described the frisson of emotion that the bittersweet melody evoked. "Despite her tender years, this child is destined to be a musical giant, comparable only to Mozart and Mendelssohn in precocity." Later, when he learned Alicia's true age, he had been too embarrassed to take back these comments.

Another stroke of luck was that a new talent show – imported from abroad, like other bad habits – was being launched by a local TV station. "Ruritania Shines" promised to bring every week an alliteration of talents, such as daring dancers, jaunty jugglers, vapid vocalists, voluble ventriloquists, even canine coteries, all competing for fame and prizes. Alicia's mom was contacted by the producer of Ruritania Shines, who declared that a genius of Alicia's magnitude must be displayed before the entire nation, nay, the whole world, and what better vehicle than the show to let her unique talents "shine for all Ruritania to see". Bursting with maternal pride, Alicia's mom gave her consent without even consulting her daughter.

Alicia was nonplussed by the sudden attention. She had written *Nostalgia* to voice her adolescent angst, and even though she thought the piece was pretty good, she had no expectation that it would be the launch pad from which her fame would take off. And she felt she was only an adequate pianist, so she fretted about performing the piece before seasoned critics. The night the show was taped, she was so nervous her mother had to help her dress – in a short pink dress and matching bow that were more appropriate for an elementary school child than a teenager – and had to give her a double dose of tranquilizers to get her steady enough to appear before the panel and the ready to adore audience.

Later, she would not remember anything about the fawning introduction by the master of ceremonies, the low-ball questions by the panel, or even how the grand piano was ceremoniously rolled onstage. The banquette was too low, the lights too bright, and as she sat before the keyboard the gleaming black and white keys seemed like teeth threatening to rip her apart. Alicia swallowed hard, shook her head to clear her mind, and soldiered on.

Next she knew she was standing in front of the panel of judges, where each of the "experts" took turns to grovel in admiration of her musicality, the beauty of her tone, and of course the haunting melody. The last one, an oxygenated matron who would never see fifty again, grasped Alicia in her arms, pressed the child to her bosom, and declared in barbaric French: "*Ma cherie. Tu es ravissant.*"

Alicia was unanimously declared to have passed the preliminary phase of the competition and was invited to return two weeks hence for the "final contest." Alicia took the news well, at least outwardly, but as she smiled and curtsied and offered her thanks in a very small voice her heart trembled with fear at the thought of having to go through the ordeal again.

Her misgivings were amplified when, a day or two later, the producer of the show came to their apartment to check on things and almost casually suggested that the audience and the judges were looking forward to another performance, "perhaps of a new or different composition" by the child prodigy. This was the first, but not the last, time a chill ran up and down Alice's spine, and an inexplicable dread positioned itself in her gut, never to be dislodged. For Alicia did not have other compositions to offer. Yes, she had composed other pieces, but those were student exercises, arid as sand dunes in the Sahara. What was she to do?

She sat solidly at the piano for most of the next two weeks, playing idly with the keys, running scales, attempting to draw a fresh melody out of a brain that seemed as empty as her late father's bank account. Finally, in desperation, she set pen to paper and produced something she titled "*Variations on an Original Theme*" that was a collection of thinly modified versions of *Nostalgia*. Since there was no time to get it printed, she arrived at the taping of the final Ruritania Shines contest clutching the manuscript in her sweaty hands.

This performance she later recalled much better than the earlier one. In response to her complaints, they had provided a sufficiently high banquette, and when her turn came, after the ventriloquist and the dancing twins and the tumblers and the performing poodles, the lights were dimmed in the hall. This added an extra touch of suspense to the audience's anticipation, which had been heightened by the master of ceremonies hailing the debut of her new work as "a momentous occasion, comparable to the premiere of Beethoven's Emperor piano concerto in Vienna in 1812." Alicia had shaken her head in denial, which everyone interpreted as a showing of modesty, and the master of ceremonies had escorted her to the piano, paternally holding her slight shoulder.

The playing had not gone too badly, she decided. She had made a couple of mistakes sight reading her own manuscript, and the tempo in some places had been slower than she originally intended, but nobody seemed to notice. Later, the recording that was made from the soundtrack of the program would become the official version of the work.

Tumultuous applause broke the moment she played the last note and rested at the keyboard to catch her breath.

She got up slowly, faced the panel of judges, and curtsied prettily. The acclamation continued, growing if anything louder as the minutes went by. The chief judge, a curmudgeon who was the terror of contestants for his snide disassembly of most performances, cleared his throat and loudly demanded silence from the audience. Turning to Alicia, he said: "Our producers like to build viewer anticipation by delaying the announcement of the panel's decision until the end of the program. We will not do so this evening. I have consulted with my fellow judges and am proud, indeed honored, to announce that you are the winner of this year's Ruritania Shines contest. You play like an angel and your music is incomparably beautiful. I predict you will bring fame to yourself, and enhance Ruritania's reputation among the artistic capitals of the world. Congratulations!!"

The other judges attempted to embellish on this speech but their voices were drowned in the maelstrom of cheers, whistles, stampings of feet, and other expressions of acclaim. Alicia kept taking bows and even blew a few kisses at the audience. She felt this was her finest hour, and she was not mistaken.

***

The prize money from the Ruritania Shines contest was nice, but soon paled in comparison with other commercial opportunities that followed. There was a hastily produced album in which Alicia played *Nostalgia*, the Variations on an Original Theme, a new but hardly novel set called "*Second Variations*," and old chestnuts by Liszt, Chopin, Debussy, Lecuona and others. In three weeks it reached platinum status and provided her with a nice stream of royalties for the following year. An international record company, bemoaning the dearth of new classical material, signed her up for a two-year contract to exclusively record any new compositions that were sure to follow. A similar deal was struck with the TV network that produced "Ruritania Shines," guaranteeing a sizeable honorarium for her future appearances on the program. To cap all of it off, a famous British publishing house signed her up for a ghost-written autobiography provisionally entitled "A Nightingale Sings." The advance on that book would sustain her for many months thereafter.

The two years that followed were ones of continuous frustration for Alicia. Her status as a "child prodigy" had been burst by an expose in a tabloid revealing to its inquiring readers the "long hidden secret" of her true age and had suggested that she might be trying to conceal her having an out of wedlock child. The flow of royalties slowed down to a trickle, and no more advances against future work were forthcoming, because Alicia had bumped into a seemingly unmovable obstacle: writer's (in this case, composer's) block. Hard as she tried, no new ideas came to mind, no ingratiating tunes dripped from her pen, no irresistible Caribbean rhythms were struck by her fingers as she pounded the keyboard. In a 2040 interview that became immediately famous, her erstwhile music teacher sought to defend the drying up of her production as only a symptom of people's inflated expectations: "Everyone expected a Mozart, who could turn out masterpieces in less time that takes most people to have lunch. In reality, Alicia is like Beethoven, who carefully and painstakingly crafted his compositions, sometimes spending a couple of years before turning out an immortal work like the Eroica Symphony. We need to give our home grown genius more time to mature and enchant us with her art."

Others, however, were less charitable. A strident article in an entertainment magazine called Alicia a "One Hit Wonder" and pejoratively dubbed *Nostalgia* "the *Volare* of the 21st Century." The refutations that flew from every quarter did little to reassure Alicia, who in her heart of hearts tended to agree with the harsh assessment.

Thus stood matters as 2041 rolled in. It was an important year to music lovers worldwide: in December it would be the 250th anniversary of Mozart's untimely death, and hundreds of special events were planned to commemorate the occasion. Mozart's music filled the airwaves, bringing further desperation to Alicia by reminding her of her artistic (and by now personal) failure. She was twenty years old, unemployed, nearly broke, and unloved. She had shed most of her childhood friends and the rest had deserted her. Her mother and main supporter had died the year before, leaving her daughter alone in an apartment that was too large for a single woman and too full of mementos of her meteoric rise to be comfortable.

In April, as spring warmed the Northern Hemisphere, Alicia made a momentous decision: she closed her apartment, emptied her bank accounts, collected some monies people owed her, and set out for Vienna. If she could not find inspiration in that most musical of cities, she would hire herself as a piano teacher or a secretary, or whatever.

***

Vienna in 2041 was of course much different than it had been in the days of Mozart. Its population had grown from less than 300,000 people then to over 3 million. Its denizens lived in relative luxury compared to the population in less prosperous countries like Ruritania, and enjoyed a relaxed lifestyle that made Vienna a desirable place to call home. However, with affluence comes a high cost of living, as Alicia learned almost immediately. She realized that her limited funds would not last past the end of the year unless she made a drastic change in her ways. After much searching, she found a guest house where she could rent a garret at a less than ruinous rate. The accommodations were basic – the bathroom was at the end of the hall – but in most respects Alicia was not your typical tourist. She was there to soak up inspiration, to breathe the air that had nourished the talents of scores of great musicians like Mozart, Haydn, Beethoven, Schubert, Brahms, Mahler, and Schoenberg. In short, she went to Vienna to waken her dormant muse. She found a studio that would let her use a piano for a few hours a day and began sampling the cultural opportunities that the once capital of the Habsburg Empire had to offer.

She visited various museums, went as regularly as her means allowed to the Wiener Musikverein to hear the Vienna Philharmonic and to the Wiener Konzerthaus to hear the Vienna Symphony. She visited the former houses and apartments of Beethoven, Mozart, Schubert, Strauss, and Haydn. She went to the collection of composers' graves in the Zentralfriedhof, the main cemetery of the city, and reverently visited the tombs of Beethoven (his third), Brahms, Johann Strauss Sr. and Jr., and Schubert. She went to the St. Marx cemetery near the Musikverein to visit the alleged tomb of Mozart and found the little graveyard an oasis of calm in the noisy city. Mozart's grave was tucked away, under a short white column with a simple inscription on the pedestal: "W.A. Mozart, 1756-1791," next to which was a statue of a fat little angel. A bed of tiny red flowers was the tomb's only other decoration. It was a pretty but uninspiring place.

Spring led into summer and then to fall, and Alicia was not making any progress in her quest. The city, however, was becoming more and more alive as the 250th anniversary of Mozart's death approached. As was the case in 1991 on the occasion of the 200th anniversary, Vienna was commemorating the composer with concerts, recitals, opera productions, symposia and other events. Large crowds were descending on the city to visit exhibitions that featured manuscripts, pictures and diverse memorabilia assembled from all over the world. Hardly a day went by without a concert of some sort, often including the performance of one or two of his operas, a concerto, his string quartets and piano sonatas, and so on. The relentlessness of the musical assault was leaving the locals oversaturated but happy with the extra income, and was grating on Alicia's nerves since the overexposure was doing nothing to revive her art.

The Requiem was scheduled to be performed on December 5, the anniversary of Mozart's death, in St. Stephen's Cathedral. The event was oversubscribed and Alicia did not try to get tickets. As the gloom of winter descended on Vienna, Alicia stayed more and more in her tiny room, contemplating in lonely desperation how all her hopes of glory turned to dust. Starting on the last week of

November, she only ventured outside to go to the bathroom, or to get some pastry and coffee at the bakery next door. She was thinner and weaker by the day, and increasingly delirious.

The night of December 4 Alicia lay in bed, tottering between wakefulness and a sleep that was more of a trance. As she lay there, she dwelt on the misery of her life and how fortune had turned from friend to implacable foe, and what was she going to do with herself when she had to return to Ruritania. She was not religious; however, in a fit of self-pity, she raised her thoughts (and perhaps her voice) heavenwards and prayed to the man whose life and works were being celebrated: "O, Mozart, please help me. You are the greatest genius that mankind has ever known. Please come to me, whisper in my ear, sow a few ideas in my barren mind so that I can regain my self-respect and my place in society. Please, I beg you..." She swooned.

She woke up with a start as something told her she was no longer alone. She cautiously opened her eyes and was astonished to find a very plain, short man standing at the foot of her bed. He was a little pudgy, was bewigged, and dressed in a tomato red topcoat, a gold waistcoat and white linen breeches, and wore a large lace neckerchief. He seemed utterly out of place yet comfortable with his surroundings. Before she could say anything, he greeted her in heavily accented Italian (a language that Alicia's mother had insisted she learn): "Good evening madam, actually good morning. I am sorry if I startled you, but I am answering your call. My name is Johannes Chrysostomus Wolfgangus Theophilus Mozart, though my friends call me Wolfgang, or even Wolfie. How can I assist you?"

Alicia was at a loss for words. Was she dreaming? Had an insane person broken into her room? Was this to be the tragic end of her career? She collected her wits and said in a tremulous voice: "Look, I have no money. You can take my purse, right there on the table, but please don't hurt me."

"As I said, madam, I am here to help you, as you requested."

Seeing that the strange little man did not appear aggressive and remained immobile at the foot of her bed, Alicia calmed down somewhat, and asked, less shakily: "Are you really Mozart, or is this some charade?"

"I am, or better said, I once was, Mozart."

"But that is impossible. You have been dead for two hundred and fifty years."

"Exactly. While I was alive and was a man of means (only for a short time, I assure you) I did a number of good deeds, helped sick and destitute people, and things like that. As a reward, my spirit is allowed to return to the world one night every ten years, on the anniversary of my death. On that night, like this one, I roam through Vienna and revisit the places I knew and loved and those that have been erected since my death: the Schönbrunn, the Hofbrau, the Belvedere, even my own Mozarthaus. I go through Theater an der Wien, the Staatsoper and the Volksoper. I amble through the boulevards and the alleys and the beer halls and churches and the parks and the Vienna woods and even the Danube, which is hardly blue, as one of my successors imaginatively dubbed. In short, I can go everywhere I please, but as morning rises I must leave for another decade. And I am expected to help anyone I can during my brief sojourn. This visit is a difficult one, for there are a number of people in town that are trying to channel me, and in just every case the channeler is doing so for trivial or illegitimate purposes. I have ignored all those demands for my attention but I could not help noticing that your plea was genuine and you were seriously in need of my help. So, I ask again, how can I help you?"

This was a disconcertingly long speech and Alicia did not understand parts of it, but she captured the essential message: Mozart was really before her and was offering to help her. So she sat on the bed, squared her shoulders, and declared:

"Herr Mozart, I hardly need to tell you that my admiration for you and the music you wrote knows no limits. Like most educated people, I am familiar with many of your works, which are perfection itself, for the gracefulness of the melodies, the originality and logic of the structures, the drama that pervades from the simplest sonata to your great operas. But unlike most people, what astonishes me the most is the speed with which you composed your works, the fact that they were produced with almost no second thoughts or corrections, in an unending stream as if the angels dictated the music and you wrote it. I have struggled in vain over the years to create something beautiful, something that will transcend my existence and will provide enjoyment for generations to come, like you have done. However, unlike you, I have no ideas, I sit before the piano for hours on end and nothing comes to me. Can you help me?" There was undisguised desperation in her question.

Mozart's specter was silent for a moment and then inquired: "Have you written anything?"

"Oh, yes, three years ago I composed a short free-form piece, like a rhapsody, entitled *Nostalgia*, which was very well received and caused me to win prizes and achieve notoriety in my country and abroad. But I have done nothing of significance ever since."

"I remember my first pieces, three little piano sonatas that I whipped up when I was five. I started composing nonstop from then on. In some ways, I wish I had not been so prolific."

"Why? I would kill to be able to do that."

"Well, when you are so prolific and write so fast, people tend to value less your effort. Look at that man Beethoven who came just after me. He was uncouth and his music was atrocious, but he wrote so slowly that he got the publishers and the public to eagerly await every morsel he dropped on their laps, whenever he got around to finishing it. But I digress. So, if I understand your problem, you once wrote something that was very good and have not been able to follow up on it for several years. Am I right?"

"Yes."

"Have you heard of what I understand people in your generation call 'one hit wonders'" I mean, artists or composers that produce one very successful musical effort and are unable to match it for the rest of their lives?"

"Yes, of course."

"Isn't it true that the work continues to be enjoyed even if the artist fades into obscurity?"

"Yes."

"Listen, there was this minor composer just before my time called Johann Pachelbel. He wrote a short piece called Canon which drove me crazy because it repeated its simple melodic line continuously for I don't know how many bars. Everyone loved it, everyone thought it was great. Herr Pachelbel never wrote anything else of any note, and yet I bet his Canon kept on being played long after his death. Do you know what I am talking about?"

"Yes, Herr Mozart. I know the Canon. It is played at many weddings, and it is still quite popular among music lovers."

"Well, there you have it. You may be another Pachelbel. My recommendation is that you enjoy what you have accomplished, and if you cannot produce any other great works, change your field of endeavor."

"No, no, no. I was born to be a composer, and will die that way."

"Well, I am sorry for you. Talent can't be forced, and it is best to be a one hit wonder than no wonder at all. Please try to be happy with what you have accomplished."

"You say that because everything came easy to you. If you had written only those three little sonatas at the age of five and then nothing else, you would be singing a different tune."

"Perhaps. But I was also a great violinist and the best pianist of my generation. I would have made ends meet, somehow." Mozart's specter closed arms around his chest, seeming annoyed.

"I am sorry, I didn't mean to be disrespectful. I was only disappointed that you could not help me."

"Well, perhaps there is one thing I can do. Do you have music paper handy?"

Yes, quite on top of my desk."

"Pull out a sheet or two, and I will dictate something for you."

Alicia did as ordered, and Mozart's specter directed: "This is going to be a Rondo in D Major for piano. Ready?"

Mozart's specter called out the notes and at the same time hummed the melody, in a weak but pleasant tenor voice. He dictated so fast that Alicia thought she would have trouble keeping up with him but, somehow, she managed. A few minutes later, she and Mozart were done. "It is very difficult" she concluded plaintively. Mozart shrugged his spectral shoulders and declared: "It is one of several pieces that were floating in my head as I lay dying. I was trying to finish the *Requiem* and never had time to transcribe it. But this is pretty much finished, trust me." Then, after a sigh, he thrust his arm out in a wide, grandiose arc and told the astonished girl: "Use it well and in good luck."

The first light of the morning shone through the garret's window, and Mozart's specter became dimmer and disappeared without waiting for Alicia's thanks. No sooner was he gone than Alicia dropped back in bed and fell into a stupor.

When she regained consciousness hours later, she was disconcerted to find several sheets of music scattered on the floor. As she picked them up placed them in some order, she tried to remember where these came from. It was a manuscript for a piano piece which she had clearly penned, but she could not for her life recall when or how she had come to write this music. She silently read the score and marveled at its complexity. How could she have written this? She was musically trained, but this was a cut above anything she had ever produced. Was her creative drought over? Was it time to give fame another try?

***

Two weeks later Alicia returned to Ruritania. She had made minimal structural changes to the score, slowed the tempo a bit, and tried as best she could to make the work sound like her former compositions. She contacted "Ruritania Shines," now in its fourth triumphal season, and was invited to appear in the next taping session, two weeks hence. That left her enough time to find a modest apartment, rent a piano, and leave word with her agent and the record company that she was back in town and had some new material that she expected would be well received. Somehow the news got to the local press and the taping of Ruritania Shines was accompanied by a great deal of speculation and the presence of several reporters among the packed audience.

She came onstage wearing a simple dress, making no attempt to disguise her age. Not that doing so would have been an easy task: she was looking gaunt from her months of privation in Vienna, and her thinness and the hollowness of her cheeks made her look even older. Gasps of surprise and a murmur of commiseration provided a background to the master of ceremonies introduction: "Ladies and gentlemen, our own star, Ruritania's most beloved artist, has finally returned. She has been a tireless ambassador of our country in the capitals of Europe and has brought honor and recognition for Ruritania wherever she has appeared. But now she is back with us again." (Deafening applause, whistles and stomping of feet).

"She will be playing a new composition that will again fill our hearts with awe, with joy, with patriotic pride. Please give Alicia a warm round of applause." (More clapping and shouting).

Alicia bowed soberly twice, sat at the banquette, and announced in a firm, self-confident voice: "This work is a modern homage to the Western musical tradition from which our own arises. It is a piano piece entitled '*Rondo in the Classical Style.*' I wrote it in Vienna, under the shadow of all the great masters who worked there." And then she played.

When she finished, her performance was greeted with polite applause instead of delirium. Puzzled, she got to her feet and took a bow. The applause got no louder; in fact, it diminished somewhat and had almost vanished when the panel's chief judge commented: "Well, that was .... *interesting.* I am no expert, but I found the piece somewhat lacking in the tropical fire that made your earlier works so delightful. It sounded a little stiff and out of fashion, like the three-piece suits that men used to wear last century. Let's see what my colleagues have to say."

The other judges were kinder in their words, but their message was essentially the same: Alicia's new composition was surprisingly lifeless, particularly for a rondo, and without expressly saying it they declared it a bore.

Later in the evening, the panel determined that a ballad singer, a flaming torch juggler, and an acrobatic dance troupe were being invited to the final round of competition. Alicia did not make the cut.

Her disappointment grew in the next few days when reviews by musical experts began to file in. One brought up the fable of the mountain giving belated birth to a mouse. Another declared that sabbaticals don't work for everyone. The cruelest of all reviewers reminded readers of Mozart's proclivity for playing practical jokes and suggested that, had this been possible, Alicia could have been the victim of the immortal's heavy-handed sense of humor.

It took Alicia many months and hours of psychotherapy to recover from the humiliation. She still hurt from the failure, but reveled in the satisfaction of being a latter-day Pachelbel and having at least one solid hit under her belt.

She also realized that one must learn to live with one's limitations. She enrolled in paralegal school and in a couple of years had secured a well remunerated position with a major law firm, where she spent the rest of her working life. She continued to play the piano, but no longer performed in public. And she never set foot in Vienna again.

The Hungry Wolf and the Maiden

The girl burst out laughing; she knew she was nobody's meat.
Angela Carter, The Company of Wolves

It had been a tough year for all living creatures in the valley. A wet spring that stunted crops had been followed by a hot and dry summer that withered them. There had been a frost early in the fall that had killed most crops that had survived the growing season. Now, in winter's grip, gelid winds blew down the mountain, turning the landscape into a desolate waste. People and wild things were cold and hungry and many feared they would not live to see the crocuses raise their yellow and purple heads through the snow.

Wolf was as hungry as anyone, if no more. The last rabbit he had devoured was but a fading memory – even though just skin and bones, it had been a reprieve from the disgusting diet of earthworms and frozen berries that winter had forced upon him. Now even those were hard to find.

His need had driven him close to the hamlet. The place was a jumble of wattle and daub huts, rancid with the reek of humans. There once had been a communal pen in the village, but the sheep that had been there had long disappeared, consumed by their owners. Wolf scowled, remembering how his last foray into that pen had been met with sharp things being thrust or flung at him. He still bore a couple of scars that ached dully when the weather got as cold as it was now.

Wolf was circling the village, always keeping a safe distance from the huts, when out of the corner of his vision he caught a motion on the road leading to the hamlet. It was getting dark, but it had 24-hour eyes, adapted to seeing during day and night. He discerned that the movement belonged to a young human, heading for the huts and carrying a large basket under one arm.

Wolf cut across the field at full speed and ground to a halt in front of the human. She was a small thing, but would make at least one meal. Salivating in anticipation, he got ready to attack, baring his teeth, raising his hackles, and moving towards his target slowly. She dropped the basket and covered her mouth in a gesture of surprise.

"Well, Sir, you startled me." She made sounds in human but her thoughts somehow conveyed to Wolf's brain. "I am on my way to visit my grandmother, who is ill, in that hut over there." She pointed to one of the poorest dwellings. "My name is Pyrrha, which means "Fire," and that is why I wear this red coat and hood. What's yours?"

Wolf was taken aback by the girl's lack of fear, and managed to respond (that is, to form in his head) the word "Gunnolf." He added (again in his head): "they named me so because I was always fighting with my brothers and sisters, and even challenged my father, the leader of the pack. That's why I got to live alone."

Pyrrha thought that was far more information than she required, but kept that judgment to herself. Politely, she replied: "I'm sorry to hear that you were mistreated. However, I must reach my grandmother right away. Please let me pass."

Gunnolf said (thought) brusquely: "Not so fast, human. I'm about to eat you." Pyrrha replied, still without a trace of fear: "That would be *so* impolite. We are on a first name basis, and you are talking about murdering me? Where are your manners?"

At this, Gunnolf became rather confused, and raised his hackles in order to appear larger and more threatening. His yellow eyes took on an angry expression and his lips curled back to expose the fangs and gums. He fixed his gaze on the human and said:

"Why should I have manners? I am a hungry wolf and you are my next meal. Prepare to die." Gunnolf crouched and readied to jump on his prey, but his initiative was cut short when Pyrrha issued a sharp command: "Stop all that! You are NOT going to attack me!"

Gunnolf was frozen in place by the command in the girl's voice. He took a defensive stance, assuming an ambivalent facial expression while attempting to stare down his opponent. "That is much better," commented Pyrrha evenly. "Now, let's talk like civilized creatures. I'm prepared to share with you some of what I have in this basket, but you have to promise you'll go away and will never disturb the inhabitants of this hamlet again."

Anger returned to Gunnolf as the meaning of these words sunk in. "I am the lord of the wild, the most ferocious of all beasts. Why would I bargain with a punk like you?" He displayed his fangs again.

Pyrrha kept her aplomb. "Because that is the best bargain you will be able to strike today. Share what is in the basket or stay hungry. It's all the same to me." She shrugged her shoulders in a sign of unconcern.

"This is folly!" growled Gunnolf and crouched with tail cocked, lips pulled back, fangs bared, ears forward, and eyes wild and threatening. Then, fast as lightning, he leapt at the girl.

Rather, he tried to. While still in mid-air, he felt a whoosh of wind and was struck by an invisible force that sent him sprawling, rolling like an acorn in the snow. "What was that?" He asked himself in befuddlement.

"It was only the sign of a door opening."

"What do you mean?" Unwittingly, Gunnolf assumed a submissive posture, crouching with curled down rump and tail tucked.

"I'm not allowed to use my powers save in self-defense" explained Pyrrha. "Now that you have attacked me, you are fair game."

A chill went down Gunnolf's spine. He approached the girl timidly and nuzzled and licked at the girl's hand. She gazed ahead coolly, displaying no sign of accepting the wolf's submission.

"See," she explained. "The population here has been wary since your last attack. They have seen you roaming around this hamlet and fear that you will hurt someone. I was asked to come and help deal with you. After all, what good is a witch if she cannot help her neighbors?" She bared her teeth in a smile full of menace.

Gunnolf had never experienced panic before, and did not stop to analyze the unusual feeling. He turned around and started to run away, head lowered, tail tucked, ears laid back. But, again, his flight was cut short by an impact against an invisible wall. He fell to the ground, feeling increasingly groggy.

"I offered you a fair deal," remonstrated the girl. "Look." She picked the basket off the ground and lifted its lid as she drew next to Gunnolf. "Here is this chicken, which I was going to give you had we made a deal." She sighed with regret, lifting the bird and waiving it in the cold night air.

She went on: "The rest of what is in the basket, I brought because I feared we would not be able to come to terms. I have herbs ... and spices ... and vegetables ... and cooking implements." Her voice was becoming increasingly faint as a gray haze clouded Gunnolf's vision. "I am told that wolf meat is not as tender as dog's, but these are hard times, so we are willing to give it a try."

She picked up a large rock from the ground and, in a businesslike manner, struck Gunnolf on the side of the head once, twice, three times.

As consciousness failed and darkness surrounded him, Gunnolf had a last thought, more a fleeting sensation than anything: "It was a mistake for me to challenge a human, even a girl. Humans are the most ferocious of all beasts."

The Adoration of the Magi

A beautiful thing never gives so much pain as does failing to hear and see it.
Michaelangelo

Luigi Andreati threw himself on the floor, cowering, as the Austrian cannon shells hit the roof of his home, the ancient Andreati Palace on Mantua's Via Cairoli. On impact, portions of the palace's roof fell in, covering the public rooms with a layer of plaster, wood debris, and broken tile. Andreati was not injured but, as he got back on his feet, he surveyed with tearing eyes the magnitude of the disaster. It would take a lot of money to repair the damage, and he did not have it.

Shortly after the bombardment ceased, summer rains began. Water began pouring into the foyer, the reception room, and the ballroom, and soon the elaborate wooden floors were buried under a layer of stinking sludge. Andreati sought refuge in his private quarters, which like the chapel had escaped intact from the shelling; he was shivering with cold and fear, for he was certain that the Austrians would soon march into Mantua to retake the city from Napoleon's troops and he could lose his life in the door to door fighting that was about to break out.

His life was spared by the French commander's negotiating surrender terms so that by the end of July the French had marched out of Mantua. The ruined city, weakened by war, hunger and plague, was again occupied by the Austrians.

Escaping with his life was little consolation to Andreati. He was ruined and his palace was in shambles: a particularly grievous casualty was extensive water damage to a large Bernardo Bellotto oil depicting Venice's Grand Canal, which had been the main decoration of the southeast wall of the reception hall.

Luigi was the last surviving member of the Andreati family. He was a bachelor nearing fifty years of age and had no sentimental attachment to the palace or its furnishings. He was not particularly aggrieved by the damage to that painting, which he found uninteresting except for its ornate gilded frame, but knew it was a very marketable piece. If he sold it to one of the galleries in Paris or London, he could raise enough funds to finance repairs to his home.

But the damaged painting was unsaleable, so Luigi needed to find someone right away who could restore the Bellotto painting. In war-torn Italy in 1799, however, it was difficult to find competent restorers, and at any rate he could not afford to travel anywhere to find an artist that could bring the work back to its original condition. So, he visited Giacomo Gatti, a local painter, and asked for his help in restoring the Bellotto. Gatti demurred, for he was just a landscape painter and knew very little of art restoration. Andreati insisted, pointing out that Gatti could not ruin what was already a ruined work, and offered to pay him ten Florentine scudi for his efforts. Gatti was as hard pressed as everyone in Mantua those days and accepted the commission.

The first thing Gatti did was study the condition of the Bellotto. Two things were obvious: first, the beautiful gilded frame had escaped damage; second, water had found its way into the picture and had already caused mold to form in several places and produced significant discoloration in others. Turning the picture around, he noticed that the frame's backing was soaking wet and threatening to seep moisture into the back of the canvas and further affect the work. He decided that replacing the frame's backing was the most urgent task that needed to be accomplished. However, because of the war he could not get backing of the quality used by the original framer decades earlier, so he decided to substitute a local material. Shortly afterwards, while Gatti was starting to go over the mold-damaged areas, the new backing began to shrink and squeezed the front, including the painting, causing it to crack all over. The Bellotto was now damaged beyond repair.

"What a catastrophe!" exclaimed Andreati when confronted with the ruined painting. "Is there anything you can do to remedy what you have done?" Gatti was contrite; after offering a thousand apologies, he mentioned that the cracks on the picture had revealed that there might be another picture underneath, which had been covered by Bellotto so he could reuse the expensive frame for his Grand Canal scene.

Andreati was not a brave man: "I'm ruined! I may not even be able to pay you!"

Gatti blanched at the thought of not receiving his fee and replied very slowly: "*Caro* Signor Andreati, not such words, *prego*. There is one thing we can still do. Let me see if there is in fact something under this picture. If there is another picture, and it has not been ruined by the water intrusion and the shrinkage of the backing, it may be pleasing. If not, we will take everything out and at least sell the frame."

"Another canvas underneath this one? Is that even possible?"

"Very unlikely, but not impossible. Artists of the past were known to reuse valuable frames like this one. Sometimes, instead of removing an existing picture, they would use it as additional backing and superimpose a new blank canvas on top of it. They got the idea from medieval monks who wrote devotional works on parchment or vellum, which very expensive. To inscribe the new writings, they removed existing text using milk and wrote over it."

"Can you uncover the hidden canvas without ruining it?"

"Well, I can very carefully apply solvents, a little bit at a time, to loosen and ultimately remove the canvas containing Bellotto's painting and see what we find. I dare not rip the canvas out lest it damage the painting underneath. However, I do not know what damage the backing may have done, or if the Bellotto has bled through onto what lies below."

Andreati remained skeptical but consented. "Fine, go ahead. At this point we have nothing left to lose." He sighed. "Do it, but be very, very careful."

Gatti did just that. Using distilled water and a variety of solvents, he was able to remove first the varnish and then the paint of the Bellotto cityscape. As the

Bellotto canvas became blank, he was able to very gingerly lift it in a series of steps. He first focused on a small section on the lower right corner of the work and, after a week of trial and error, was able to peel off an area roughly the size of a pocket Bible. And yes, there was definitely a different canvas with a painting under the one that showed the turbid waters of the Grand Canal. "What is it?" asked Andreati eagerly. "I don't know" replied Gatti. "All I see is a dark patch that could be the ground. We probably need to remove the Bellotto canvas in its entirety before we can make sense of what the other one shows and determine its condition."

"All right, go ahead" urged Andreati. "Be as quick as you can, but still be very careful." The moment he said it he realized he was not making sense, but he was getting anxious – they were in mid-October already and his meager funds were being depleted quickly.

The palace was almost the only asset left in Andreati's possession; the other property he still held was a vineyard south of town, where the family had for centuries grown the Viadanese grape that was the main component to the Lambrusco Mantovano, a delightful red wine that was much sought after for consumption with cold cuts, pizza, and pasta dishes. The vineyard was Andreati's sole source of income.

The Viadanese grape harvest was concluded and the grapes had been crushed by the time Gatti removed two hand-widths of the Bellotto canvas. He had switched to work on the lower left corner, and what he had uncovered appeared to be the hind quarters of a white palfrey and the rump and back legs of a large dog. The colors were vivid and the figures seemed ready to leap out of the frame. Better yet, by some miracle the hidden painting seemed to be undamaged.

"Oh, that looks good," admired Gatti. "Whoever painted this knew what he was doing. Notice the delicate shape of the horse's legs and the detail on the dog's coat."

"Please, please," implored Andreati. "Can you finish uncovering this work? I get a good feeling about it."

"I do too" replied Gatti. "But we must take extra care to do this right and not damage the painting. I will go as slow as it takes," he vowed.

Andreati's impatience almost got the better of him, but with an effort he restrained himself from any further demands.

This was the time of the year when he had to take a trip to the *azienda vinicola*, the winery where his harvested and crushed grapes would be blended with other grapes in the process of making the Lambrusco Mantovano. The ostensible purpose of his trip was to collect from the winery owner the agreed upon price for his grapes. However, Andreati was hoping to negotiate an increase from what had been agreed in the spring. 1799 had been a fine weather year except for the summer downpours during the siege of the city, and the Viadanese grape crop from his estate had been abundant and of apparently high quality, so Andreati was hoping to get a better deal.

The winery owner, Fausto Pezzetti, immediately disabused Andreati of any notion that he would get a higher price for his product. Yes, the grapes looked and tasted great but the year had been terrible for business with the French and Austrian armies trotting up and down the countryside and shaking down landowners for all they could get. Pezzetti finished his tale of woe dramatically: "I may not even be in business next year."

Andreati and Pezzetti knew each other well, having done business together for many years. Thus, they engaged in a friendly but protracted negotiation that lasted a couple of days, during which Andreati was seething with ill contained impatience fearing the worst for having left Gatti alone with his picture. At the end, Pezzetti relented and offered a somewhat higher price than he had given earlier on, and he and Andreati shook hands and parted company.

Thus, it was an afternoon in the second week in December that Andreati rode back into Mantua. Upon arrival at his palace, he rushed immediately to the reception room where an absorbed Gatti was cleaning and slightly retouching the newly revealed picture.

And what a picture it was! Andreati gasped as in one glance he took in the colorful array of human and animal figures that crowded the canvas. It was obvious that the picture represented the Adoration of the Magi, the arrival of the Three Wise Men at the manger where Baby Jesus lay on Mary's bosom. But saying that did not quite do justice to the spectacle on display in the newly revealed oil.

The left half of the picture was taken up by several gaudily attired noblemen, their horses, esquires, and onlookers. At the center, the three kings from the Orient were offering their gifts; one of them, knee on the ground, was presenting a covered cup to Jesus, who sat placidly on Mary's lap as she showed the infant to the visitors. To the right, peasants on bent knees or holding lambs completed the tableau. The background was a serene landscape; every one of the figures had an individualized countenance and expression. Mary, in particular, was breathtaking in her ethereal loveliness; the composition was such that the eye of the beholder was immediately drawn to her and the infant she held. Indeed, those figures in the picture that were not looking away seemed transfixed by the scene that was presented before their eyes.

"It's beautiful" whispered Andreati in awe.

"And it's miraculously intact. I saw a picture like this one at a church in Perugia" said Gatti, wonderstruck. "It was by Raffaello Sanzio, one of the greatest artists of his time. But it was part of an altarpiece, and was rather small, although exquisitely detailed. This may be a later version by Raffaello, or a copy by one of his disciples, or a work by some other painter seeking to profit from the genius of Raffaello."

"Could it possibly be an original by the maestro himself?" wondered Andreati.

"No way to know. A painting like this should be in a church or in the vault of some moneylender in Firenze. It defies imagination how it could have ended in the hands of some ignoramus who would replace it with a banal scene like the Bellotto."

"Do you think I would be able to sell it for a good sum?"

"No doubt that you would be able to sell it in Milano or Venezia, and probably would fetch a decent price. But everyone would discount it as being the work of a disciple of Raffaello or some unknown third party, so you would never get as much as the Bellotto would have commanded."

"What are we talking about here? What is your best guess as to what this picture would bring?"

"Alas, I'm no expert on the sale of art, but judging from the prices that my landscapes are getting, you would probably be able to get at most a couple of hundred scudi for it."

Two hundred scudi. Financing the repairs to the dilapidated Andreati Palace would run to four hundred scudi or more. Two hundred was not enough.

Andreati had another idea: "Is it possible that we could find still another picture under this one?"

Gatti gave him a dirty look. "I would hesitate to damage this magnificent work, even if it's only a copy, on the remote chance that something better might lie underneath. See, it seems almost as if this picture wanted to be found and was protected from damage by the hand of God. I'm sorry, I will carry out your wishes if you ask me to tamper with it, but I will do it with a heavy heart."

Andreati stood silently in front of this probable imitation of a masterpiece by Raffaello. Suddenly, he felt how he was getting on in years, and shuddered at the prospect of poverty in his old age. Selling this picture would alleviate his predicament. He experienced the dilemma that many a gambler faces at the table: walk away with meager winnings, or put it all back on the table, casting caution to the wind and hoping for the best.

Except that here the gambler's impulsive behavior would mean getting rid of the marvelous work of art in front of him. Did he even have the right to sacrifice an object of great beauty just to help getting out of financial trouble? And what if the painting was indeed by Raffaello? Would that not be a crime?

He brushed those concerns aside as his pressing financial needs became again paramount. What did he care about one painting or another? It was only something to hang on a wall as evidence of your wealth. He was not wealthy and there was nobody he needed to impress.

Then, as his tired eyes were drawn to the Virgin Mary in the painting, Andreati realized that for the first time in his life he was in the presence of real beauty. He loved that painting and did not want to part with it. Life was ebbing away and he had little to show for his years on this world. If he kept the painting, he could give himself every day the satisfaction of owning a great work of art (whether original or not) and pretending that he owned a real Raffaello, something potentates all over Europe would wish they could say. More importantly, he would enjoy what nobody else could: admiring the beautiful Madonna who was there for his eyes only, like the adoring figures in the picture would be forever doing.

Besides, it was almost Christmas. What better present to give himself this holiday season? It had been a cruel year, but this belated gift made up for many months of suffering.

He decided to visit Pezzetti again and find out if the merchant would be interested in buying his vineyard. He hoped he could get a decent price for it.

Pezzetti agreed to buy the vineyard, but could not offer much. Andreati was thus faced with a dilemma: sell the vineyards for a song and spend the rest of his life in dire poverty, watching his palace fall into ruin; or sell the painting and live off the proceeds. It was a difficult choice to make, but the magnetic attraction of the picture prevailed.

In the summer of 1801, torrential rains drenched Northern Italy. During a vicious storm in August, the roof over the living quarters of the Andreati Palace collapsed, as did much of the rest of the once sumptuous structure.

Scavengers seeking to recover anything of value in the ruins discovered the emaciated corpse of Luigi Andreati under the rubble that once had been his bedroom. He apparently had been dead for quite some time, but the body was essentially intact, with little trace of corruption. The entire room had collapsed around him, but on the only wall still standing hung a magnificent Renaissance picture that seemed to shine with a light of its own and showed no damage from the elements.

"*É un miracolo!*" marveled the rescuers.

The picture was reverently taken down and sent to Milano for assessment. It was determined to most probably be a copy of a Raffaello miniature by some unknown artist, and thus have only scant market value. It was donated to the Church and placed behind the altar in a church in Mantua, where it is to this date the object of veneration by the faithful, in a manner not unlike the adoration it received from the late Signor Andreati.

The Lunar Moth

"What color moth do you want?"

The old man and his visitor sat on hassocks covered with a leather that was dark and cracked with age, in the spare mountain hut. They sipped autumn flush tea, savoring the amber liquid's musky flavor, while the old man readied himself to deliver his lecture for the thousandth time.

"I don't understand" replied the visitor, confused. "I want the best quality moth that you can sell me so my son will be a worthy successor. As I told you already, I am prepared to pay your price." He was attired in the costume of a Mongol fighting man: a heavy fur-lined green coat fastened at the waist by a leather belt encrusted with jewels, from which hung his sword and a dagger. The man was young, but projected power and ferocity.

"It is not a question of price, and all my moths are of the highest quality. The color of the moth signifies the virtues that it will confer on a newborn. There are four moth types. The red moth is called Fafnir. The gold moth is Smaug. Nithogg is the name of the black moth, and the jade one answers to Hydra."

"But what are their virtues? I want moths with the best virtues." The visitor was visibly impatient.

"Let me explain, your Grace." The old man got to his feet with some difficulty and poured some more tea into the visitor's cup. "Each moth can confer an excellent virtue on the boy or girl to whom it is offered. A red Fafnir provides courage and strength. A gold Smaug bestows the gifts of concentration, persistence and devotion to one's goal. A black Nithogg grants self-assurance and steadiness. The jade color in Hydra is the symbol of purity and restraint. So it is a matter of what virtues you would rather have your heir possess."

"I want them all!" cried the visitor. "Give me all four!"

A smile grew on the old man's face. "You don't understand. Each of these moths is a powerful entity that must be mastered if it is going to be useful. Failure to subdue a moth causes you to become its thrall and its virtues become vices. For example, a controlling Fafnir will turn those he inhabits into reckless and prideful beings. So, you must consider what virtue is most important to you and, having obtained the right moth, must be careful to nurture your child so that the moth does not become dominant over him."

"Does that mean that if I don't buy a red moth from you my child will be a coward?"

"No. Each child is born with his own set of inner moths. Even if you do not get a Fafnir from me your child may turn out courageous and noble. But buying my Fafnir moth guarantees that the virtues associated with it will be greatly enhanced."

The visitor's irritation grew. "I have traveled across barren steppes and endless deserts, I and searched for this valley for months, and all you offer me is something I already have? I should slay you for wasting my time!"

The old man shrugged, unfazed by the threat. "Tell me, was your wife pregnant when you left her?"

The visitor was taken aback by the question. "Of course not. I want to have a moth or two with me before my bride and I seek to make a baby."

"All is well, then. You can take a moth egg with you and deliver it before you make a child with her."

Curiosity got the better of the visitor's anger. He asked: "How will that work?"

The old man went to a cupboard behind a hanging bear skin, rummaged through shelves, and returned holding a bright red object the size of a tiny quail egg. "My moths are very small, as this egg demonstrates. All you must do is bring the egg back home and have your wife swallow it whole, washing it down with salted milk tea or airag. The egg remains unfertilized within her until you have coupled and a new life has been produced. At that point, the egg will enter through the baby's mouth just in time to hatch when the baby is born. It will then reside beneath the skin, on the base of the child's skull for the rest of his or her life."

"Will it become large, like a growth?"

"No. The moth will never be bigger than a baby's little finger, and his presence will be undetected by all, especially its host."

"If I take more than one egg, will the process be the same for each egg?"

"Yes, but do not to tempt fate by giving more than one egg to your wife. If you take two moths and they remain untamed, their character flaws will feed on each other. In addition, having two moths sitting next to each other in one's skull will cause headaches and other discomforts."

The visitor continued to be unhappy by these restrictions, but finally shook his head resignedly. "My father traveled to see you many years ago. He was the one who urged me to seek you out. He claims that I have a red moth in my head, and thanks to his oversight during my early years I have grown as fearless and proud as he is. I will follow your advice and take only one egg."

"Wise move" agreed the old man. "What color moth do you want?"

"Ours is a nation of warriors, and is always in need of heroes. I shall take a red."

Without further ado, the old man deposited the small red egg on the visitor's hand. "Beware. These eggs are very sturdy and are protected by magic, but still can break. Carry it in your undergarments, close to the warmth of your body, and make sure you do not take a fall or otherwise drop it. Now, for my payment...." The old man extended a hand and the visitor extracted a vial from his silk undershirt, replacing it with the egg he had just purchased.

The old man took the vial and asked with a mixture of greed and suspicion: "Is this fresh?" The visitor pursed his lips with disgust and replied: "Yes. I drew it this morning. Do you want to see the arm from which I took it?"

"That will not be necessary. Thanks. Your offering will sustain me for many months." Then he gave a formal bow to his customer. "Happy roads and good luck to you and your family." The visitor returned a curt bow, turned, and whisked away into the darkening afternoon.

***

Over the course of generations, the moth merchant exchanged thus his wares for blood with those who risked the perilous trip to his abode. Most of his customers bought Fafnirs or Smaugs, a few chose Nithoggs, almost none fancied Hydras. The results of their selections were for the most part predictable. Seldom did the Fafnir buyers succeed in imposing discipline on their offspring, so the ruling classes continued to be full of prideful men who led their subjects into bloody wars. Those Smaug children that were properly reared became renowned scientists, prolific artists or prudent and crafty rulers. Less fortunate Smaug children became misers, unrestrained collectors of trinkets, alchemists in endless search for the philosopher's stone. Well-raised Nithoggs grew to be diplomats, compelling figures on the stage, magnetic preachers. Unrestrained Nithoggs were melancholic souls, often led to suicide or destructive behaviors such as addiction. Successful Hydras becoming revered religious leaders, even saints. Failed hydras reveled in sex, food, drugs, gaming, and dissolution.

The moth merchant seldom followed the trajectories of those receiving his wares. The only cases that attracted his interest were those in which a buyer had insisted on getting pairs of moths, because those instances always resulted in noteworthy calamities. Children with Fafnir and Smaug moths invariably became ferocious, greedy rulers bent on conquest and pillage. He could recall three of those, and each had brought about the end of a period of civilization. Fafnir and Nithogg combinations led to people who were anti-social, disdainful of others, and heartless; the recipe for a criminal, and the merchant could trace two of the worst among these monsters to his clients. Fafnir and Hydra combinations led to overbearing pleasure seekers; Smaug and Hydra produced notorious libertines; and so on.

But business is business and the merchant pursued his trade without considering the consequences of the sales he made. "There will always be misery and sorrow, yet the world endures, and so do I."

***

Yet there came a time when heroes and sages were no longer valued. The number of visitors to the secluded hut decreased, and ultimately stopped altogether. Deprived of sustenance, the merchant felt himself growing older and weaker, and began to experience fear. What was he to do? He experimented drinking blood from goats and sheep, but animal blood barely nurtured him and did not stop the ravages of aging. He prepared himself to die.

He was lying on his cot one night, half dreaming of flying astride an eagle that was carrying his body through a cloudless sky towards Heaven, when a noise shattered his stupor. Someone had entered his hut.

With difficulty, the old man forced his rheumy eyes to focus on the newcomer. It was a woman, veiled and dressed in a white robe adorned with delicate pink trimming, wearing a formal white headdress with a pink peony in the middle: the funeral garments of a Chinese dowager.

"Are you coming to claim me?" he asked, trying to steady his voice.

"Your fate is unimportant. What matters is the business that brings me to you."

"What is that?"

"I come to offer you a bargain that you may not refuse."

After a silence, she continued: "I will extend your life for a thousand years in exchange for a service."

"What kind of service?"

"I want you to breed a new kind of moth."

"A new kind? There are only the four kinds I sell."

"You are a powerful wizard. You must use your magic to create Pai Lung, the lunar white moth of death."

"What sort of moth is this, and how do I create it?"

"You have to combine the properties of your moths in such a way as to make the resulting moth make his host wish to terminate all human life and be powerful enough to accomplish it."

"Terminate all human life?"

"All."

"Will this moth kill me as well?"

"You will survive for the period I offer you. Perhaps you will be the last man left alive."

"But why would I agree to something so terrible?"

"Because if you do not, you will die this very night. So, choose: instant death or a thousand-year reprieve."

It was a dilemma. The old man loved life, and had clung to it for centuries by drinking man's blood. What if the world was destroyed?

But he did care. His Fafnirs and Smaugs and Nithoggs caused pain, misery and carnage, but their effects were transitory. Pai Lung's effects would be drastic, and much as he disdained mankind, he hated the idea of bringing death to everyone on earth. He queried:

"Why do you want to extinguish all human life? Isn't it enough for you to take us one at a time?"

"My motives are not your concern. Maybe I am just tired of my job."

The old man then tried to play for time:

"How long do I have to decide on your offer?"

"When the first light of the new day seeps under the door of your hut, you shall die unless you have agreed to my proposal." With that, she vanished.

It was the longest night of the old man's life. Conflicting memories struggled for his attention. The women who had spurned him. Serving a cruel master who rained blows and lashes on him, not caring for his suffering. His humiliating banishment from society for practicing his art. The kindness of a beggar who had shared a bun with him, when he was an abandoned orphan. A wedding ceremony in which the couple's love for each other shone with a light brighter than a thousand torches. A man, during an earthquake, running into a collapsing building to rescue a child and tossing her into the safety of her parents' arms as he was buried under a torrent of brick and mortar. After the same earthquake, the looters that ransacked the ruins and robbed and slayed the survivors. On and on: glory and shame, good and evil.

Finally, the decision was made for him through his overwhelming tiredness. As the first light of the morning seeped under the skin that served as door to his hut, he faced the reappearing figure in the white shroud and declared in a weak voice: "I will do it."

***

He spent many months applying his magic to the task of transforming one of his eggs into that of a lunar white moth. At the end, he succeeded in turning a Nithogg egg into the pale white moth egg with the properties he sought. He was pondering how to let Death know of his accomplishment when the skin at the entrance to the hut was drawn aside and a young woman walked in.

She was beautiful, with milky white skin and glossy raven hair that cascaded down her neck. She wore a yellow gown of the purest silk and, except for a gold pendant with a large inlaid pearl, wore no jewelry or other adornment. Even though it was a cool spring day, she wore no outer garments. The old man wondered how she had managed to make it across the mountains.

"I have come for the Pai Lung egg" she declared, without preamble. The old man nodded, silently greeting Death's emissary. He ambled to his cupboard and returned with a round egg, white as snow except for a few dark speckles like pinpricks. "Here it is."

"It is imperfect" declared the girl, eyeing the speckles warily.

"I am sorry, it is the best I was able to do. If your mistress wishes to wait, I can spend more time trying to come up with a more perfect specimen. But be assured it works."

After a long pause, the girl held out a small hand. "I accept it. It will be my companion until my nuptials, and then we shall become one with each other. I will raise my child with this egg in him, all its powers unchecked."

"And when will I get the promised compensation for my efforts?" asked the old man testily.

"Here" said the girl, handing him a flask full of an amber liquid. "Drink this. You will never experience hunger and will never need to feed again."

The old man seized the flask, tossed away the stopper, and drained the liquid in three long gulps. "It does not taste all that …." He never finished the sentence, and dropped in a heap to the hut's floor.

"Nobody said Death plays fair," said the girl and disappeared.

***

Folk tales from that period tell of a beautiful princess who had a most wonderful child, a son who was pale as the moon and handsome and strong and clever, and grew to be the ruler of his country. As the prince came of age, however, he became heartless, tyrannical and obsessed with power, and soon proclaimed his intent to dominate the entire world and bend it to his will at whatever cost. He launched one war of conquest after another, until the remaining nations banded together and raised the most powerful army ever to be gathered under one flag. There was a titanic battle between the prince's forces and those of his opponents. The battle lasted for weeks, and took the lives of thousands. At the end, though, the prince was defeated and had to seek refuge in his underground stronghold, with the enemy in hot pursuit.

He was prepared for the possibility of this final encounter. Together with his wizards and scientists, he had developed a weapon of unimaginable power. Once unleashed, this weapon would extinguish all life for many leagues and its vapors would rise in a mighty column that would pollute the air as it traveled around the globe, poisoning all lands which it touched. "If the world is not mine, it will belong to nobody," he declared.

As the enemy's charge broke through the barricades that protected the stronghold, the prince sat alone in his command room and grasped the lever that would ignite the weapon and destroy the world. The Fafnir in his soul growled with rage. Smaug pressed him on towards the culmination of his plans, and Nithogg shouted with dark despair his hatred for mankind. Yet a small voice in his heart pleaded for the preservation of all that was beautiful and good and deserving to live. It was a tiny bit of Hydra that the old man had smuggled into the egg, causing the speckles shown on the its surface – a Hydra that, unlooked for, had escaped the warping of the prince's soul and now sowed doubt into his plan.

The prince debated with himself only for a few seconds, before the other moths drowned the pleas of the Hydra. But these seconds were enough: before he could press the lever and activate the weapon, an enemy soldier broke into the room and thrust a lance into the prince's heart.

No human ears could perceive the keening screams of the dowager, nor could mortal eyes see her figure as she bent over the fallen prince to claim him. And it would have taken superhuman discernment to understand Death's reproach: "That old merchant did not play fair, either."

Gwarwyn Goes Fishing

Gwarwyn was a *bwbach*, a humanoid known outside Wales as a brownie. He dwarfed other creatures of his kind, and thanks to his keen senses of sight and hearing he could perform for his human hosts tasks not usually given to *bwbachs*, such as protecting domestic animals from wolves and other predators.

Early on Whitsuntide evening, Gwarwyn had gone fishing on the river Neath, taking advantage of the summer weather. The Neath ran a meandering course through southwestern Wales until it plunged into the Horseshoe Falls, not far from where Gwarwyn had positioned himself. He stayed on the bank, because although the river bed was gravelly and gave good purchase, the current in the stretch leading to the falls was swift and there was always a chance of slipping.

As he sat on the river bank, the evening sky darkened and threatening clouds rolled in from the west. Gwarwyn was unaware of the change in the weather, because his eyelids had turned heavier and sleep had overtaken him.

He looked up with a start. His keen hearing had detected, some distance away, the sound of cries. The sounds were approaching, so he moved back from the bank a little trying to get a view of whatever was causing the commotion.

Finally, the source of the disturbance became visible: a raft was heading down the river, coming in his direction. The cries were emitted by a human female that was clutching a seat on the center of the structure as it moved randomly, drawn here and there by the current.

Despite the darkness, it took only a glance for Gwarwyn to recognize Anwen – the daughter of Tudur ap Gruffydd, a wealthy landowner in the kingdom of Dyfed. Tudur was one of the humans for whom Gwarwyn worked, tending to his fields at night and protecting his lambs from predators.

Gwarwyn had sometimes spied on Anwen when events drew him abroad during daytime, like county fairs and religious festivities. She was always nicely dressed, always smiling. A couple of times they had run into each other in the manor house's kitchen, where every evening Gwarwyn was left on the hearth food (oatmeal cakes were his favorite), clothing items, and other presents, all intended to entice him into staying at the estate.

In each occasion they met, Anwen had averted her face with disgust and left without addressing him. Gwarwyn had greenish skin, was very hairy, and had a wrinkle-covered face, all of which made him unsettling or frightening to some humans.

Gwarwyn had secretly longed after Anwen. He often admired from afar the perfect oval of her face, the softness of her body. Yet, he knew she loathed him.

As the raft approached, Gwarwyn noticed that Anwen's auburn hair, which he had always itched to caress, was shooting in all directions, buffeted by the breeze. She was pale as if she had seen a ghost, and trembled as the raft made steady progress towards the falls.

Gwarwyn jumped into the river and, as he did so, a strong wind began to blow, gathering intensity until its blasts swept the countryside. The wind roiled the waters and impeded his progress as he swam towards the raft, which was rising and falling with loud splashes, its timbers lifted and tossed by the force of the storm. Gwarwyn's considerable strength served him well, as he was able to overcome the tumbling of the frenzied Neath as he approached the vessel.

At last, Gwarwyn seized the side of the raft, coming close to being brained by a sudden jolt of the structure. He clung to the slippery logs for dear life and, with a wrenching effort, pulled himself onboard. In the back of the raft, Anwen watched him in horror, her fear of the elements eclipsed by the sight of a creature in soaking rags that came tumbling towards her with obviously evil intent. She recognized Gwarwyn, and seeing him brought back the memories of their meetings and the multitude of folk tales she had heard about brownies' malevolence.

Gwarwyn reached her and extended a hairy hand, beckoning the girl to join him. "Come on, lady, let me carry you out to safety," he grumbled. Anwen did not move but rolled herself into a defensive ball as he approached. "No, go away, dirty *bwbach*, leave me alone!!" she cried, clutching desperately at her seat.

"Come on, please, there is no time to waste!!" Gwarwyn insisted, and reached out to seize her arm. She pushed him away and got up, lurching towards the side of the raft, intending to go in the river.

As Anwen readied to jump off, Gwarwyn thrust headfirst at her, trying to stop her from plunging to a certain death. She flung her arms out at him in a protective move. They collided and catapulted together into the water. The impact with the water drained at once all resistance from Anwen, who clung to Gwarwyn, gasping.

Gwarwyn looked at the girl and then at the raft, whose surface had almost disappeared from sight. There was a crushing sound: the raft had been propelled against a protruding rock and had splintered into a thousand pieces, disintegrating from bow to stern. Gwarwyn clutched Anwen's body closer to his and covered her body with his to protect against the flying wreckage.

The forward pull of the river as they approached the falls became stronger. Gwarwyn made out a disturbance in the waters ahead, a vortex into which the floating detritus was being drawn. He put his left arm around Anwen so that he could steer them both clear of the raft remnants that sailed past them in the current. He tried to push the floating objects away with his one free hand as the river thrust them against him. The ones he could not avoid hitting he met with his body to save the girl from injury.

The falls came into sight. Gwarwyn looked around anxiously, searching for a way out. The river banks were near but out of reach, for the current kept him, burdened by the girl's weight, from making headway towards the shore. There was nothing left to hold onto; even the wreckage from the raft had gone into the abyss. Gwarwyn stretched his legs as far down as he could, but failed to touch bottom.

The waters became white with froth, and broke into an irregular circular motion. Gwarwyn could tell from the mist rising about the surface that they were about to start gyrating and plunge down the falls to their deaths. The maelstrom was only twenty feet ahead. Then, he saw something that stuck out of the water from a pole at the shore to another in midstream -- a thick rope net strung just above the whirling surface of the river. Wreckage from the raft, tree limbs, roots and rocks were caught in the net's webbing, as well as countless dead fish.

Gwarwyn felt relief rise in his chest, to be squelched by the realization that they were likely to be impaled on a sharp piece of flotsam or a nail-covered board. He maneuvered with inhuman strength, further increased by desperation, to find a relatively empty corner of the net. He found one and allowed himself and the girl to be slammed into it.

The ropes that formed the netting gave a little so their impact against them was not too painful, but the strain of the rushing waters pushing around them towards the falls made Gwarwyn feel as is his flesh was being strained into a liquid mass that would be sucked in by the net and then released into the maelstrom.

With a supreme effort, Gwarwyn began to advance towards the shore along the netting, holding onto one of the tie lines. He had to let go of Anwen's body, who mercifully continued to cling onto him. Hand over hand, inch by inch, he made the excruciating trip along the rope, resisting the push of the stream that drew them towards the falls. Twice he faltered and almost let go; each time, Anwen's groans gave him renewed strength and saved them both from certain death. He continued advancing until at last his feet found the gravel at the river bottom. He half walked, half propelled himself and Anwen towards the river bank.

Before reaching the safety of the shore, they came upon a large moss-covered boulder by the water's edge. Gwarwyn laid Anwen down on the rock, prying her fingers loose, as she would not let go of him. With an exhausted sigh, he collapsed on the rock next to her. He could go no further.

They lay there for a very long time, recovering from the shock and the pain that throbbed through their bodies. At last, Gwarwyn turned over on his side and contemplated the girl. She was wearing a jerkin over a plain blouse, loose fitting brown trousers and leather boots – not unlike his own uniform. Her jerkin was torn and open, and her breasts heaved up and down under her blouse with her irregular breathing. She was slowly regaining consciousness, shuddering from the cold.

Anwen's hair was matted and covered her eyes. Gwarwyn ran his hand over her forehead to straighten it out, and halfway through his gesture it became a gentle touch. Unable to control himself, he let his hand slide over her cheek and traced with his index the curve of her upper lip.

Anwen opened her eyes and looked vacantly into Gwarwyn's face, just above hers. "Are you hurt?" asked Gwarwyn in a soft voice, holding her chin in his hand.

Anwen then gave a start and came awake. She said nothing but put her arms around Gwarwyn's neck, as if seeking reassurance after their near-death experience. Gwarwyn pivoted on his free arm and let his body drop carefully beside Anwen's. They stared at each other without words, still prey to the terror they had just shared.

On a sudden uncontrollable impulse, Gwarwyn pressed his lips against the girl's in a stream of kisses, at first soft and then increasingly more passionate. Anwen did not resist but responded in kind: she tore away at his tunic, which bunched up over his shoulder blades exposing his bruised and wounded muscles.

Regaining his senses, Gwarwyn sought to restrain himself. It was not right to take advantage of their ordeal to abuse this human girl who abhorred him. He flexed his arms and raised his body to walk away. Yet, Anwen pulled him in, and sought to resume their kissing.

The surprising way Anwen was behaving caught Gwarwyn in a surge of desire. They embraced again and then undressed hastily, fingers fumbling over buttons and clasps. When their bodies were freed from all bonds,

Gwarwyn seized Anwen's wrists and held her outstretched arms above her head as he entered her.

Joined, they rose and fell in a wild, arrhythmic concert. Their faces pressed against each other, now rubbing tenderly, then bumping at random. At last, they sighed and embraced one last time, eyes closed; they then passed out, dead to the world in their ecstasy. Around them, the rain stopped, the river grew calm, and only the crashing sounds of the falls and the calls of night birds broke the evening silence.

When Gwarwyn rose from her body, it was dawn and the moon was starting to sink below the horizon. He lifted Anwen's head up and brushed her eyelids with the tip of his tongue. Her eyes opened and he kissed her slowly, all urgency gone, savoring the taste of salt, blood and sex in her mouth. As their lips separated, Gwarwyn ran his hands on her wet hair, finally completing the gesture that had initiated their lovemaking.

Gwarwyn reached over his side and groped for his tunic, which he took in both hands and wrung out, releasing as much of the filthy water as he could. He sat on the boulder and found Anwen's own blouse and jerkin, which he wrenched dry and handed over to her, repeating the operation with their trousers. Not a word was exchanged while they were getting dressed.

When he was ready to speak, a multitude of questions assailed him. "What were you doing alone on a raft in the river in the middle of the night?" He asked softly, to avoid sounding reproachful.

She gave a rueful smile. "I was running away from home. I was intending to float only a few hundred yards until I reached the landing at our neighbor's estate, where I meant to steal one of his horses. Once in the raft, I discovered I could not guide it because the current was too strong."

"Why were you running away from home?"

Anwen's reply was full of bitterness. "My father wants me to marry Ormund Rhys, a swine if there ever lived one... I'd rather die than live with him. But, of course, now ..." She broke off.

"Now what?" asked Gwarwyn anxiously.

"Now I don't have to worry about marrying him, or anyone else. I hope my father will allow me to hide in a nunnery to wait out the rest of my days. When he dies, I will be free to do as I desire."

"But Anwen," protested Gwarwyn. "I love you and will marry you and will make you forever happy as my mate."

"Me marry YOU?... My family would never consent, and we would face universal rejection. ... And ... me marry an unclean *bwbach*?! How could I live with you, who are not even human? What would happen when we had our first fight and you turned into an evil *boggart* bent on hurting me?" She seemed so vehement in her rejection of the marriage proposal that Gwarwyn did not have time to get offended.

Finally, he shook his head with a grimace. "I would never have hurt you. It's not allowed to those of my kind to commit physical violence upon humans. ..." He tried to say much more, but words stuck in his throat. "But you're right. I am a *bwbach* and can't wed a human. Let's get you back to your family." He helped her out of the rock and together they waded towards the bank of the river.

As they got to the shore, their wrenched garments were starting to dry, clinging to their bodies. They halted for a moment to rearrange their clothing.

"Well, we best go on our separate ways," he declared. "I won't tell anyone what happened, but will remember you forever. Please try to be happy."

"I'll have to tell Father that my maidenhood is lost, but won't say it was you who took it. Go in peace." Anwen turned around and started to draw away. Then, suddenly, she came back and kissed his cheek. "I'm sorry. I'll always remember you. You were kinder to me than any man I've known."

She walked away without looking back again.

Gwarwyn sat on the ground, his breast heaving. He had known love and tasted despair. He bent the head on his chest, and uttered a disconsolate moan. The memory of an unrealized dream, of lips that had passionately touched his, would remain with him for a long time.

He glanced around. The morning was advancing and there was not a cloud in the heavens. The Neath ran placidly as it flowed towards the falls.

He gathered his pole and fish basket. His fishing trip had ended leaving him empty-handed and with an ache in his heart. It was time for him to move.

The Girl, the Wyvern, and the Talking Ape

"Magical pendants are so overrated" bemoaned princess Adelfa as she rubbed again the iridescent stone that hung from a chain around her neck. "Can't get this one to do anything for me."

Adelfa glanced around and pressed her stuffed monkey against her chest. She declared, a bit melodramatically: "Why should I, a princess, be imprisoned in a filthy tower like a criminal?"

She knew the answer only too well. Her father had been a just king, who had tried to do his best for his subjects. His care for the common folk had placed him at odds with the aristocracy. When a spate of noblemen led by that despicable earl had revolted against him, her father had been defeated and slain. She had been seized and confined to this tower. Only the earl's ambition had saved her life: His plan was to force her into marrying him, thereby quelling popular unhappiness, and allowing him to become the legitimate ruler of the country.

Of course, she had resisted his advances and spent the last three months languishing in prison. Bread and water and a cot hard as stone had been her fate. Other than the guards who came twice daily to bring her food and empty her chamber pot, she was alone, her stuffed monkey her only companion. She could look out of the barred window of her cell and watch life go by, but nobody could hear her cries for help and probably would have done nothing to assist her even if they could. She was alone and desperate.

"Oh, Bananas, why did my fairy godmother give me this pendant if it was going to be of no use? I'm supposed to get three wishes fulfilled by rubbing on the stone. But I rub and rub, to no avail. I ask for this tower to crumble, for the doors to my prison to open so I can get out, and it's all for nothing. What am I doing wrong?"

Bananas did not answer, but for one fugitive second Adelfa thought she saw a gleam in the toy's glass eyes.

Adelfa pouted. (She was already fourteen, but had not yet abandoned a tendency to pout for which she had been often scolded by her tutors.) Then, willfully, she seized Bananas with one hand and rubbed the pendant with the other, repeating the incantation her godmother had taught her: "O, holy stone, grant me a boon. Make Bananas able to talk to me, so I will have a companion in my misery."

There was a brief flash of light, as if a thousand candles had been lit and then gone out. Before her astonished eyes, the little cloth monkey shook itself from her grip, dropped to the floor, and began growing until it was almost Adelfa's size.

"Oh, Bananas!" cried the princess. "What happened to you?"

There was no immediate response. The creature before her stretched and contorted, adapting to its new size, and then grimaced, as in the grip of some inner pain. Finally, it looked at Adelfa and declared in a husky voice:

"Nothing, my Lady. Thanks for liberating me. I feared I would never regain my true self."

"What do you mean, your true self?"

"Please allow me to introduce myself. I am Cymon, prince of the clan Ouroborus."

"No!" she cried in shock. "You are Bananas, my toy monkey."

"Excuse me, my Lady, but I am actually a chimpanzee, an intelligent ape never to be referred to as 'monkey.'" His broad mouth curved down in disapproval.

"I beg your pardon. What I meant is that up to a moment ago you were a felt toy no larger than my arm, and now you are almost as big as I am. What happened?"

"You did this yourself. You asked the pendant to make me capable of talking. It did that, and it also reverted me to my natural form. The pendant does more than just what you ask."

"But I did it only as a joke. I' have asked a thousand things from the pendant, and it has done nothing."

"Yes, I have been watching. My impression is that you have always asked the pendant to do physical things, like crushing stone or moving objects. I think it only works at modifying living beings like you and me."

"What a worthless piece of junk!" retorted Adelfa angrily. "That's of no help in my situation!"

"Perhaps," said Cymon. "But maybe if we can get out of here, your remaining boons may prove useful."

"But how am I going to get out of here!!?" cried Adelfa.

"There may be a way. The guard that brings your evening slops, he comes around sunset, is that right?"

"I think so."

"Next time he comes, I'll create a distraction so you can slip out of your cell. Once you are out, you may be able to escape. I'm sure someone will give you shelter."

"I don't know, it seems risky."

"Yes, but what do you have to lose?"

"I guess nothing. If I stay here, I will die or, worse yet, be forced to marry that monster."

"So there. Better dead than a slave, I say."

Adelfa was not happy with those choices, but reluctantly nodded in agreement.

Getting out proved easier than Adelfa had expected. As she heard footsteps approaching, she placed herself behind the cell door. When the key rattled on the lock, she held her breath in anticipation.

Cymon stood two paces back from the entrance. And as the guard entered carrying a tin plate and an earthen cup, the chimp jumped up and down and made guttural noises that rattled the surprised soldier.

The guard cursed and made a pass at the crouched figure, dropping the plate and cup with a crash. Cymon was too fast for him, though, jumping up and down and sideways to all corners of the cell, foiling each attempt at capture. Meanwhile, Adelfa quietly slipped out of the cell door and marched quickly down the corridor towards the stone stairs at its end.

Before she reached those, Cymon emerged from the cell with the guard in hot pursuit. Adelfa began racing down the long flight of stairs as fast as her body allowed. She was reaching the bottom when Cymon caught up to her, running with inhuman speed.

The guard had stopped chasing after them and, instead, was blowing a whistle to summon help.

Adelfa and Cymon reached the courtyard and were heading for the forest across from the tower when several soldiers emerged, merged from all corners of the castle, carrying swords, pikes and other weapons.

Cymon, who' had been looking in all directions seeking an escape route, caught the girl's arm and forced her to make a sharp left turn in the direction of a donkey that stood grazing on the sparse grass of the yard, unperturbed by the commotion.

"What...?" began Adelfa. Cymon did not give her time to complete her question. He pointed at the donkey and said: "That ass. Ask your pendant to turn it into a swift steed."

"But..."

"Do it, there is no time to lose."

Adelfa rubbed the pendant and said, panting as she tried to catch her breath: "O holy stone, grant me a boon. Turn this donkey into a gallant steed that can carry me away, fast as the wind."

No sooner had she finished uttering the words of the incantation, the twilight gloom became bright as day and the donkey, braying in surprise, was enveloped in a cloud from which emerged a dragon-like creature, the size of a horse, hovering in the air above them and landing with a thud in front of the princess.

Adelfa was petrified with fear at the sight of the beast. It was metallic gray in color and had enormous wings that flapped constantly in the afternoon air. Its two stubby legs did not provide support for its body, so it balanced precariously on the ground with the aid of a long tail that ended in a sharp tip. As it opened its snout it showed two rows of sharp teeth and a deep throat from which drooled greenish saliva.

Adelfa turned around to flee, but Cymon seized her arm, dragged her towards the apparition, and commanded: "Sister wyvern, bend down so we can mount you!" The wyvern growled but obeyed, and girl and ape climbed with difficulty onto its hard, scaly back as the first of the guards reached them.

The soldier grabbed Adelfa's leg and tried to unseat her, but the wyvern flicked its tail and gave him a vicious lashing that sent him sprawling several feet away.

"Well done," encouraged Cymon. "Now take us down that road, as fast as you can."

The wyvern wasted no time. Flying so fast that it became only a dark blur, it sped away, with Adelfa and Cymon hanging to its scales for dear life.

"Where to?" inquired Cymon.

"Let's head west. My uncle's domain is that way. If we can reach him, he will protect us."

"How far do we have to go?"

"I'm not sure. I' have been there only once, when I was very young. We went on a carriage driven by four identical black horses .... The ride seemed to take all day, but I slept through much of it. In any case, we need to follow the westward road."

"Great," sneered the ape. "We don't know where we are going, nor how long it will take us to get there." The wyvern made no reply, as it continued to dart away.

They flew through the night, and well into the morning hours. Finally, Adelfa cried with a voice made hoarse by exhaustion: "We need to stop and rest. I can go no further and it does not appear that anyone is following us."

Cymon thumped on the wyvern's neck and directed: "Sister, take us to that copse of alders and drop us there. Gently."

"We need to give this dragon a name. What should we call him?" asked Adelfa as she gingerly dismounted, every portion of her body sore from the uncomfortable flight.

"Her. It' is a female wyvern, not a dragon."

"Why did the pendant give me a wyvern? I would have been content with a horse."

"I don't know. There must be something about a wyvern that makes her preferable under the circumstances. You saw how she dispatched that guard."

"Let's call her Lightning, because she moves as fast as anything I've seen."

Adelfa turned to the wyvern, which was looking at them attentively, as if following the conversation. "Wyvern, from now on you shall be known as Lightning, and I will sing your praises to all we meet."

Lightning growled.

They found a nearby stream and Adelfa rinsed the dust off her face as best as she could. She and Cymon drank deeply but their thirst was replaced by a growing hunger.

"How far are we from your uncle's land?" queried Cymon.

"I don't know," replied Adelfa uncertainly.

"We best get going, again" replied the ape. They remounted Lightning and headed again towards the lowering sun.

As night approached, it became obvious that they were lost. The road they were following for so many leagues had narrowed to a dirt track and the landscape had become more barren, with no farms or other signs of human habitation within sight. "On my trip here, maybe they made a turn while I slept, and I missed it," acknowledged Adelfa ruefully.

"Let's find a safe place to spend the night and wait until the morning to decide what to do," suggested Cymon.

There was no shelter to be found so they slept in the open, Adelfa resting her head on the ape's shoulder. They had no food or fire and it was bitingly cold. Adelfa had never felt so miserable.

As the first rays of the sun broke over the horizon on the east, Adelfa struggled herself awake and rose, chilled to the bone and stiff as if her body had turned to leather. Cymon was already up and presented her with a handful of berries. "This is all I could find," he said apologetically. Adelfa took the berries and chewed on them. They were sour and tasted of wilderness, but she ate them anyways. They barely made a dent in her hunger.

"How about you, Cymon? Did you find anything to eat?"

"No, my Lady. But do not worry. We Ouroborus are a very sturdy breed."

"What are we going to do? I fear that forging ahead on this road is insane and may be our death. We have no food, no warm clothes, and no idea of what lies ahead."

"I hate to say this, my Lady, but I think we must go back. Maybe before we get to the castle we'll find the turnoff we missed."

"Back to my prison?" asked Adelfa, disconsolate.

"Remember the old saying – where there is life there is hope."

So, they climbed again on Lightning's hard back and Adelfa told the wyvern in a whisper: "Please take us back. Sorry for all the trouble." Lightning snorted and started flying back the way they had come.

They had been on the road half a day when Cymon got up with a start on top of Lightning's back (a maneuver that almost tumbled Adelfa down to the ground) and pointed at something ahead of them. "What's that?"

Soon Adelfa saw what had got the chimp so excited – a large cloud of dust, moving in their direction and approaching rapidly.

"Horses, many of them, coming at us in great haste."

"Can we hide somewhere?"

"No. The shrubs in these parts would not shelter a cat, and Lightning is too large to conceal."

Soon the riders came close enough that they could see their faces. The earl was at the head of the party, grimy with dirt and sweat. He was handsome, though cruelty had left a permanent grimace on his face.

He reined his horse when he was under Lightning and inquired, with evident irritation. "Princess Adelfa! What is the meaning of this escapade? Aren't you liking my hospitality?"

Adelfa scowled at him and spat her reply: "You murdering thief! I wish you were dead!" As she was not grasping her pendant, the wish was not granted and the earl's demise was not forthcoming.

The earl uttered a derisive laugh. "My pretty thing. Soon I will make you my bride and teach you who is boss."

"Never!" Anger colored her shout.

"We shall see. For now, let's get you back to your quarters. I have a special treat in store for you."

The nature of the treat never got revealed, for in that moment Lightning shot down and took a huge bite of the withers of the earl's horse, just before the saddle. The wounded horse collapsed to the ground, carrying the earl down with it in a tangle of human and animal limbs. The earl lay under the horse, unmoving.

Every man in the earl's coterie advanced threateningly towards Adelfa, weapons drawn, ready to face off to Lightning.

Clutching the pendant, Adelfa spoke: "O holy stone, I seek one final boon from you. Please make all the men here love and cherish me and offer me their allegiance as their rightful sovereign."

The flash of light that ensued after these words did not seem as bright as the previous ones, and Adelfa wondered whether the plea had been effective. She needed not have worried. One by one, the soldiers lowered their weapons, dismounted, and bent one knee on the ground in recognition of her majesty.

Adelfa waved her hand acknowledging their vow. Then, turning to Cymon, she asked quietly: "The earl is still alive. Should I order him killed by his own troops?"

"Not yet, my Lady. Let's see what he does."

The earl was visibly hurt. One leg, trapped by his falling horse, appeared broken, and he had cuts and bruises all over his body. Laboriously, he got up, bracing himself on the chest of Lightning. In a faltering voice, he hailed Adelfa: "Alas, sweet princess. How badly I have used you. Can you possibly find it in your heart to forgive me?"

Adelfa became torn between conflicting emotions. A moment ago, she had hated this man who had wronged her so deeply, who had taken away her father and her kingdom, and all the happiness in her short life. Now, however, he was broken and begging her forgiveness. What to do?

Cymon came to the rescue. "The greatest rulers are those that temper justice with mercy. If you set him free, you will have shown yourself to be a worthy successor to your father, and will set you on the course to a happy reign. Slay him, and his friends and allies will fight you to the end."

Adelfa turned her attention to the earl, who was gasping for breath and appeared near fainting. "Earl, I am willing to forgive your misdeeds as long as you swear your fealty to me and promise to make your supporters do the same. Is that agreeable?"

"Yes, Your Majesty," said the earl with a faltering voice.

Adelfa patted Cymon affectionately. "Thank you." Turning to Lightning, she declared: "I don't know where you came from, but I shall be grateful to you forever."

"My Lady, we only did what a friend would do," replied Cymon. "Your gratitude is accepted but not required. But watch that earl carefully, in case he changes his mind in the future."

"But how could he do that? Isn't he compelled by the pendant to stay loyal to me forever?"

"Ah, but who knows?" responded Cymon, with a mischievous wink. "How long will the pendant's gifts last? For all I know, I could turn back into a toy any minute!"

"Oh, Cymon, nooo," groaned Adelfa.

"Pardon me, my Lady. I was only jesting. But grant me a lifetime supply of bananas, and I'll stay like this forever." And he winked again.

Whistles in the Forest

Bigfoot exists, along with Nessie and the Jersey Devil. Their formal discovery will happen tomorrow, next week at the latest, and won't you feel silly when they are?
Thomm Quackenbush, Holidays with Bigfoot

His small frame and the green scales that covered his body blended with the foliage of the tall trees; even his flaming orange hair would pass for a clump of bright flowers. It was good camouflage, and this was fine by him, for he enjoyed being left alone, invisible to the humans.

Sure, sometimes there were sightings. On occasion, a woman washing clothes on the river bank would catch a glimpse of him as he moved swiftly to rescue an animal caught in a snare or a bird about to be devoured by a caiman. When that happened, he would flee rapidly, leaving confusing prints on the muck, for his feet were set backwards.

"It was a *curupira!*," the woman would shout excitedly to others in her Tupi language.

But, for the most part, he and humans did not interact and he was able to carry out his mission of protecting the animals and trees that inhabit the jungles of the mightiest of all rivers.

Things changed when a different sort of humans, pale skinned and hairy, arrived in the jungle. They carried metal rods that spewed thunder and lightning and went on to kill or enslave the Tupis. From time to time, he would observe the newcomers' murderous actions; they disgusted him, but they did not cause concern, as human affairs are unimportant.

But more pallid humans kept arriving, bringing darker humans as their thralls. The masters and their slaves felled trees and burned wide swaths of jungle to clear the land and make room for their plantings to grow and their strange animals to roam. Forests started disappearing and, with no trees to release their moisture into the passing clouds, rain became scarcer, causing more plants – and the animals who subsisted on them – to perish.

He did all he could to oppose these destructive men. He was not a violent creature, and limited himself to playing tricks against the invaders. His whistles could resemble the calls of birds or the noises of animals; hunters would follow these sounds and get lost in the woods. Loggers would run away when he imitated the growls of jaguars and other ferocious animals. He could also emit eerie human noises that scared the colonists.

Sadly, his efforts failed to impede the spoliation of the land. The virgin woods were assaulted by the human *marabunta*, even more destructive than the army ants they resembled. He grew afraid that the humans' appetite for destruction would extinguish millions of plants and animals and turn the jungle into an arid wasteland. He had to do something.

***

He inflated himself to a size that would resemble that of an adult human and walked into a settlement in broad daylight, taunting the inhabitants to capture him. At first, the villagers ran away, hiding inside their cocoons, the smell of their fear burning his nostrils. Finally, the bravest among them approached, armed with fire sticks and other weapons. As they gathered around him, he spoke. His words were in rudimentary Tupi, a language to which he had been exposed for many generations. None of the villagers understood Tupi, but as they continued to encircle him they fetched someone, a very old and wrinkled female that belonged to that nearly extinct variety of human that had been around for as long as there had been human life in this jungle. Their conversation, such as it was, went as follows:

[He]: "Do not fear me. I come in peace with an important message for you and your kind."

[The woman]: "What are you?"

[He]: "I am the *curupira*. I am the guardian of the woods and the streams and all the plants and animals that populate this domain."

[The woman]: "But you don't exist. You are just a legend we use to keep our children from misbehaving."

[He]: "I am real. I have come to tell you and your kind that you must cease what you are doing. You are killing this forest and leaving behind a wasteland. You are blindly causing innocent animals and plants to die, fertile soils to turn to sand, rivers and streams to dry out. If you continue, the young among you will grow into misery and poverty. I command you to stop."

[The woman]: "I am only one of the few survivors of what was once a large and powerful tribe. These people killed us off, as they are killing the land. I can convey your message, but they won't believe the truth of my words. Even if they believe me, they won't do anything about it. Their hearts have turned to stone, and they don't care what they do to others or themselves as long as their desires are satisfied. Yet, your words and mine are being recorded. I hope against hope they will listen."

[He]: "I do, too. And now I must go."

Then, the *curupira* sought to break through the knot of his would-be captors and disappear into the jungle, but he could not outrun the firing sticks. Four bullets pierced through the cryptid's scale-covered skin. He halted, ran his hands over the holes where the shots had entered, took one last ungainly step, and fell to the ground.

His pursuers approached the *curupira*'s body, which still convulsed but finally stopped writhing altogether. One of the leaders among the villagers turned the corpse over with his boot: the protector of the wild's open eyes stared blindly at the vast canopy of the forest. The leader gave one last casual kick at the cadaver, as the rest of the villagers crowded around it.

"What was that?" asked someone.

"Who cares?" replied the leader. Then: "We need to get moving. This section needs to be cleared by the end of the week."

There was the shuffling of dozens of feet. Later, except for the cries of an old Indian woman, the forest became silent. But soon would be reawakened by another creature that would continue the fight against the invaders.

The Mapinguari

Here comes the Mapinguari singing aww
"So Long Old Bean" by Devendra Banhart

For time beyond memory, a giant stood guard over the vast expanse of the Amazon River basin. His seven-foot body was covered by a thick, matted layer of greenish fur that had the texture of wild grass. He lacked a mouth, but had an eating orifice in the center of its torso, containing three rows of serrated teeth. His feet turned backwards, ending in claws that left groove marks on the ground. His rigid face was dominated by an enormous, single eye. As he lumbered about the wilderness, he occasionally uttered a deep roar that resonated like the sound of faraway thunder.

The primitive humans that inhabited the Amazonian jungle called him the *mapinguari*. When alerted of the cryptid's proximity by his overwhelming stench, they shied away lest they be caught in the beast's deadly grip. He, for the most part, ignored the two-legged apes and devoted all his attention to protecting the animals and majestic trees in his domain.

The *mapinguari*'s attitude towards humans changed when a new kind began to appear, a few centuries ago. These were mainly pale creatures who set out to raze the jungle. The cryptid then started going after the trappers, the loggers, the cowboys, the farmers, and others who committed acts of desecration against the land. When he corralled a human walking alone in the forest, the *mapinguari* would seize the man's body and bring it to the gaping mouth in his midriff, from which emanated an unbearable odor of decaying flesh that was the last sensation the man would experience before being crushed by the monster's teeth.

As the number of his victims grew, fear rose in the hearts of those trying to tame the forest, and they reacted by organizing hunts to destroy the monster. The *mapinguari*, however, knew intimately each corner of the wilderness. Men would see him only when he chose to reveal himself, and this usually occurred when an opportunity for slaying one or more of them was available.

One day he found himself surrounded by an angry mob of settlers. They lunged at him with torches, and shot at him with firing sticks. The bullets, however, ricocheted off the dense fur of the *mapinguari* and the fire from the torches only left smoking patches on the cryptid's skin, releasing a fetid odor that nauseated the men. The *mapinguari* then charged back at the humans and slayed most of them, letting only a few escape to serve as a warning.

In a later encounter, the *mapinguari* came upon one of the leaders of the men who were bringing down the forest. The man was armed with a rifle and a bull whip, and frantically used both weapons in an attempt to arrest the monster's attack. However, as bullets whizzed by and the bull whip's sonic boom resounded, the cryptid advanced rapidly on the man, hoisting him in the air and crashing him on the ground, an action he repeated until the man's body had been reduced to a pulp. The *mapinguari* then bit off the head of the corpse and carried it away.

The *mapinguari* then went to the village where that band of settlers lived. He was carrying as a trophy the severed head of the man he had just killed. He intended to confront the villagers with the gruesome evidence of his revenge, but could not do so because the village was deserted, its inhabitants having fled in fear of the cryptid's attacks.

The *mapinguari* discovered, at the edge of the village, the hut of an old Indian woman who was too infirm to escape. She lay on a pallet, breathing laboriously, impending death showing on her features. For a moment, the *mapinguari* felt a touch of pity. However, he put feelings aside and addressed the woman in broken Tupi, the Indian's language:

[He]: "Hail, human."

[The woman]: "If you are Death, hurry up and finish your work. I suffered enough already and was left to die by all who knew me."

[He]: "I am not Death, but a living creature. I have come to let your kind see how I avenge myself of their crimes against this land."

[The woman]: "They are all gone."

[He]: "Yes, but they will pay for their arrogance with their lives. I shall continue to chase and slay everyone I find."

[The woman]: "Please do not take your vengeance on every one, deserving as they are of punishment. Just give them a warning. Maybe they will listen."

[He]: "There will be no more warnings. You humans are destroying the world and deserve to be exterminated."

[The woman]: "At least dump the head you are carrying on the village square. Maybe those who return will understand your message and act on it."

[He]: "I do not expect they will change, but I will do as you ask."

The Indian woman closed her eyes forever and the *mapinguari* walked away from her hut. He leveled every dwelling in the village save hers and left the severed head protruding from a sharpened stick, buried in the ground in the middle of the square.

The cryptid then retreated to the heart of the forest. He knew his mission might eventually have to come to an end, because he alone could not stem the tide of devastation that humans, like fire ants, were visiting on the Amazonian jungle.

Years have gone by, and a standstill of sorts has been reached. Development ground to a halt in the corner of the river basin patrolled by the *mapinguari*, but men continue their path of destruction everywhere else.

The cryptid now realizes that, other than protecting the sanctuary he has established, he cannot chase away the humans that continue to arrive. But he is not discouraged and feels that his fight must continue. If at the end all resistance fails, he will at least have the bitter satisfaction of knowing that, in destroying the greatest forest in the world, men are be bringing utter ruin upon themselves.

The Tenth Symphony

If you give me five years to write a symphony, I'm still going to be asking for more time two days before its due.
Darren Criss

Death comes knocking at your door at the most inopportune times.

Take the case of Dmitri Ivanovitch Petuleff. Not that he was young when the black robed skeleton appeared before him; no, he was in his sixties and had known for months that his liver cancer was fatal and his exit from this world was approaching. Yet, the specter's appearance took him by surprise, as he crouched at his piano trying to milk a few more notes off his tired brain.

"Go away" he challenged the visitor. "I'm busy."

"It does not matter," replied the phantom inexorably. "Your heart is about to fail. Come!"

"Please, not yet! Wait just a couple of hours! I'm nearly done here!"

"Death waits for no one. I hear the same plea from just about every mortal who faces me."

"My case is different. I'm on the verge of completing a monumental achievement!"

"Which is?"

"I'm composing the last few bars of my tenth symphony. I have most of the phrases figured out in my mind. I only need to flesh them out and complete the orchestration…"

"And why can't someone else do this after you are gone?"

"Because what I want to do will provide a sublime, unexpected ending that will bind together all the main themes of the symphony and render it unforgettable. Nobody else can do this but me!"

"Assuming that is true, why does it matter? What is so special about this symphony of yours?"

"Look, I've written a lot of music in my life, including nine other symphonies. I have met some recognition and success, but I'm no Beethoven or Mahler. This work will raise me to the rank of the immortals. It will be listened to centuries after I am gone, if only I can complete these last few bars!"

"So, your vanity is what is at stake here. Right?"

"Not just my vanity. Great music elevates the souls of the people, makes their existence better while they wait for you. I'll be forgotten shortly after I am gone, but this symphony, if I get to finish it, will endure. You owe this small gift to the multitudes you'll be taking after today. Just give me at least a few more minutes!"

"I said I do not wait. But a war plane just dropped an incendiary bomb on a hospital. Many are dying in terrible agony. I must prioritize collecting those casualties. You have a few moments respite. Use them well!"

***

He sat at the keyboard and focused on the love theme from the third movement, recalling how he meant to integrate the delicate melody into the crashing finale he envisioned. His progress, however, was interrupted by a rush of memories of his beloved wife and children, lost one way or another in the tides of the years. He recalled the tender embraces, the whispered words of passion, the glowing logs in the fireplace casting points of light and shadow on their faces, the one perfect summer afternoon all five of them had spent at the shore…

He shook himself away from those thoughts and started drafting a rising motif for the strings, underscored by the brass and the timpani, when again other memories intruded: his bitter fight for acceptance at the conservatory, a fight that had ended with the grudging recognition of his talent by director Smolensky; recognition, but never full acceptance due to his mixed race, rural background, rustic manners; his eventual success…

He was still lost in reminiscences about his triumphs and failures, his loves and losses, when there was a chill in the room and the hooded figure reappeared to stand in front of the composer, still bent over the piano, his fountain pen scribbling on the manuscript paper.

"Let's go!" commanded the figure, raising a skeletal finger to summon the composer.

"No! I need more time!" implored Petuleff.

"There is never enough time!" replied Death, making an irrevocable summoning motion with its outstretched arm.

"Oh, well, maybe the memories were worth the loss..." started the man. There was the shadow of a smile on his lips as he clutched his chest and tried in vain to right himself up.

***

The nurse found Petuleff on the floor. There were cuts on his face and hands from his fall to the ground; his body was cold and rigor mortis had set in. Also on the floor was a jumble of papers, the manuscript of a score he had been working on when he suffered the fatal heart attack. One of his students picked up the loose sheets reverently and arranged them in proper order. The last page showed an irregular diagonal ink stain that ran down from the middle of the page to its edge. Upon review, it was determined that the stain originated on the incomplete last bars of the Finale, and appeared to be the start of a variation on a theme from the preceding Adagio. It was not obvious where the composer was going with this when death overtook him.

Efforts were made to correct a few errors on an otherwise polished score and add a coda, a short climax to the main body of the movement. The codas that were generated by composers and conductors were either trite or bombastic and did little to enhance Petuleff's music, other than putting a final period on an interrupted sentence. One critic likened the efforts to complete Petuleff's final symphony to adding the missing arms to the Venus of Milo: workmanlike, but uninspired attempts to match the scope of the original artist's conception.

Petuleff's tenth symphony received its premiere three months after the composer's passing. The work was well received but, perhaps encumbered by its hobbled ending, never found a place in the pantheon of everlasting classics. In generations to come, only musical archeologists would dig up the memory of Petuleff and his many compositions, including his unfinished tenth symphony.

It would never be known whether Petuleff would have succeeded in achieving a brilliant ending for the work. Perhaps the world was not all that worse off for the loss, in comparison with the joy the composer experienced in the last moments of his life.

Alfhildur and Posthumous

The unicorns were the most recognizable magic the fairies possessed, and they sent them to those worlds where belief in the magic was in danger of falling altogether.
After all, there has to be some belief in magic — however small — for any world to survive.
Terry Brooks, The Black Unicorn

The mythical creatures sat around the Great Mage's banquet table for a final gathering before dispersing throughout the universe. Their host raised his cup of ambrosia and toasted:

"This world has failed us. Humans no longer believe in magic. We must abide elsewhere until their folly has come to an end and man regains his sense of wonder. But we will leave one of us behind to serve as our sentinel. He will send us the signal to return when the time is ripe." He motioned for his underling to rise. "Alfhildur, one of my assistants, has agreed to become our secret eye on earth for however long it takes for the change to come about. Let us drink a cup in his honor." He took a sip of the pinkish liquid, and all others who had mouths did the same. Alfhildur, a slender, youthful-looking *ljósálfar* with a luminous face so beautiful that those who looked at him had trouble staring away, bowed slightly at his master and joined in the toast.

The Great Mage continued. "But his wait may be a very long one, so I propose we give our elvish emissary a companion. One who will be his friend and supporter, who will carry his load and give him counsel and succor in an hour of need." He halted again and pointed to a gigantic iridescent egg that lay on the center of the table. "I give you Posthumus, the last unicorn, destined to be born in a world that no longer believes in his kind." There was a murmur of approval throughout the hall.

"As soon as he breaks out of his shell, we shall all leave this Earth – minus Alfhildur and Posthumous, that is."

Two days later, Posthumous cracked open his shell and emerged into the world. Although relatively small at birth, he was soon to grow into a magnificent stallion, the color of fresh fallen snow. He was swift and graceful, and when let loose on the castle's yard, he started to run in excited circles, impatient to go out into the wild and explore the land beneath the tor that held the Great Mage's castle.

At this point the Great Mage came out into the yard and issued a calming gesture with his right hand. Immediately, Posthumous stopped and inclined his head in homage to his master. The Mage addressed elf and unicorn:

"From this moment on, you will become friends and constant companions. Alfhildur will lead and Posthumous shall obey. The labor that has been assigned to you may be of long duration and will at times prove tedious and dangerous. While you are in the air, you will look like just another moving cloud, invisible to those below. Once you land, however, you will be visible and draw instant attention. Be wary: humans tend to attack those they do not know and may try to cause you harm. Remember: your job is to see and listen, not to engage. Do not get involved in the affairs of mortals and at the first sign of trouble you must retreat. You may use magic for your protection, but only as a last resort. Travel safely and come back to us when your mission is completed. Have a safe journey, and fare well!" The Mage bowed his head in salute and retreated.

Alfhildur got on the unicorn, and together they rode out of the castle's main gate, into a world from which all other magical beings had already departed.

***

Alfhildur and Posthumous then engaged in a melancholic task that extended through years and then centuries. They would travel across the world, seeking for a spark of understanding in minds that had become obsessed with power and greed, too full of themselves to extend beyond the limits of their ignorance.

The pair did not touch the ground except to satisfy their corporeal needs. Food was often scarce, shelter perilous. Through luck and skill, they escaped many a close encounter with death at the hands of bandits or when they found themselves unwittingly enmeshed in a battle between opposing armies. Each traveler provided aid to the other in escaping these threats, which became more difficult to avoid as the humans devised increasingly effective ways of doing harm to each other. They frequently felt weary, but soldiered on to carry faithfully the work that had been assigned to them.

***

They went over tall mountains that seemed to nearly scratch the heavens, crossed deep rivers and sand-covered deserts, and at length arrived at a plain where bright wildflowers dotted the ground and tall trees swung in the summer breeze. *Let's rest here for a bit* suggested Alfhildur into the mind of his steed. *I am tired of witnessing the horrors of human behavior.*

Posthumous descended in a slow spiral towards a brook whose waters flowed gently towards some distant sea. As they approached the ground, they became aware of a discordant note in the pastoral harmony: a small girl, wrapped in colorless rags, was heaving up and down by the edge of the stream. Coming closer, they could hear her desperate sobs – all the woes of the world seemed to have coalesced into a figure that was too tiny to contain them.

Alfhildur dismounted and approached the girl. He could read the girl's mind and, roughly understanding all at once the nature or her grief, sought to console her, using his seldom employed human language: "What is your name, little one?"

The girl interrupted her sobbing to respond in a single breath: "Aleida."

"Why are you grieving, Aleida? What have you lost?"

The girl stopped sobbing once more and replied: "My little dog... was snatched away by a bird of prey" and resumed her desperate crying.

"Oh, that is so sad" replied the elf. "But perhaps you will get another dog."

"I can't!!" cried Aleida in despair. "Spark was not just a dog. He was my friend, my faithful companion, my eyes!!"

"What do you mean your eyes? ..." started Alfhildur, but the question died on his lips as he felt in his mind the explanation in the unicorn's thoughts: *She is blind!*

Alfhildur came next to Aleida and she grasped the elf's legs, seeking comfort from her grief. As the elf tried to free himself gently, the unicorn spoke in his mind again:

This one is pure of heart and has experienced a real loss. Can we do something for her?

Alfhildur rejected the compassionate thought, as he done other times: *We are here only to observe and report. We must not become involved with the tragedies of humankind.*

For once the unicorn rebelled against his companion's admonition. *You may be allowed only to act as an observer, but I am not entirely bound by your rules.* Coming closer, he entered Aleida's mind and offered, more in the form of an emotion than through words: *Here, take my gift!*

Posthumous then projected his consciousness into the girl's mind and deposited his sight into her brain. Immediately, Aleida opened her eyes and in one glimpse captured the beautiful panorama around her and, further, as far as the horizon and beyond, the multitude of images stored in the unicorn's mind as they were emptied into hers.

You cannot do that!! screamed the elf silently. *Have you gone mad? I command you to cease helping her!*

Posthumous considered whether to disobey his master, and realized he was not permitted to do so. He uttered the equine equivalent of a sigh and withdrew his senses from the girl's mind, perhaps expecting that she would become blind again.

However, the unicorn had left a trace of his visual ability behind, and an unexpected compromise was achieved: the magical horse's sight was almost entirely restored, leaving him a little nearsighted; Aleida was now almost blind, but could see a short distance into her surroundings. She uttered another cry, this time a mixture of awe and pleasure. Enjoyment of her newfound vision was only tempered by lingering grief over the loss of her faithful dog, for some losses are too grievous to ever be entirely overcome.

Why did you do it? remonstrated the elf.

The girl was innocent and her grief sincere. What is the purpose of having magic if it cannot be used to help those who merit it?

Alfhildur did not agree with his companion's deviance, but let it pass, considering that their mission would not be harmed by an occasional transgression. He shrugged his shoulders and bounded atop the unicorn. They were almost immediately gone from the girl's presence, but not from her memory.

***

Aleida became a famous artist who, time and again, would transform the brief vision of the world granted to her by Posthumous into paintings that superimposed figurative images of a unicorn or an elf against a moving, colorful abstract background that reflected her emotions at her newly-discovered world. Her art evoked strong positive reactions from its viewers and she became one of the most popular painters of her era.

She was once asked in an interview why she kept including in her painting fantastic figures with no connection to the real world. Her answer was emphatic:

"I paint what I believe in. There is magic hidden in this earth, and it's the duty of each one of us to seek it, and find it if we can. If we all do this, sooner or later magic will be with us again and the world will become a far better place."

***

Sometime after their encounter with the blind girl, Alfhildur and Posthumous found themselves crossing a mountain range in the northern corners of the Earth. A fierce ice storm was raging, pelting the travelers with pellets of frozen rain. Seeking shelter, the unicorn's senses detected the existence of a cave on the side of one of the mountains, and the steed and his rider barged into the cave to wait out the storm. No sooner had they entered, they realized they were not alone: several humans were massed against the far wall of the cave, seeking to share their body warmth against the gelid wind and rain that blew in through the opening.

They were two families: four adults and six children altogether. They wore animal coats, but were shivering, panting, and clinging to each other. Alfhildur dismounted and approached the group. Standing by a bearded man who seemed to be their leader, he asked in one of the tongues that humans used in those parts: "What are you people doing in this cave? Did the storm catch you outdoors?"

The man shook his head and responded to Alfhildur's question with another: "Are you a demon, come to finish us off? Can't you just wait a little bit until we all die from the cold?"

"I am not a demon" replied the elf. "Just a visitor from far away. But tell me, you are unarmed and are accompanied by several young ones, so you do not appear to be part of an army."

"We are no army. We are farmers from south of here, trying to escape from a band of lawless men that has been moving through the land sacking, burning, and murdering everyone. My neighbor and I saw them coming towards our farms and took our families and the few things we could carry and tried to cross the steppe and these mountains to reach a village on the other side. Our mounts died from the cold and we stopped in this cave two nights ago and then the storm caught up with us. We are done!"

Pothumous stood by the entrance of the cave, but projected his mind onto that of his companion. *Are we going to help these people, or let them die?*

Alfhildur frowned. *You know the answer to that question. We have been through this before.* His thoughts, however, bore a slight tinge of uncertainty.

The unicorn insisted: *Six children! What wrong have they committed?*

Do not try my patience! You know my orders!

Posthumous did not repeat his plea, but a few moments later came back with a new thought: *Say, I am feeling a bit cold. How about you?*

The elf knew magical creatures like Posthumous were impervious to heat or cold, and detected the subterfuge embedded in the unicorn's thoughts. He winced and replied: *Fine, I will give us some warmth.* Pointing to the ceiling of the cavern, he muttered a few words. Instantly, a wall of flame appeared on the rocks, as if they had turned into burning timbers. A pleasant warmth filled the air, extending through the entire area – including the corner where the humans were huddled.

The humans turned their heads to the flames with an amazement that soon turned to joy. Then, following the example of their leader, they cast themselves to the ground in adoration, exclaiming excited words of thanks and praise.

The storm abated several hours later and Alfhildur motioned the unicorn towards the exit. *Let us go, now. I have had it with hiding in this hole like trapped mice.* And then he remarked to the leader of the humans: "You are safe to go now. Good luck!"

The unicorn, with Alfhildur on his back, took to the air before the astonished eyes of the knot of humans. As their figures below became smaller, Posthumous praised his companion: *That was a good thing you did.*

The elf's response was a bit surprising: *I have been mulling in my mind for some time whether following your instincts is a better approach than strictly adhering to our mission. It is. We were asked to look for signs that humans were finally ready to believe in magic. Those people below are now believers, because we used a bit of magic to assist them in their plight. I will report my observations and suggest that, if humans are to go back to believing that magic exists, we must give them some evidence that such is the case. I hope they will agree.*

The Fractious Familiar

A familiar is such a creature, an animal or bird that sees inside
to the very soul of its human companion, and knows what others might not.
Alice Hoffman, Magic Lessons

Bronwen was going to be late for the coven, and this upset her.

It was her familiar's fault that she would be tardy. He, a black goat named Raven, kept importuning her with pleas for attention, butting his horned head against the lower extremities of his mistress and bleating raucously. Raven could not speak, but was so closely in touch with her soul that Bronwen could easily understand the animal's demand to be taken to the meeting.

"Disruptive animals like you are not allowed at the Witches' Sabbath," Bronwen vocalized. Then, entering the simple mind of her companion, she promised: "If you behave, I'll bring you crunchy leaves and a carrot or two."

Raven resisted his mistress' entreaties. An image formed in his mind that Bronwen, after puzzling for a while, was able to interpret. "You want to fly with me!?" she asked, incredulous. "You are too heavy to be carried on my lap and everyone knows that goats can't fly."

Raven was strong willed and not so easily dissuaded. An intense emotion flowed from his mind to hers. "Teach me how to fly, then!!"

Exasperated, Bronwen shoved the familiar away and replied brusquely: "That's impossible! Now, go to your bed and wait for me! I won't be gone long!" She opened the door of her hut, dragged out her armchair, sat down, and uttered in her mind the familiar spell. In a moment, the chair took off, carrying her into the gloomy night.

***

The objectives of the witches' meeting that evening were resistance and revenge. The country's king had ordered the extermination of all witches in his domain, and armed soldiers were already marching through the land seeking the hideouts of the worshipers of the Enemy. The witches that were captured were killed on the spot; if there was any lingering doubt about the culpability of a suspected witch, she would be tried and burned at the stake, to join her martyred sisters.

"We have to do something to stop the carnage!" declared one of the younger witches. "But what?" queried another. Finally, one of the older members turned to Bronwen and whispered: "What do you think we should do, sister?" Bronwen, who had remained silent up to that point, rose from her chair, cried out for attention, and addressed the gathering: "Rulers only acknowledge their errors when truth bites them on the rear. We need to hurt the king badly so that he will learn to leave us alone!" A witch interrupted her with a question: "Hurt him how?"

Bronwen threw her hands in the air and continued: "I will turn my familiar into a fire-spewing dragon and bring death and destruction upon the king's palace. With luck, the oppressor will die in the attack. Death to the king!"

"Death to the king!" bellowed the entire congregation.

***

As the armchair flew her back home, Bronwen began harboring misgivings about the undertaking she had promised. Raven was a mild animal, though often wayward and stubborn. He might not be fierce enough as a dragon to accomplish his mission and slay the king. Worse yet, his attempt could result in his death at the hands of the king's soldiers. If that happened, she would perish as well, since no witch can survive the death of her familiar.

She reached a wrenching decision: she would ride Raven on his quest and guide his actions. They would succeed or fail together.

Meanwhile, Raven was chagrined at being abandoned by his mistress and having his yearn to fly denied. He raced back and forth the four corners of the hut, trying to find respite from his discomfort. One of his gyrations had him stop before the table where Bronwen's open spell book rested. A vague idea took hold of him: the recipe for flying was in those papers and, if he consumed them, he might learn how to course in the skies without need for his mistress' intervention. He approached the volume and began chomping his way through its age-embrittled pages.

He was still noisily devouring the treatise when Bronwen opened the door and came in. She noticed immediately the ravaged book and the bits of paper lying on the table and the floor and hanging from Raven's beard, and realized the magnitude of the disaster. She let out a scream and, with a wave of her hand, blew the goat away towards the rear wall, into which he crashed with a bang. He remained there, whimpering.

Ignoring her familiar's distress, Bronwen picked up the remains of the book. Only a few, half devoured pages remained between the calfskin covers. The words of all her spells were gone, save for those still present in her memory.

She experienced another shock when she thought of the transformation spell she would need to use to turn Raven into a fierce dragon. She had never needed to cast a dragon transformation spell, though she had used similar ones to make spoiled meat edible and turn rats and other vermin into specs of dust. Transforming a goat into a dragon might require the exertion of more power, but should be the same process.

She summoned Raven and led him outside the hut to a nearby clearing. There, she ordered him to be still and started pronouncing the ancient words of the spell as she remembered them, while at the same time focusing her mind on the creature she desired to create.

She finished the spell and looked at Raven, who regarded her back curiously. He had not changed at all.

Frustrated, she tried casting the spell again, increasing somewhat the emphasis she lay on some of the most critical phrases. Again, nothing happened. Without the spell book at hand, she was hostage to her memory, which had obviously deteriorated over the centuries. She would have to go to another witch, perhaps Orenda, and ask for help. But this would be embarrassing, so she would make one last try first.

She repeated the words of the spell slowly, dropping them one by one, closing her eyes and making a maximum effort to concentrate on her desires: creating a dark, horrifying winged beast that she would ride to make battle with the king.

When she opened her eyes, Raven was gone. Bronwen let out a desperate cry and dropped to the ground, expecting to die any moment, victim of the miscast spell that had also slayed her closest friend and companion.

A few moments passed. Then, Bronwen heard a persistent buzzing overhead. She looked up and, circling above her head, flew a large black moth, flopping its dark wings vigorously. Her mind contacted that of the tiny insect and Raven's consciousness melded with hers.

There had been a change, though. Raven now flew deliriously back and forth, letting himself at times be carried by the night air. Her familiar no longer felt like a goat and seemed to be enjoying his new condition better than his former life.

Could Bronwen attempt again to transform Raven into the dragon she wanted, or try to return him to his original shape? If she tried and failed, she might kill them both. She could no longer rely on him to behave as a fierce dragon and, if Raven returned to his former life as a goat, he might resent Bronwen for taking his new freedom away.

Bronwen returned to the hut. She would visit Orenda and the two of them might come up with a new plan for dealing with the king. For the moment, she felt that respecting the feelings of a lower creature, even one as humble as a moth, was an important aspect of her mission in life.

She would, however, have to find a way to retain a flying bug as a familiar, or persuade Raven to accept returning to his former shape. But those were problems for another day.

End of Term

From the ashes, a fire shall be woken, A light from the shadows shall spring...
J.R.R. Tolkien, *The Fellowship of the Ring*

Bennu, the bird with a soul of fire, flew to the shrine of Sun God Atum-Ra in Heliopolis and prostrated himself before the unseen deity. It had been a long flight across the sands and the dark waters and Bennu was exhausted, but it was fear more than fatigue that made him drop his wings and shiver in the presence of his master.

"You have summoned me, O Lord, and I have rushed to come before you. What is your command?"

The response from Atum-Ra came out of the air like a burst of thunder that shook the walls of the ancient structure. "You know well what I desire." There was a momentary pause, as if the God allowed Bennu to acknowledge his understanding; but the bird remained in sullen silence. The voice then continued: "You have served me well for five hundred cycles of the seasons, carrying my commands to man and beast and seeing to it that I am properly worshiped throughout creation. You have grown old in my service and now you must come to rest. You will be consumed by my fire, and out of your embers will rise your successor, to continue your mission for yet another term. Make yourself ready to disappear into the eternal void."

"But Lord" countered the bird, finally regaining his voice despite the terror that paralyzed him, "I do not want to burn. If I turn to cinders, I will be gone for good, and there will be nothing left of me."

"Not so," replied the voice of Atum-Ra. "I shall cause a new phoenix to rise from your ashes, fresh and young, identical to you down to the tiniest tail feather, except for his renewed strength and vitality."

"Maybe he will be *like* me, but not *me*. *I* will still be gone. There will be no resurrection for *me*."

"Bennu, how dare you defy the laws that I have set in place to govern the world's existence? Have you forgotten that your duty is to serve at my pleasure for as long as I command it, and not beyond?"

"I know my duty, but I'm not quite ready to discharge it to its ultimate conclusion."

"Why not?"

"Every day I have spent in my service to you has filled me with pleasure. I have watched humans raise tall temples and humble tabernacles in your honor, and witnessed and partaken of the sacrifices that they have offered in their altars to placate you and the other Gods. I have soared through the skies in the soft mornings of spring and the warm summer afternoons. I have eaten the sweet fruits of the earth and drunk its nourishing waters. I have felt the caresses of the breeze, the gentle kisses of the rain. I have endured high winds, crashing thunder, and blinding lightning. I have savored living in all its manifestations.

"My heart still beats strongly in my breast. My feathers are brittle and faded, but they still gleam at the touch of the rays of the sun as I wander aloft. I know the paths I must follow and am familiar with the ways of men and the gentle or fierce disposition of the beasts in the field. Please let me stay around a bit longer!"

The unseen deity spoke again with a stern voice that was a touch less peremptory than before. "What you ask for is not possible. Everything mortal has a destiny that must be fulfilled: a beginning and an end, a course to be completed and ended with nothing to follow it. I will, however, grant you a boon. You may take to the air one last time and fly as long and far as your wings can carry you. When you touch the ground, I will smite you and create a successor from your ashes. He will bring your remains to me and I will hold them next to my throne forever, and that will be your measure of immortality. Fly away, take a last look at the world — and then you must go."

Bennu uttered a grunt that reflected his dismay and inclined his body forward in obeisance. Then, forgetting for one moment his weariness, he rushed out of the temple and rose into the air, experiencing again the gentle touch of the breeze and the sights and sounds of the vast world that opened beneath his body. Alas, fatigue soon returned and, after two or three circles around the human habitations of Heliopolis, the bird began losing altitude and, despite beating his wings feebly, dropped to the ground.

Bennu felt a sudden burst of gratitude for being granted this last flight. Then there was a sharp snap, like a whip being brandished in the air, and the firebird burst into flames and was consumed instantly, leaving only a mound of ashes to mark his passage through the world. There was another snap, and some of the ashes rearranged themselves into the body of a large, beautiful bird with a prominent fiery crest, red, orange and yellow plumage, and bright blue eyes that shone with youthful intensity.

The newly risen phoenix punctured a wound on a nearby myrrh tree to bleed its gum, and shaped the liquid, as it hardened, into a waxy shell. The phoenix gathered the cinders that remained of his predecessor, dropped them into the shell, and flew back to the temple in Heliopolis to deposit the remains before the presence of the sun god.

The new phoenix then withdrew to carry out his duties for the first time, armed with a knowledge and dispatch that were imparted on him by the one left behind. For he retained all the memories of his predecessor, and in so remembering him at every turn, kept him pretty much alive.

Another chapter in the eternal cycle had just started, yet the progression of phoenix deaths and rebirths would continue for as long as the Gods ruled this earth.

Henrietta: A Fable

The amorous rabbit kept his hold and remained where he was, but then the moment of her being conquered was come; she squatted herself as all hens do, which after having run away from the cock, consent at last to admit his caresses; she let the rabbit put himself in what position he pleased; he left his two hinder-paws on the ground, and laid his body all along the back of the hen, whose tail was removed to the left side by the pressure of the thighs of the rabbit; the hen in short became a perfect doe to him; he remained active upon her four or five times longer than a cock would have done.
Ferchault de Réaumur, Memoire, 1751

From the moment I was hatched it was clear that I was an unusual chicken. My mother was an ordinary hen, but there was nothing ordinary about me, one of many eggs she laid over several spring mornings. The down covering my body at birth soon became fur, instead of feathers. I grew long ears and whiskers. From the wings back, my body became long and devoid of any tail. My feet had four toes and were entirely covered with hair. Indeed, I could be described as a combination of a rabbit and a hen.

How I came to be like this was never known. As hens often do, my mother would sometimes stray into the woods, away from the coop and the farm's yard, but did not reveal what adventures she pursued that might have led to my coming into the world. Needless to say, I never knew my father; he was certainly a wild buck rabbit running around in the woods. My mother named me Henrietta and, perhaps due to my dubious origins, never gave me the kind of attention she lavished on her other offspring.

In time, the physical and behavioral differences between me and other chickens became more pronounced. I was smaller than my contemporaries, but quicker to move, more active, and much, much faster on the ground. I was also more sociable and tried to become friends with other chicks, pullets, and hens in our community. Those efforts were uniformly rebuffed: most of us chickens are independent creatures that do not make friends easily. Plus, of course, I was different in many ways, and my very presence created suspicion and disdain all around me.

The most significant form of disapproval by other members of the flock was in the pecking order. I grew into an existing social structure ruled by older hens, led by a white named Gertrude (Gertie, for short) with a broad, deep body and an oblong and brick-like overall appearance. Gertie enforced a rigid procedure for eating treats and other goodies dispensed by our human owners: the roosters came first; she and the other dominant hens and their favorites followed; the less favored among us would have to settle for whatever scraps remained. I was the lowest one in that pecking order; if I got too close to those above me in the hierarchy, I would be chased away.

Another manifestation of the disaffection of the members of the flock towards me was their standoffish behavior. They co-existed with me, but never joined me (or allowed me to join them) when small groups of us gathered at feeding times or when we rested in the shade in the warm afternoons. I was also kept apart from the others when I roosted at night.

When I matured, I was largely ignored by the roosters. I mated a few times, but the males seemed put off by my strangeness and neither they nor I enjoyed our couplings very much. The eggs I laid as a result of these encounters were always sterile.

Thus, I grew up alone, often hungry and always ignored. But I chose to stay close to the flock because I enjoyed the company, such as it was, of those of my kind. Yet I became increasingly distressed. I would pluck at my fur, wander around restlessly, or lay about disinterested, often lacking energy to move. I might have perished from apathy but for the incident that changed my life.

***

One night during the warm season, I and the other chickens resting in our coop were awakened by the sound of a warning call issued by one of our roosters. The call was loud and insistent and alerted everyone to get out and run for safety.

Our coop is enclosed by wires erected all around and above the roosting area where we perch to sleep. The ground, however, is not covered by anything, and is just unimproved dirt. Some predator had dug its way under the coop and was emerging from the earth, making threatening noises and getting ready to attack us.

The coop has windows covered with screens that let in the cool night air. Alarmed, the chickens in the coop flew to the windows and burst through the screens to escape danger. The attacking beast broke through one of those windows chasing after them.

I was one of the last chickens to escape the coop and, as I reached the yard outside, I noticed that the intruder had already slain two members of the flock and was trying to seize other chickens that were running or skimming all over.

It was what humans call a fox. He was long and slender, with an orange coat, a flattened skull, upright, triangular ears, a pointed snout, and many sharp teeth. His tail was long and thick and helped him to pivot high in the air. I realized I did not have a chance of escaping him if I attempted to fly away.

I had a burst of inspiration. Instead of trying to join the rest of the flock, I planted my feet on the ground and began cackling insistently as loud as I could. My efforts to attract the predator's attention were successful, for it turned around and faced me, so I could see him in full for the first time.

His eyes had vertically slit pupils and seemed to glow in the dark. He looked at me with great intensity and, for a moment, left me paralyzed with fear. I then shuddered and broke into running as fast as I could, away from the carnage in the yard and into the forest.

Had I been a "normal" chicken, the fox would have caught up to me in three strides or less. I was, however, part bunny and was running for my life, so I could run very fast. The fox seemed to have been surprised by my burst of speed, but almost immediately started running after me.

I had a small advantage: I knew every step of these woods, and was able to twist and turn in ways that made it difficult for the fox to follow. Nonetheless, it was only a matter of moments before the fox caught up to me.

In desperation, I jumped into a rivulet that ran behind the farm and started drifting away. The fox approached the edge of the water, getting ready to jump after me.

There was a loud noise and the fox issued a loud yelp and fell to the ground. A few steps away, a human then appeared. I immediately recognized him: he was the owner of the farm that I and the other chickens inhabited. On his right upper extremity, he held a smoking black tube.

***

I let myself float away in the water for a bit, trying to quiet my fast-beating heart and seeking to regain my composure. When I finally came ashore, I realized I had landed in an unfamiliar area. I started calling out, hoping some flock members would hear me. I heard no response, which added to my distress from the close encounter with the fox.

I began walking, near the edge of the water, trying to orient myself. After a while, familiar noises began filling the night. Other members of the flock were in the vicinity, searching for me.

Sometime later, our two roosters, Gertie, and five hens came through a clearing and approached me, making all kinds of noises that I interpreted as being joyous. They escorted me back to the farm, clucking, chattering, shrieking. Gertie was the loudest among the group.

Since that memorable night, the flock has treated me with respect and attention, and I have risen higher in the pecking order. I now sit amiably in the middle of the groups that gather under the trees after eating, and am surrounded by many new friends as we roost for the night.

***

I should not have needed to perform a heroic act and put my life at risk for the benefit of the others as the price for getting their acceptance. They should have recognized that, while different, I was as legitimate a member of the flock as any other chicken. We all have good traits and bad ones, and there must be room for chickens of all types, for that will preserve our flock and make it stronger.

The Ugly Fairy

Someday you will be old enough to start reading fairy tales again.
C. S. Lewis, *The Lion, the Witch and the Wardrobe*

Florandel was convinced it was the ugliest of all fairies in the world. This was perhaps an unusual concern, for fairies are hazy, shapeless clouds of diffuse matter with just a small, better-defined nucleus where their essence resides. They lack any color and resemble pulsating, featureless bursts of gas. Yet, once Earth became ruled by humans, fairies found the need to interact with the smart apes and began to assume more distinct shapes that would be recognizable by the men and women with whom they dealt.

They developed a standard "body," subject to variations to account for the local customs and traditions of the folk of particular areas. Traditionally, in its human contacts, a fairy would appear small and thus less intimidating; it would mask its shimmering nature by adopting a delicate form along the lines of that of a human female clad in transparent, flowing robes, and in some localities would be endowed with large, colorful wings that made the fairy more pleasing to the human eye. All these features were mere appearances, and could be changed at will by a simple gesture.

The ethereal nature of fairies does not mean that they are lacking in the ability to experience thoughts and emotions. They once were half-way fallen angels, exiled out of the gates of heaven but not rebellious enough to be cast into the abyss. They were allowed to dwell on Earth, charged with maintaining the balance of nature, protecting its fruits, keeping the air pure and the water in springs and streams clean, guiding many processes such as evolution of organisms, growth of plants, the spread of animal life. They were made the invisible husbandmen of the planet.

A group of fairies, including Florandel, dwelt in a vast forest, having only limited contact with each other and with the scarce human population. The fairies, however, gathered occasionally to consult about matters felt to be significant. In those encounters, they often took counsel from one fairy, wiser perhaps than the rest, Gloriana, whose advice was invariably followed.

It was to Gloriana that Florandel carried the misgivings about its appearance. As they met in Gloriana's underground dwelling, the sage listened attentively to Florandel's tiny energy discharges that serve for words among the fairy folk. Gloriana was bemused: "Your concerns are unfounded. You can assume any appearance you choose, and can be as fair as you desire, and as beautiful – however you measure it – as any of your sisters."

"Not so, Mother," replied Florandel, utilizing the form of address that the fairies in this community chose when "speaking" to Gloriana. "We fairies are bound to adopt a certain appearance when making ourselves visible to humans. This appearance can vary depending on the skills and physical characteristics of each one of us. Thus, we all appear to a human as if we have a face with eyes and a nose and a mouth, and limbs and a body, but what they see when they look at us is different for each fairy. I can tell, for instance, when humans of tender years look at me, their faces distort in disgust or fear, but if they see Orianda or Luminaria they smile and their eyes widen with excitement."

"So, you are judging your beauty by the reaction of young humans when they meet you?"

"We have no other standard by which to judge. Appearing before a horse or a rabbit yields no results."

"My daughter, there are two flaws in your self-evaluation. First, we cannot read the minds and feelings of humans, and therefore cannot use their facial expressions, or even their words or actions, as measures of the opinions they form of us. Second, and more important, you are letting the judgment of inferior beings be used to assess your worth. If you are really concerned about what you call your beauty, you need to measure it yourself."

"But how can I do that?"

"It so happens that the issue has come up before, in another situation. Let me show you something." Gloriana glided to a dark corner of the cave and returned holding a thin gold necklace from which hung twenty-eight bezel-set colorless gemstones. "Put this around what, in your human form, would be your neck, and wear it continuously through one complete cycle of the moon."

"What does it do?"

"Each morning, as the moon sets, one of the gemstones in this necklace may become shining like a diamond or turn dark red like a ruby, or maybe none will change. At the end of the twenty-eighth day, look at your reflection on the stream that runs past the waterfall east of here. The image that you see will be your true self, and you will be able to determine whether you are indeed beautiful or ugly."

"What does the coloring of the gemstones mean?"

"A gemstone turning bright like a diamond means that you have become more beautiful than the previous day. One gemstone turning dark red warns that your beauty has decreased. A day in which no gemstone changes color your beauty has remained the same."

"Do I have to wait a full lunar month before I can learn the results?"

"You can gaze at your image on the stream as often as you wish, but the true result, containing the necklace's final judgment on your beauty, will only be reached on the final day."

"Seems like a cumbersome way of finding out what a mere glance should reveal."

"You would be surprised how much true beauty depends on things that can change in very short order. In any event, this method is a far more accurate way of discovering a fairy's beauty than relying on the reactions of humans."

Florandel uttered the fairy equivalent of a sigh, thanked Gloriana, and departed, the necklace dangling from its "neck."

***

That very afternoon, as Florandel was making its rounds of the border between the forest and the human settlements that lay at its edges, its attention was caught by cries arising from a hollow in the uneven terrain. Approaching, the fairy noticed that a fawn had been caught in a snare and was wailing in pain. Floarandel moved swiftly to force the snare open and rescue the animal, which limped away, bleating to evince relief, or perhaps to give thanks to the fairy for its rescue.

Nothing else of any significance happened that day, but the following morning as it bent over the clear waters of the stream, Florandel noticed that its ears, which heretofore had been – in its estimation – too large, appeared to have shrunk slightly. Also, one of the gemstones hanging from the necklace was shining brightly.

***

The second day went by without incident, and there were no changes in the fairy's reflected appearance or the necklace's condition. On the third day, however, Florandel ran into a gaggle of boys who were playing wheelbarrow races on the meadow by one of the farms. The children were so intent in their play that they did not notice the presence of the fairy, which all of a sudden felt a bit upset at being ignored. Florandel turned itself into a hummingbird, an eye-catching metallic green speck of feathers with a bright red throat, and began whirring its wings rapidly as it flew above the heads of the children.

Several of the children were drawn to give chase to the bird, who would fly tantalizingly close and then move away just enough to let them come near and almost touch it. The chase went on for quite a while, with Florandel luring the kids farther and farther into the forest. After a while, the chasers got tired and began dropping out of the pursuit, but one towheaded, freckled faced seven-year-old persisted and went on and on, chasing the elusive bird, until they reached a dark, remote corner of the woods. There, the hummingbird hung high in the air, forcing the boy to stop. He then realized, for the first time, he was in totally unfamiliar surroundings and had become lost.

Florandel's initial impulse was to guide the boy back to safety, but then the fairy reflected: "Boys should learn not to chase after little creatures and possibly harm them." It flew away, leaving the boy alone. He became increasingly afraid as the afternoon wore on and night approached.

The fairy came back hours later and, after some searching, found the boy sitting on a fallen log, whimpering disconsolately. It realized the prank had gone a bit too far and, changing back into a fairy's human appearance, approached the terrified child and greeted him: "What are you doing, young man, sitting by yourself in the dark?"

The boy was too scared to reply, and Florandel asked again: "Would you like to go home?" This time, the boy managed to reply haltingly: "Yee... ah, ye...aah, pleeease!!"

Florandel led the boy back to the meadow where they had first met. It was later discovered that he had developed a permanent stutter.

Florandel also learned, the morning after this encounter, that one of the necklace's gems had turned dark red, its ears had gone back to appearing unusually large, and its nose now was a bit crooked.

***

The days advanced in quick succession, sometimes holding new adventures, others passing uneventfully. Florandel had several opportunities to be helpful to humans and beasts, extricating a cart stranded in the mud, shining a guiding light that allowed a traveler to find his way out of the forest, leaving a pot of fresh milk at the door of an elderly couple, guarding a sparrow's nest against a marauding murder of crows. The fairy was also mischievous from time to time, pinching cows to set a stampede that interrupted their grazing, luring a passerby into an elaborate maze where he would linger for hours, imitating the growls of ferocious animals to scare hunters away, stealing eggs from a chicken coop and pies left on a window to cool.

At the end of the lunar month, Florandel's enchanted necklace sported over a dozen sparkling diamonds, seven dark stones, and a few dull, colorless gems. As for the fairy's reflection on the stream, some aspects of its looks had improved: the eyes now shone bright green, the curvature of the lips was more perfect, the blond hair shone like gold. On the other hand, the ears were now longer, the nose more aquiline, and the skin had acquired a bluish tinge instead of the pink hue Florandel favored. Overall, the changes did little to alter the overall balance of the fairy's human appearance, which seemed to be sort of pretty, but not outstanding.

Bitterly disappointed, the fairy paid another visit to Gloriana's cave. "Look at me!" Florandel complained. "This necklace is worthless! The image of me it shows is almost the same that humans see! Am I that ugly?"

Gloriana smiled. "Perhaps your true self is not that different from the image humans perceive when they look at you. Do not blame the necklace, for it is not meant to improve your appearance but reflect your true self. The colors of the gemstones in the necklace reflect your character. You tend to be helpful and compassionate, but at the same time cannot resist performing pranks that are hurtful to others. You are like all creatures, a mixture of good, bad, and indifferent. Be thankful that the good predominates, and that on balance you do make a positive contribution to the order of things."

"But..."

"No more buts. Lead your life the best you can, and your true beauty will shine through."

"I don't want to be better, just more beautiful."

"Sorry about that. You are beautiful enough as it is, in my book. Now be gone!"

And Florandel realized it was time to accept its looks, such as they were, and disappeared in a cloud of mist to float around the forest.

The Dopey Lion

The Umba region is a beautiful hidden corner of Tanzania. Bounded by forests on the east and north and a placid stream on the west, it is almost isolated from the rest of the Serengeti. It is a peaceful place, except at the end of the rainy season, when its expanse of grassland witnesses the raucous passage of hordes of wildebeest, gazelles, impalas and zebras that come from the south in search of greener pastures.

At the time of this story, a pride of lions under the leadership of an older male named Bemba with a carefully groomed tawny mane had established itself as rulers of all that lived, transited, and often died in the territory. Bemba had come to power by out-roaring competing males and females over the course of several challenges. The pride now consisted of Bemba, several sycophantic males, and a good number of females (including his attractive mate), plus youth and cubs.

Bemba slept through much of the day, but was active in the early morning and had most of his activities (which consisted of abusing everyone in his domain) at that time. He left hunting to the females, and concentrated instead on preening, walking about, and defecating. He did not get enough exercise and eating was his favorite pastime, so he had become fat over the years, and now weighed over 500 pounds.

His governing style consisted of making grandiose, self-praising pronouncements and issuing orders suggested to him by his underlings. After a while, nobody paid attention to the pronouncements, which often made no sense. His orders, however, needed to be obeyed if one wanted to stay in his good graces.

From the start, Bemba's orders had sowed discontent among his subjects. A case in point: shortly into his rule, an outwardly healthy male had dropped dead without visible wounds. Later, as the vultures cleaned the carcass, it was discovered that the lion's intestines were rife with tapeworms, and other remains in the animal identified antelope meat as being part of his diet. Some of Bemba's advisors concluded that antelopes were carriers of disease. Bemba immediately ordered a ban on the entry of antelopes into his domain, and the expulsion of those present. These orders were difficult to administer, since antelopes came in great numbers during the migration at the end of the rainy season, and were largely circumvented by those already in his territory, who took flight when those charged with enforcing the expulsion approached. Nonetheless, the orders caused resentment because they often deprived lions and other predators of a prized food source.

One evening, Bemba was breakfasting on a wildebeest that one of his wives had just slain. The corpse was so fresh that a small bird was still pecking at the hide, eating ticks. Bemba was familiar with birds like that one, for they often traveled alongside the ungulates that migrated through the savanna each year. Like many of its kind, this specimen was small, and had a short, thick, red bill. His large eyes were red and unblinking and were surrounded by bright-yellow circles. The head, neck, wings, and tail were brown-gray; the undersides were pale yellow. It stared curiously at Bemba but did not appear scared of the predator.

"Get away from my meal" growled Bemba. "Why?" replied Oxlicker, for that was what many called the bird. "I'm doing you a favor. I eat ticks, fleas, and insects infesting wounds of animals like this fellow. You should be grateful that I get rid of those vermin for your convenience."

"Ticks never bothered me. But YOU are starting to annoy me. Get out of here unless you want to be part of my breakfast."

"Now, wait..." Oxlicker jumped off the carcass and flew around the lion, keeping a safe distance from his jaws. "I've traveled all over the world and have a lot of information that could be valuable to an eminent animal like you."

"What information could I need from you? I am Bemba, king of the savanna. I am feared and respected by all."

"Yes, but I bet you don't know that you have many enemies, like the antelopes you tried to ban. They, and others who don't like you, are amassing at your borders bent on ousting you."

Bemba took the threat seriously. "Really? I must alert the pride so we can defend ourselves."

"Just one second. The threat is serious but not imminent. We're in the middle of the dry season. The attack will take place during the great migration moons from now, at the end of the rainy season. We have time to prepare."

Bemba, being dim witted, had no idea of how to prepare against the impending attack. "What do we have to do?"

Oxlicker appeared to ponder for just one second. Then he declared: "Hire me as your advisor and promise to let me feed on this pride's catch for as long as I want, and I will tell you what to do."

"As long as you eat only ticks and fleas, that arrangement is fine with me."

"Deal."

So Oxlicker became one of Bemba's most trusted advisors. He promptly recommended measures to improve internal security and "make sure there were no disloyal subjects lurking behind the king's back that could assist the enemy." In this category were included the herds of baboons that roamed throughout the savanna. Bemba disdained baboons because, with their hairless red bottoms, they did not look like the other animals. Also, they lived by themselves and had strange habits. They were extremely difficult to catch, for when chased they climbed up trees, out of reach. Oxlicker hated them because they ate insects that could have been part of his diet. In other words, they were a disfavored minority group, prime targets for discrimination.

Bemba ordered all herds of baboons out of his territory, and further ordered that they, like the antelopes, be denied entry into the portion of the savanna he controlled. These orders were carried out with limited success by packs of wild dogs that roamed the savanna all through the year. Baboons often held their ground and fought the wild dogs, or escaped them by climbing into acacias or baobabs. For that reason, Bemba's eradication efforts were often bloody and lingered on for many months without getting rid of the pestilent animals.

In addition to fighting the perceived internal disloyalty, Oxlicker recommended to Bemba that he built a high palisade along the southern boundary of his domain. Such a palisade, he argued, would stop incursions and delay any attacks. Bemba, who was given to boasting, embraced the idea and vowed publicly to build a beautiful palisade, the tallest and greatest palisade the world had ever seen.

This was, however, not such an easy task. He would have to engage the elephants that lived in his kingdom, and maybe invite others from abroad, to fell trees, carry them to the border area, and stack them on top of each other to a sufficient height. It would take forever to get the job done, and since each elephant consumed many pounds of vegetable matter daily, all other animals in Bemba's domain would need to be mobilized to gather feed for the workers.

Nonetheless, Bemba was too dim to understand the difficulties of the project, and too arrogant to go back on his promise to complete it. "We will build the palisade, make no mistake about it. Sooner or later, we will get it done" he would repeat to everyone, over and over, despite the indifference or resentment of his subjects.

But he did not get to build it. That, and several other costly plans proposed by Oxlicker, failed to materialize after being bombastically announced, and caused Bemba's rule to become more tenuous and his kingdom more divided. And the threatened invasion – which had been only an invention of Oxlicker – did come about because prides in other parts of the savanna took notice of the decline and stormed across the border, leading to a ferocious fight between Bemba's forces and the interlopers. Oxlicker flew away early in the conflict and was never seen again.

It was only through great pains, suffering and bloodshed that dominion over Umba was maintained by Bemba's pride. But not with him at the helm: a younger and more sensible lion challenged Bemba and deposed him with relatively little effort. The older lion justified his demise to having become tired (as he was wont to say) of winning and deciding to rest on his laurels and bask in the veneration of his subjects.

But no veneration was ever granted; he was reviled as the worst ruler Umba ever knew, that is until, later, another egotistical beast took the throne. But that is a story for another day.

Blame Rupert

> *Life is not complex. We are complex.*
> *Life is simple and the simple thing is the right thing.*
> Oscar Wilde
>
> *Toto, I've a feeling we're not in Kansas anymore...We must be over the rainbow!*
> Dorothy, The Wizard of Oz

As he reached thirteen years of age and attained puberty, Sean felt he was a poster boy for faggotry. He kept his feelings to himself, of course, but the self-loathing was always there, inches from the surface, raising its ugly head whenever the boy thought of himself as, to use his father's expression for the likes of him, "a damned queer."

He had revealed himself only to his next-door friend Lindsay, who was almost his same age but very different in personality. Where Sean was reserved, Lindsay was pleasing, friendly and outwardly charming. They had known each other since infancy and, to Sean's surprise and delight, their playful roughhousing as children had slowly given way to a sort of intimate touching that revealed that they shared a bond of sexuality that would soon bloom into a relationship.

One Sunday afternoon, after a day at the cinema in which they had explored each other's body in the darkened theater, Lindsay proposed: "Sean, how about us becoming boyfriends?"

Sean smiled, and then recoiled at the invitation. "Yes, Lindsay, I really would like to be your boyfriend, but not in secret. I would have to reveal myself. I can't continue to keep my feelings hidden from everyone, particularly my folks. I'd have to come out to them before I announce we are a couple." Lindsay embraced his friend and, right in the middle of Belgrave Square, planted a wet kiss on Sean's mouth. "Then you need to come out, pronto!"

Sean pushed Lindsay away. "Come on, Linny. Not in public!"

Lindsay insisted: "I have the hots for you and don't care if anyone knows about it. You have to open up! Being gay is not a crime anymore!"

Sean took leave from his friend and went into hiding in his room. Should he tell his mother? What would she say? Lucinda was a strict Catholic and frowned on any form of immorality. Homosexuality was seldom discussed in the household, but Sean was sure she would be horrified at his disclosure. And his father... there was no doubt what Angus O'Leary would say and do, and it was not pretty.

Over the next few days, Sean tried to avoid Lindsay while he attempted to sort out his conflicting emotions. Lindsay soon caught on to his friend's ploy and confronted him: "Why are you giving me the cold shoulder? Don't you like me anymore?"

Sean was apologetic. "I'm almost ready to come out, although I still worry about what will happen. But I just can't bring myself to do it. I don't know how to let my family know without hurting them and myself..."

Lindsay then made a suggestion. "You need to talk to an expert."

"Do you know someone who can tell me how to do it?" asked Sean. "And don't mention any teacher from this school." The faculty of their middle-school was old fashioned, to say the least.

"Why don't you have confession with one of the priests at Mary Immaculate?"

"Oh, please.... You know I'm not religious."

"OK, how about this? My cousin Roddy once told me of a rumor that has been going around Dublin for some time..."

"What kind of rumor?"

"Well, it's sort of a fairy tale, but who knows? Are you familiar with the sculpture of Oscar Wilde they put up in Merrion Square in the late nineties?"

"I haven't seen it, but I've heard the way it is described, something like The Fag on the Crag. Is that what you are talking about?"

"Yes. Well, Wilde was a famous Irish queer that went to prison for messing with boys over a hundred years ago, are you familiar with the story?"

"I vaguely recall hearing about it, but don't know the details."

"Never mind. The rumor is that if you go to Merrion Square at midnight and come to where the Wilde statue sits, you can ask him any questions and he'll answer them for you. In life, Wilde was very smart and thought he knew all the answers."

"I don't believe it."

"Well, it's incredible, but what if it is true? I bet Wilde could give you advice on the best way to come out."

"That's just ridiculous. I'm not going to go to a park in the middle of the night to talk to a statue!"

"Look at it this way. The worst that can happen, you won't get an answer to your question, but I'm sure Wilde won't tell anyone. So, what do you have to lose?"

"Only feeling stupid, that's all."

"Well, it was only an idea. Anyhow, I really have the hots for you, so you better find a way to give me satisfaction or I'll have to look for someone else, maybe that cute Barnwell kid..."

***

As days piled on each other, Sean's anxiety mounted. Lindsay was making good on his threat and was hanging out with Cillian Barnwell, who was younger than Sean and very pretty. Sean started twice to have a talk with his mother about his "condition," but dropped it. Lucinda suffered from a weakened heart and was feeling arthritis pains in the shoulders and hips, and Sean felt reluctant to take a chance of aggravating her maladies. Sean became sort of constipated, his secret trying to burst out into the open without his being able to release it.

The boy only shared his anxiety with his dog. Sean had been eleven when his family acquired Rupert, a shaggy wheat-colored Cairn terrier, left behind when Uncle Seamus packed up and left Dublin for a job in Saudi Arabia. Seamus hardly had said goodbye to the dog, who had barked and wagged its tail in great agitation and had tried to climb up its master's leg without success.

Sean had felt sorry for Rupert after its abandonment and had taken it upon himself to adopt the scruffy animal and make it his pet, but had trouble getting accepted by Rupert as its new master. As most terriers, Rupert was clever, quick to bark, lively, feisty, and stubborn. It probably still felt it belonged to Seamus and resisted Sean's orders, challenging his commands at every turn. Sean, who was not bossy by nature, had to discipline Rupert constantly just to prove he could make the dog do things as he ordered. After a while, however, Rupert had bonded with his young boss and, while still independent, became an impulsive and intense friend who seemed to understand the boy's feelings.

As he dwelt on his dilemma about coming out, Sean had become irritable and short with everyone, even Rupert. The dog, however, had displayed surprising forbearance at its master's moodiness.

Then came one Thursday in late April. It had been cold and windy most of the day and Rupert, reflecting the nasty weather outside, had barked constantly at every noise, getting increasingly on everyone's nerves. Finally, after dinner, Sean made a snap decision. This was as good a time as any to pay a visit to Mr. Wilde, and Rupert's antics provided cover for what otherwise would have been odd behavior on his part.

As bedtime approached and Rupert continued to bark and growl, Sean turned to his parents and declared, feigning exasperation: "I'm going to take this dog on a long walk so he will let off steam and quiet down. We'll go to Portobello for a while."

"Don't go there" retorted Lucinda. "It's getting pretty late and at this hour Portobello will be full of drunks and perverts."

"All right, then" replied Sean, pretending to give in. "I'll go towards Trinity instead. It should be quieter as long as I stay away from the campus."

"But..." started Lucinda, but Sean put his overcoat on quickly, tied a leash around Rupert's neck, and rushed out before she could raise any more objections.

***

It was a long walk from the family's apartment in Rathmines to the Merrion Square, near Trinity College, where the sculpture of Oscar Wilde sat. Sean tried to make haste out of fear that he may get there too late and miss a séance with Wilde's statue. Rupert trotted happily along, sensing that they had embarked on some enjoyable adventure. The last few blocks, coming up Fitzwilliam Place, Sean and Rupert were literally sprinting, both panting from the unusual exercise.

The park was not large; soon after entering the square from its southern end, Sean could make out by the light of the moon and the nearby buildings that there was a mound of rocks near the northwestern end of the square. He cast hesitation aside and, holding firmly Rupert's leash, approached the structure.

There it was: a life-size rendering of a long-haired middle-aged man, dressed in green, pink and grey clothes, all made of various stone materials. He was reclining in a casual, haphazard way on a large boulder, and displayed a sardonic expression on his face. His eyes focused on another statue, a nude bust of a man; a third statue of a pregnant woman sat nearby, forlorn.

Sean had no trouble figuring out what the grouping of statues represented. Wilde had been full of himself. He cared little for women but was attracted to males, and had a condescending attitude towards other people. Had he met Wilde in person, Sean would have found him intimidating.

The boy got so nervous that he almost turned around to return home, but managed to keep his emotions in check and placed himself right in front of the stone curb that separated the statue from the path where he and Rupert stood. In a small voice he started: "Mr. Wilde... Mr. Wilde?"

He could have sworn that the stone eyes of the statue turned away from the nearby nude and looked down on him. The leer in his expression changed to interest as he the reclining figure seemed to be focusing on Sean, perhaps sizing up the boy.

There was a pause as Sean, petrified with fear, tried to figure out what to say. The statue arched its eyebrows as if getting annoyed at the wait, and for a moment Sean feared that the interview would be over before it even started. He forced himself to continue.

"Mr. Wilde, Sir, I came to ask for your help with a very important question about my life. I am gay and would like to let my family and friends know about it, but don't know how to do it. What would be the best way for me to come out?"

The stone eyes of the statue seemed to roll in its sockets and its mouth spread wide open in mirth. An unearthly voice, resonant like a rumbling of distant thunder and at the same time dripping with irony, sounded inside Sean's head:

"I never voluntarily revealed myself as a gay man. To the contrary, I was denounced as a sodomite by the father of my lover, sued him for defamation and lost, and then I was charged with moral turpitude and put in jail for two years. I only dealt with my true nature when I was in prison. I spent most of my life trying to avoid having to do what you are so keen on doing. Why are you bothering me with this?"

Sean broke down in tears, shaken by the denunciation. He hunched his shoulders and turned around as if to retreat, but the statue continued, now in a kinder tone: "But, if for some reason you need to confess your true nature, the best way to do it is to keep it simple. Write a short note making a complete disclosure. Keep it next to you when you go to bed and read it again the following morning to make sure it says exactly what you mean. Then go to your parents and read it aloud."

Sean started to thank the statue for what, in retrospect, was an obvious piece of advice, but at that point Rupert began barking loudly and attempted to reach the rock slab where Wilde's statue rested. Sean was almost unable to control his pet and, as they struggled, steps were heard approaching from the other end of the green. Sean pulled on the leash viciously and yanked Rupert away, and the pair managed to leave the square undetected. It was not until they were halfway home that Sean realized he had failed to thank Wilde for his advice.

***

At home, they found Lucinda awake, sitting by the front door on her armchair. She greeted them angrily: "Where have you been? It's nearly two in the morning!!"

"Sorry, mum" apologized Sean, catching his breath. "You won't believe this, but Rupert was still barking like a dog possessed until only a few minutes ago!" Beside him, Rupert looked up sheepishly.

Sean was always a good boy and Lucinda had no reason to suspect he had done anything wrong. "You'll be the death of me! Go to bed! We'll have a talk in the morning!"

As he took off his sweat-drenched clothes, Sean reflected on the odd adventure he had just gone through. Talking to a statue was far-fetched enough; receiving personal advice from a long-dead man of letters was totally incredible. *Wait until I tell Lindsay. He won't believe it either.*

He was putting on his pajamas when he recalled Wilde's advice and remembered he had to write a note to his parents before going to bed. He was undecided as to what to say, and even whether to write anything at all. Then he concluded that it would be ungrateful on his part not to follow Wilde's instructions. Taking a pen and a sheet of paper from the nightstand drawer, he scribbled the following:

"Dear Mum and Dad: You are very important to me, so I need to tell you that I am gay. I have been gay all my life, and will continue to be gay until I die. There is nothing you did that has driven me to fancy boys rather than girls. I hope you can accept me as I am and continue giving me your love and support.
Your son,
Sean"

He read the short message over and over, and was unsatisfied with it. Should he say more? Should he make any promises? Should he offer to move out if the family chose to disown him?

He found no answers to those and many other questions that suddenly assailed him, but he was dead tired and decided to let these matters remain unresolved until the morning. He fell into a deep sleep the moment his head hit the pillow.

When he woke up, his first impulse was to throw away the draft he had written and revisit the entire issue again. Maybe he would not need to come out at all. He was going to do it mainly for Lindsay, but his friend had proved less than trustworthy. Maybe he should not inflict pain on his parents. Perhaps he would wait until he was of age, or one day leave town the way Uncle Seamus had, and would not need to come out until then, if at all...

He was still ensnared in those confusing thoughts when he reached for the note he had written and left on top of the nightstand before going to bed. It was not there.

He began searching frantically for the note, on the floor, behind the night table, and under the bed. He was on his knees when the door to his bedroom opened and his parents walked in. Lucinda was holding the note in her hand. She had been crying.

"Couldn't you at least have told us directly?" she asked, reproach and disappointment in her voice.

Sean was at a loss for words. His father then piped in: "It was quite craven to send Rupert as your messenger instead of telling us face to face yourself!"

"I didn't send Rupert to carry that note... I was thinking of throwing it away!"

He looked down and there was Rupert, hiding behind Lucinda's legs.

"Rupert! Bad boy! Why did you do this?!!"

Rupert barked just once, in a low tone that seemed almost contrite.

"What possessed you to do this?" he asked again, and the implausible answer came back immediately. "You talked to you-know-who, right?"

Rupert shook its head up and down once.

Sean realized that this was an impossible conversation to hold with Rupert, particularly in front of his folks. "Alright, I'll get you later." Then, facing his parents, he asked the truly important question. "Never mind how you got my note. What did you think about it?"

Lucinda took two steps forward, lifted him off the floor, and clutched him in her arms. "Sean, you are my only son and the light of my life. I don't understand it, but if you choose to lead your life that way, I'll give you my blessing and all my support." Her embrace was so tight that Sean could hardly breathe.

Raising his head, Sean's eyes locked on his father's. Angus O'Leary's face was a rigid mask. "I think you are a degenerate" he said in a low, dangerous tone. Then he went on: "But, as your mother says, you are *our* degenerate. I will not condone your behavior but will support you no matter what you do, provided it is not criminal." This, Sean surmised, was as close to acceptance as he would ever get from his dad. And that was good enough.

Freeing himself from his mother's grip, Sean got on the floor, grabbed Rupert and whispered: "You are smart, but this is a bit much. I reckon you let him know that I was torn by indecision I was and he directed you to help carry his instructions out and you did. That turned out fine, but please let me make my own decisions, will you?"

Rupert averted its eyes and yawned.

The Yellow Butterfly

Before the sacred box/jar was opened by Pandora, there were not any bad things roaming the world and it was a fortunate place. After her Pandora's box incident, the world was never the same again nor will it ever be.
Anne Rice, Pandora: New Tales of the Vampire

I am Calliope, poetess and sometimes scrivener. My cousin Pandora begged me to write down her story, for falsehoods are being spread about her. I am not always as accurate as my sister Clio, and my memory is not as good as that of my mother Mnemosyne, so there may be an error or two here and there. But what I am about to tell is essentially true.

Long ago, there was a war between the old gods and the new ones – a squabble in which almost all deities and their allies were involved. One of the old gods, called Prometheus, fought on the side of the new gods and assisted mightily in the defeat of his relatives, for which he won praise from the victors. My father Zeus, the leader of the new gods, promised to grant Prometheus any wish of his as a reward for his help.

Prometheus, seeing that the earth was barren, asked Zeus for the ability to create life to populate it. Zeus asked how Prometheus proposed to do this, and Prometheus replied that he had some ideas and hoped that neither Zeus nor any of the other gods would interfere. My father declared: "By my sacred thunderbolt, I vow that the Gods will not interfere with your creations, save in case of dire need."

So, Prometheus made the animals and the plants, and fashioned man out of a mixture of clay, water and fire. He endowed animals, and even plants, with instincts that assisted them in their quest for survival. However, he was not satisfied with the man he created, Epimetheus, for he was a dullard and lacked initiative. In order to improve his handiwork, Prometheus stole a spark from Zeus' thunderbolt using a giant fennel stalk and, upon touching the stalk to Epimetheus' brow, granted him intelligence and spirit. Touching the stalk to the ground, Prometheus started a fire and taught Epimetheus how to kindle and extinguish it. This was the beginning of the human as it exists today.

Zeus was extremely angry at Prometheus for stealing a spark from his thunderbolt and at man for daring to use it. Fire, up to that point, had been the exclusive property of the gods. Prometheus was seized and chained to a rock in a remote mountain for all eternity. Every morning an eagle sent by Zeus descends on him and eats his liver bit by bit. As night falls, the liver regenerates, so it can be ravaged the next day.

Zeus was also angry at Epimetheus, but recognizing that man was innocent of Prometheus' deeds and remembering his oath, decided that his revenge on man had to be subtle. Zeus ordered that a maiden be crafted from earth and water by his son Hephaestus and be endowed with beauty, grace, and intelligence. That was Pandora. She came out of the depths of the earth in a trance, carrying with her a lidded jar. As she completed her ascent to the surface, she became conscious. She then heard a thundering voice that ordered her to guard the jar but never open it, for terrible things would happen if she did. Zeus was perhaps expecting that Pandora's curiosity would drive her to open the jar immediately, but she did not do so.

Pandora became Epimetheus' wife. They had many children, who in turn coupled with one another and had a multitude more. The land was plentiful, and could support the increasing human population.

Epimetheus remained vigorous and, when the bloom of his marriage to Pandora wilted, he began lusting after his daughters and grand-daughters, and started neglecting his duties to his wife. As time passed, Pandora became unhappy with Epimetheus' lack of affection and constant betrayals.

It was then that Pandora had an unexpected visitor. He was tall, handsome, glowing with vitality; he wore winged sandals and a winged cap, and carried a satchel and a winged staff on which two snakes were coiled. He announced himself self-importantly: "Greetings, mortal. I am Hermes, messenger of the Gods."

Pandora was terrified by the appearance of a deity, and remained silent, shaking like a leaf in a storm. Hermes noticed her terror and continued in a somewhat less portentous tone: "The Gods have seen your suffering and sent me to offer help."

"What... what do you mean?"

"It is well known that your husband Epimetheus is behaving badly, taking his pleasure with younger women and forsaking his duties to you. Is that not the case?"

"Yes, but..."

"The solution to your problem lies in your own hands. Within the jar that has been entrusted to you there are many things, good and bad. One of the good things is Fidelity, a blessed spirit that protects married women from neglect from their husbands. If you release that spirit, harmony will return to your household and those of your daughters, and the sacred link between spouses will forever remain unbroken."

"But how do I set Fidelity free? The jar is lidded and, as you said, is full of things that should remain captive."

Hermes gave her a tight smile. "You will have to be very careful. First, you must go to the river, capture a crab, and tear off one of its pincers. Then, lifting the jar's lid with the pincer just a tiny bit, you must summon Fidelity and, when she shows her head, grasp it gently, pull her out, and immediately close the jar. Release Fidelity so she can fly into the air, and she will do the rest."

"It does not sound too complicated. Are you sure it will work?"

"I give you the word of Hermes that if you do as I described, Fidelity will be released and will help you and all of womankind."

Pandora thought it was very kind of the Gods to send her their messenger with the solution to her problem, so she thanked Hermes and bid him farewell.

I wish she had talked to me before proceeding further, for Hermes is a lying scoundrel, the god of thieves and false witnesses. As it was, Pandora went to the river looking for a crab to capture, though she had no fishing experience or tools. However, she found by the bank of the river a huge oak tree whose branches almost touched the waters. Leaning on the side of the massive trunk was a three-pointed bronze harpoon fixed onto a long pole. Either intuition or a touch of divine insight told her that she could use this spear to impale a crab, should she find one. And, as if driven by the same divine forces, she saw a large crab lying immobile by the water's edge.

Pandora managed to spear the beast and puncture its carapace a couple of times. She hoisted the dead crab and, laying it on the ground, smashed it with a rock. She then tore a claw from the corpse and took it back to her hut, where she kept the jar with her other possessions.

Remembering Hermes' instructions, she lifted the jar's lid a little and called out: "Fidelity, come out to be freed." No sooner had she opened the jar, however, there was a loud rumble and a shade, made of darkness and fog, burst out and grew to fill the room.

Pandora had the presence of mind to slam the lid back on the jar, for that spirit did not square off with her expectations: she was assuming Fidelity would be a lithe, benevolent looking shade, who would spread her diaphanous aura around her and cover the entire world. Whatever this spirit was, it did not look the least bit benevolent.

"Are you Fidelity?" Pandora asked timorously. The reply came after a harsh burst of laughter: "NO! My name is Khaos. All that exists was once within my substance, and in time the heavens and the earth, the gods, and other immortals escaped from me and scattered over the universe. I have been trying to regain all that I lost using disorder and turmoil as my weapons. When the old gods sought to bring down the new ones, I fought with the old and was imprisoned in this jar. Now that you have freed me, I can seize all that exists and absorb it back into my being."

Pandora was disconsolate. Had she lost the chance of freeing Fidelity? Should she try opening the jar again, this time very, very carefully, and summon her?

Fear ant hope battled in her heart. At the end her hope was too strong, and she pried the lid of the jar just a tiny bit, while again summoning: "Fidelity – please come out! Quickly!!"

There was a hiss as of hot water escaping out of a fissure, and a stentorian cry: "I'm free!"

A column of smoke rose and coalesced into a menacing figure that held a gigantic spear. Brandishing the weapon and stabbing at the open air, the newcomer shouted: "They imprisoned me so there would be an end to War. But now I will pitch man against man, god versus man, god fighting god. There will be carnage and spilled blood until the end of time!" Then, before Pandora could do anything to stop him, he seized the jar, shook it, yanked the lid off, and called out: "Death! Famine! Anger! Hatred! Come out and join me!!"

With the lid removed, there was a tumultuous whoosh, as not only those spirits summoned by War surged out, but Envy, Lust, Greed, Malice, Arrogance, Fear, Disease, and other banes whose names the world would get to know later, streamed out and dispersed. Pandora was never able to determine whether Fidelity had been among the escapees, but to this date there are no signs that, if she exists, she is working to preserve marital harmony.

Pandora realized that she had failed in her duty as custodian and had allowed all sorts of calamities to spread throughout the universe. Fearing the Gods' retribution, Pandora looked inside the jar to see whether any captives remained. There was still something on the bottom: a large butterfly, yellow with blue fringed wings and forked hindwings, shimmering in the afternoon sunlight. It fluttered restlessly inside the jar, searching for a way out. Pandora reached into the jar seeking to grasp the insect but was halted by the familiar voice of Hermes:

"Let it be, woman, and close the jar. This butterfly is Hope and if it escapes nothing will be left to help men bear their woes."

"But if Hope stays trapped, how can it be of any help to mortals?"

"All they need to know is that Hope exists and is never lost unless humans abandon it. Humans must toughen their spirits, and Hope will help them overcome calamity."

"You lied to me, and tricked me into opening the jar so that the evils of the world would be released. Why did you do it?"

"Humans have been touched by the sacred fire, and thus gained the potential of becoming great and one day threatening Olympus. With the ills in the jar released, man will face all sorts of adversities, and will never grow too powerful. On the other hand, Zeus is stern but not without mercy. He judges that if the human race fails it will be only through its own doing. He is leaving Hope to ward you, but you must find ways to survive without further help or hindrance from the Gods."

Pandora was outraged at the caprices of the Gods, but knew what she had to do and set out to deliver this message to all her children. She is now gone but her message, as memorialized in these wax tablets, is for all to read. I am burying these tablets in a cave under sacred Mount Ossa, the site of the battle between immortals at the beginning of time. May men follow their teachings and learn to endure their ills by preserving hope.

Medusa's Stare

> *Medusa, she's staring at you*
> *Medusa, with her eyes*
> *Medusa, oh she's cold*
> Anthrax, Medusa

1

They say that some of the world's most important stories are about women, yet they are always told by men. I do not know whether my story is that important, but it has certainly been told (falsely) by one man after another. Until now.

My father Phorcys, a renowned sailor, was my first betrayer. I never learned what secrets nested in his soul, but from an early age he was eager to part company with me. I was a docile and unusually beautiful child, and loved him with the fervor only a daughter can bestow on the father she worships. Thus, I was hurt to the core when he announced that soon he would present me as a gift to the priestesses of Athena so I could become an acolyte in the new temple erected by the city in honor of its patron deity. "The Goddess can only favor us upon receiving such a wonderful gift" was his explanation. I saw my suffering reflected also on my mother Ceto's face, but she did nothing to oppose my father's designs.

Around my fourteenth birthday, my first *menses* were discharged and I was deemed to be of age, whereupon my father led me on the steep climb to the Acropolis, and together we entered the Parthenon, the great temple dedicated to Athena Polias. There, he took me before Eueris, the high priestess, and presented me to the old woman: "Reverend Mother, I am Phorcys, the sailor, and this is my daughter Medusa, a virgin just of age. I wish to dedicate her to the Goddess and enroll her in your service. It is my wish that she become your *diakonos*...."

Eueris interrupted him: "Are you seeking to expiate some sin against the Gods or ill deeds towards another mortal? Because this is neither the place nor the appropriate manner for seeking such forgiveness."

My father replied with eagerness: "No, Reverend Mother. I am not seeking atonement, but presenting the Goddess with a disinterested gift."

The priestess scowled in disbelief, but turned her attention to me. Holding my chin up with her withered hand, she declared: "Girl, you are beautiful. Your presence will lighten up the dullness of our duties." Then, to my father: "Very well. Go in peace. We accept your gift. May the Gods grant you their favor in your future endeavors." My father turned around and left without a word of farewell.

I later learned he had been harboring suspicions of infidelity against my mother, which he could not prove (as they were unfounded) and his spite against her was vented in part upon me and my sisters. Whatever his reasons, I never laid eyes on him again.

Years passed and, as I matured, I became comelier – I do not say this in vainglory, for beauty was the bane of my existence. All the men whose eyes rested on me, and not a few of the women, were charmed by my perfect white skin, my full lips, the shining violet eyes, and the wild curly hair that cascades, like an auburn waterfall, down my back. Oftentimes, I found myself needing to fend off the too friendly advances of my admirers.

I gave those encounters little thought, as an inconvenient part of existence. I felt uninterested in the passions of the flesh. Since I entered Athena's temple, I had dedicated myself to a chaste life of prayer and service.

My devotion to Athena did not go unnoticed. My offerings to the goddess – milk, cakes, the organs of baby goats – were well received, for the smoke of my burnings rose gently to the heavens, giving off a subtle perfume to the air in the temple. Eueris complimented me more than once on my piety and hinted that I might be her worthy successor once she retired.

Then, one night a few weeks after midsummer, Athens experienced one of the violent storms that are typical in our city during that part of the year. The thunder and lightning were so severe that each of us took refuge in our cells, cowering in fear. I was praying that Zeus would stay his hand and spare the temple of his favorite daughter from his thunderbolts when, framed by the livid bursts of lightning, I saw a dark shape on the threshold of my cell. I was sure I had closed the door, but somehow the figure was soon inside, approaching the *klismos* chair on which I sat. He was a giant of a man, all muscle and sinew, with a weathered face and a graying beard. He stopped in front of me and commented, in a booming voice that sent shivers down my spine: "Maid, you are as beautiful as they said!"

I trembled and, instinctively, covered my face with my hands, hoping that perhaps this was a nightmare that would vanish when I looked up again. But he did not go away. To the contrary, he lifted me by the hips, raised me to my feet, and carried me effortlessly to my narrow, skin covered bed. There, in several deft motions, he removed my peplos, lifted the *strophion* that covered my breasts, and lay on top of me, panting. I tried to resist, but he was almost twice my weight and exhibited an inhuman strength. A few moments later, he had freed himself from his tunic and pulled down my loincloth. We were naked.

My recollection of what happened next remains unclear. On the one hand, I did not welcome his attempt to possess me; on the other, I did not resist and, by my motions, facilitated his undertaking. Past the initial intense pain, I may have been enjoying the loss of my maidenhead to the virile stranger. The new sensations of pleasure and pain became so intense that I was overwhelmed and passed out.

I woke to a slap on my face by Eueris, who was hovering over the frame bed in which I lay, naked and bloody, exhibiting marks on my body that were clear evidence of recent intercourse. The priestess was accompanied by two of her young *kanephoroi* attendants; they all seemed in a state of profound shock.

As I opened my eyes, Eueris shouted a question that was more of an accusation: "Who? Who did this?"

I burst into tears. "I don't know. I don't know. He broke into my cell during the thunderstorm…"

"You are lying!" replied Eueris angrily, grabbing and pulling on my hair. "We found the door to your cell wide open, with no signs of forced entry. Whoever it was, you let him in!"

My tears became an anguished cry. "I swear for all the Gods that I did not let that man into my room, nor did I consent to be violated..." I was shaking and bawling uncontrollably, and perhaps my giving all these signs of distress made Eueris let go of my hair and pull away from me.

"Perhaps it was a God" said, timidly, one of the *kanephoroi*. "It is said that evil gods travel abroad during storms and wreak havoc on mortals."

Eueris gave me a considered look, as if weighing her options. "This is a terrible scandal. Medusa has broken her vow of chastity and can no longer remain in our service. On the other hand, she has been a favorite of Athena and, if she is an innocent victim as she claims, the wrath of the goddess may descend on us all."

She turned to me and cautioned: "I need to think and seek counsel on this grave matter. For the time being, you are to remain in your cell and not show your face in public. You have dishonored us and your presence contaminates this holy temple. I could send you back to your family, but I fear that your father would treat you more harshly than you deserve."

"No! .... Please don't send me back to my family!"

I began bawling again.

***

Some days later, Eueris returned, accompanied by a very old man dressed in the white tunic of the religious orders. He introduced himself to me with these words:

"Medusa, my name is Erimateus. I'm a priest in the service of the Oracle of Delphi. Eueris has sought the advice of holy Apollo on how to deal with you, seeing how you have profaned the temple of Athena and consorted with an unnamed man or god. I have come to relate to all of you the God's counsel."

There was an expectant pause while Erimateus prepared to deliver his message. In a slow, formal voice, he continued as follows: "Pythia, the priestess that serves as Oracle, conveyed this message from Apollo: 'the virgin who has consorted with a male must be confined forever on a remote island, away from contact with humans, for she is cursed: whoever gazes into her eyes shall promptly die.'"

With those words, my fate was sealed. Apollo was a well-known enemy to his half-sister Athena and was inflicting pain on her through the banishment of a favorite acolyte. I had been betrayed by another male, this time a god.

***

They took me to the small island of Sarpedon, a rocky outcrop of land in a remote corner of the Mediterranean. To keep me company, they forcibly brought my sisters Stheno and Euryale and the three of us made a solitary living, feeding off sea birds and fish and longing for the bygone days of our youth. No ships ever touched on our island save by misfortune: in the span of a decade only three shipwrecked vessels came ashore on the tiny bay near our hut. Each time this occurred, my sisters hid because they were ugly and feared that pity and scorn would be visited on them by the castaways. I was left to play hostess and give such succor as I could to the stranded mariners.

There were unfortunate consequences to these sporadic visits. Invariably, one or more of the sailors would become mesmerized by my beauty and would try to make love to me, despite my protestations. On those occasions, my sister Stheno came out of hiding and slew or chased away the importuning suitor. She was the strong one in our family.

One of the visitors driven away by Stheno was Agenor, the oldest son of king Polydectes of the island of Seriphos. Agenor became so heartbroken by my refusal to yield to his entreaties that, during his voyage back home, he killed himself by jumping into the sea.

Polydectes was devastated by the death of his heir and swore to take revenge against me. He commanded his future son-in-law Perseus to come to Sarpedon and kill me. Perseus, to protect his mother, who was at the mercy of Polydectes, agreed to do so. He says he never had any intention of harming me in any way.

Perseus arrived in Sarpedon a fortnight ago. Shortly after we met, he declared his love for me; in turn, I was swayed by his beauty, for he is as handsome a man as I have ever encountered. I am hoping the two of us will be able to find peace and contentment somewhere far away. We leave at high tide two days from now.

2

It is I, Euryale, who must complete the story recounted so far by my sister Medusa. Anger and remembered pain lash at my soul as I recall the betrayals she endured, and I can hardly hold the *kalamos* straight in my hand as I etch the rest of her story on the wax of these tablets. But the tale must be finished, for there are lessons in her tragedy for women to learn.

Perseus had not fallen in love with Medusa, but was biding his time for the best opportunity to slay her and carry out Polydectes' revenge. Feigning affection, he gained Medusa's confidence and was ultimately invited to her bed. After a night of lovemaking, Perseus rose before dawn and, seizing his double-edged *xyphos*, struck a mighty blow that severed Medusa's head. He ran from the scene of his crime holding Medusa's severed head in one hand and the sword in the other. At the beach, he was met by Stheno, who had been awakened by the noises coming out of Medusa's bedroom. Perseus did not hesitate for a second: dropping my sister's severed head on the sand, he squared off against Stheno, put her to death in three wild strokes, and swam back to his ship.

The rest of the story I have learned bit by bit, through the mouths of visitors to my island. Perseus' trip back to Seriphos encountered numerous delays, and it took him almost a year to appear before Polydectes. To show the successful completion of his task, Perseus displayed to the King my sister's severed head. The head was largely decomposed and emitted a loathsome odor; the abundant curly hair had become a mass of vermin and the sockets of her once beautiful eyes were bottomless pits of darkness. Polydectes stared at Medusa's eyes, trembled, and slumped from his throne, dead.

Popular imagination has woven a tale of horror involving Medusa's head and its ability to inflict death upon those who gaze at it. It is all invention; the truth is that Medusa, either dead or alive, has never hurt anyone and the accusations against her are only efforts by the men who wronged her to discredit and vilify their victim, a common tactic among males.

I, however, remain in Sarpedon. My complexion, like that of my father, is greenish; I have bulging eyes; serpents coil around my waist. Pity the man who dares to approach me, for the rage of a woman against men who wrong her is worse than that of the Furies (who are women themselves).

Killing the Jabberwock

> And hast thou slain the Jabberwock?
> Come to my arms, my beamish boy!
> O frabjous day! Callooh! Callay!"
> He chortled in his joy.
> *Lewis Carroll, Jabberwocky*

"Why am I so ugly?" asked young Godfrey, knees bent at the pool's edge, lamenting the mismatched limbs, the boil-covered face.

"You are not ugly, my boy" replied his warden, the dwarf, in a dulcet tone. "And, compared to other boys I've seen, you are positively radiant. We all display unwelcome inheritances from the poison."

Godfrey rose to his feet, nearly bumping his head against the lowest branch of a giant birch. "You only say that because you want me to feel good. And I can't. After watching my parents get the withering disease from the poison and die within a couple of weeks, I am no longer able to feel good. I hate this world, I hate having to hide day and night, I hate living off berries and wild rats. I wish an ant would come and get me!" He broke out in a stream of sobs.

"Don't you ever say that!" cautioned the warden. "And lower your voice. They might feel your distress!"

"I don't care!" replied Godfrey peevishly, but dropped his voice to a near whisper. "I can handle any of them, with this!" He extracted from his tunic the laser broadsword he had inherited from his father and made circles in the humid air with it.

"That would be just holding a pin against the ant queen, the Jabberwock. You wouldn't last a minute if she and you faced off."

"Let her come" exclaimed Godfrey, raising his voice again.

***

"You say that because you've never met her. The worker ants are bad enough, being almost twice the size of a human. The soldier ants are bigger than the worker ants. The Jabberwock is even bigger than a warrior ant; one of her legs is as large as you.

"The claws on each of Jabberwock's legs can seize your body as if it were a stick, and bring it up to her mandibles, to be broken apart and carried back to the larder in the colony's anthill. You wouldn't stand a chance against her."

***

"And you also need to be alert to the Jubjubs, the winged ants that fly out of one of the colonies to form a new one. A Jubjub will usually be too intent on her migration to pay attention to the creatures on the ground, but if she notices you, she will seize you and take you to feed the new colony. That is what happened to one of my brothers, as you know." The warden had several brothers, all deformed creatures with large round eyes and repulsive wrinkly skin the color of fresh excrement.

"I know better than to walk in the open" sneered Godfrey. "The leaves of the trees that grow in this phantom forest will give me cover as long as I stay under them."

Their conversation was cut short by a distant thumping that became a roar in a matter of seconds.

"Quick, hide" warned the warden. "That's a Bandersnatch approaching."

***

Through openings in the dense vegetation, they could see a gigantic green bug lumber towards them. The progress of the bug was ponderous, for it ate leaves, stalks and tender branches along the way, leaving behind a liquid trail of excretion that had a somewhat aromatic smell. "How come the ants have not killed all the Bandersnatches as they did to other species?" wondered Godfrey.

"The ants like eating that thing the Bandersnatches release. Both species live in close proximity and appear to get along" replied the warden.

"Will it attack us?"

"Bandersnatches eat only plant products, but will attack any human that impedes their feeding or bars the way of their progress. Best hide until this beast passes through."

***

"Anyhow," resumed the warden, "if you are so intent on setting yourself against the Jabberwock, I will cast a spell on your broadsword so that it becomes a true vorpal weapon, unerring in its reach for the heart of an enemy."

"I don't believe in spells, but you can do it if you wish." Godfrey handed the sword to the warden, who disappeared with it inside his underground warren.

***

Next time they talked about the ants Godfrey expressed an unwavering desire to find and slay the Jabberwock. "I'm not scared and the weapon you enchanted for me should be enough to dispatch the monster."

"I would be most pleased if you succeeded. My grandfather was told by his grandfather that the year of the big flashes all living things that survived the explosions started dying off, as did most of mankind. An unseen poison covers all lands and has killed most forms of animal and plant life. For some reason, the poison did not exterminate the red warrior ants, which started growing until they got to their current size. Little by little they killed most of our ancestors and took the corpses inside their anthills to feed their young. The Jabberwock's hill is vast and very old, and holds whatever non-edible human possessions like rings, jewels and the like the ants did not consume. If you killed the Jabberwock, we could enter the anthill and retrieve the lost treasures."

"I don't care about treasures, though I'll take them. I just want to kill the bitch, and won't give up until I find her or she finds me."

***

Godfrey's quest went on for several days, as he traveled across the phantom forest. Having consumed most of what was edible, the giant ants no longer foraged the forest, which extended a long distance in all directions. Godfrey had been following the paths of devastation left by the warrior ants in the wake of their raids, but the tracks of barren soil were dug a long time in the past and had an abandoned look.

As sunset approached, Godfrey felt tired and thirsty. He leaned against the trunk of a giant ash tree and started to ponder where to go next. He soon had fallen asleep.

***

Godfrey woke up with a start as a cacophony of rustling leaves resonated through the woods. A nightmarish creature with an enormous head and clicking mandibles was approaching fast, multi-faceted eyes glowing red as they reflected the setting sun. Jumping to his feet, Godfrey brandished the sword and held it before his extended arm.

The Jabberwock could not speak, but focused its full attention on the human repast that offered itself to be devoured. Its mandibles opened and closed in anticipation, in an ominous murmur that evidenced his readiness to pounce on its prey. Godfrey pressed the sword trigger, immediately releasing a blue shaft of intense coherent light. The boy aimed the light at the petiole, the narrow segment before the ant's full abdomen, as the ant drew nearer.

***

The Jabberwock tried to snatch Godfrey with its mandibles, but the boy shifted quickly aside and, in one swift motion, struck at the petiole with a laser beam set at full intensity. Snicker-snack went the light beam, cutting through the chitinous skin and vaporizing the tissues within. The Jabberwock convulsed as its body was riven, the front half flinging itself madly at its human antagonist. Using its legs to lever itself, the ant sought to throw its full weight onto Godfrey and crush him.

Snick-snack. Godfrey ran the laser blade from one side of the ant's head to the other, cauterizing the eyes and burning away the antennae. The Jabberwock sprung even higher and lunged wildly with its mandibles seeking to ensnare the boy, but Godfrey jumped back and directed the laser light at the intersection of head and thorax. There was an unbearable stench of burned chitin and the ant's head tumbled to the ground with a deafening noise.

***

Godfrey left the inert body of the Jabberwock on the ground and retreated as far away from the battle scene as he could, lest other ants come into the forest. When his energy ran out, he rested his head against a tree trunk and fell into a stupor that lasted until the following day. Once recovered, he went back to the corpse of the Jabberwock and laboriously started to drag the head of the dead insect back to the village as proof of his success.

***

The humans that inhabited that knot of the phantom forest came out of hiding and gathered at the clearing in twos and threes at the sound of the warden's joyful shouts of greeting. Godfrey approached from the far side of the clearing, dragging the Jabberwock's severe head, which he laid down in triumph before his neighbors. He was covered head to toe in a sticky yellowish substance and was panting from the effort. He was unable to speak for a few heartbeats. Finally, he declared:

"I have killed the Queen and her host is now disorganized. Neither workers nor soldiers can become a new queen themselves, nor can they raise a new queen. So, this ant colony is over. We are, at least for the moment, free."

***

The warden was ecstatic. He would have to wait a few days until the ants dispersed, but then he could lead the humans under his command to the anthill and retrieve the treasures the insects had hoarded for generations.

"Come to my arms, my joyful boy! Let me embrace you!"

Godfrey freed himself from the arms of the warden and looked askance at his caretaker. "I wasn't sure you wanted me to survive that fight" he stated coldly.

"Don't be silly" replied the warden unctuously, "you are my most favorite person in the whole world. Let's go, I will prepare a refreshing potion that will soothe your nerves. We'll drink it to celebrate this fabulous, joyous day!"

Godfrey caught the gleam of malice in the warden's eye and stood waiting at the center of the clearing. Not long afterwards, the warden returned holding two clay cups filled to the brim with a dark fluid. The warden proffered one to Godfrey and started drinking the other.

"Actually, I like your cup better." Godfrey moved suddenly, snatched the warden's cup away, and presented his to the dwarf. "Here, drink to my health, and I'll drink to yours."

"Thanks, but no thanks," stammered the warden. "I've already drunk from my cup. It would be bad luck for you to share my saliva."

"Alright. But you must drink from my cup" insisted Godfrey.

"No, no, I prepared it specially for you. It's delicious" replied the warden, starting to shake.

"You dishonor me by refusing to drink from my cup. Take it and drink it or suffer the consequences of my displeasure." Godfrey spilled the cup from which the warden had drunk and threw it to the ground, turned on the laser broadsword, and lifted it up threateningly.

The warden turned around and started running away.

Godfrey flung the sword at the fleeing dwarf. The vorpal weapon unerringly struck the dwarf on the back of the head and carbonized him instantly.

***

The warden's demise was received by the population of humans and dwarves with consternation. The warden had apprised the majority of his neighbors of the riches that would be within their grasp as long as they did not have to share them with a victorious Godfrey. Also, the boy carried a bad reputation on account of the antisocial exploits of his father and the rumors of incest in his family. For those reasons, and maybe from envy, they surrounded the proud boy and threatened to punish him for his crime.

"You must leave our tribe and never come back!" said one. Nobody dared risk the kiss of the vorpal sword, so they remained hostile but took no further action.

Godfrey was undaunted. "I will leave your company, but not on account of your threats but because I despise the lot of you. I will go to the Jabberwock's anthill and claim whichever of the hidden treasures I choose. You can have anything that is left."

He turned away from the group and disappeared into the phantom forest. His last words trailed behind him like a fatal omen:

"The Jabberwock is dead, but now the ants know that there are humans left alive in this forest. They will comb the area, find each and every one, and devour you all. I won't be around to protect you, and I expect to die myself fighting them. Enjoy your last miserable days."

The Witch and the Crows

There are no words to capture the infinite depth of crowiness in the crow's flight.
Ted Hughes

Orenda was bent over her magical herb patch plucking away weeds when her concentration was broken by harsh calls coming from the skies above. She looked up, craning her neck and hoping not to find what her eyes confirmed: a murder of crows, rapidly moving black shades set against the clouds.

The witch scowled, and her face reflected her profound loathing of the birds. She had room in her affections for most living beings, large and small, peaceful and predatory; crows, however, were disgusting creatures that managed to survive through cunning despite the enmity of everyone else.

Crows devoured vegetable life and preyed on animals that were smaller or weaker than themselves; they befouled every surface over which they flew or in which they landed; they came in large numbers, disrupting the peace. Annoyingly, they were clever and eluded all measures to scare them away.

Orenda had attempted to protect the herbs she grew by placing netting around the rows of plantings, and inserting some lavender, garlic, and citronella bushes, for crows disliked their smells. The crows, however, would station themselves on nearby trees and would wait out the witch; when Orenda turned her back, crows would crowd into her garden, cut through the netting, and peck away at the tender stalks and leaves, ignoring the plants that were supposed to repel them.

Next, Orenda tried to keep the crows away by blocking the airspace above her property. She cast a spell that created an invisible barrier high above ground that kept flying objects from passing over her hut. This strategy gave rise to two problems: first, it prevented passage by friendly birds and impeded Orenda's travel by air during her rounds; also, it did not serve to prevent invasions by crows, who adapted quickly to the situation by flying close to the ground, below the tree canopy.

Orenda tried keeping the crows away from her plantings by erecting scarecrows, which she made more impressive by using magic to infuse the dummies with threatening motions with their limbs and heads. Several crows recoiled in fear at first, but heckling from others in their company encouraged them, and then other crows, to fly over and around the planted figures, sit on the scarecrows' heads, and defecate noisily on the figures before proceeding to devastate the crops.

A different type of scarecrow -- a plastic owl with a crow attached to its talons – also proved ineffective. The owl was mounted on a weather vane, and gyrated randomly with the wind; it operated until it was attacked by a host of crows, which pecked and tore away at the device, dismantling it.

Orenda concluded that she had to do something drastic about these crows. Besides their annoyance, their plundering of her plantings was making it hard for Orenda to make essential oils for candles and ritual tools, assemble sachets, prepare magical potions, and collect items required to cast spells. She had to get rid of the crows, one way or another, and would not mind it if they all died.

With those thoughts in mind, Orenda raised the fight from deterrence to extermination. She set poisoned lures on the ground among the rows of planted herbs.

A single crow was sent out experimentally to eat one of the morsels that had been placed by Orenda. The crow ate the poisoned bit, convulsed, keeled over, and died. The other crows mourned the deceased but reacted to the sacrifice of their companion by ignoring Orenda's remaining lures.

At this point, Orenda realized she was in a war against an enemy that matched her in persistence and cunning. She decided, like humans tried to do in similar circumstances, to negotiate a way out of her confrontation with the crows.

***

Negotiation, of course, requires communication. Crows are great communicators. They have dozens of vocalizations they use to send messages to each other, the most common is the cawing sound, which conveys location information to other members of a flock, warns of potential threats, and asserts territorial boundaries. Another vocalization is rattling, a rapid series of short, staccato sounds used to challenge or to signal danger. And there is clicking, a softer and more subtle vocalization that crows use to convey specific messages to one another. And so on.

Orenda had no time to learn the specifics of the crows' complex communication system. She opted, therefore, for a more direct approach: she entered the mind of a crow foraging nearby and began displaying simple images indicative of her thoughts.

[Orenda]: (Image of a fleeing owl) ##Not enemy##(Image of a white field) (Image of a crow flying serenely) ##Friend## (Image of a green field)

[Crow]: (Image of Orenda's face) (Image of a fleeing owl) ##Not enemy?## (Image of a white field)

[Orenda]: ##Friend## (Image of a green field) (Image of a very large, powerful looking crow) ## (Boss?)##

[Crow]: (Image of a different, large, older looking crow) ##Boss##

[Orenda]: (Image of a crow flying) (Image of the older looking crow) ##Bring?## (Image of a blue field).

[Crow]: (Series of images superimposed on one another) ##Confusion##

[Orenda]: (Repeats message)

[Crow]: ##Confusion##

[Orenda]: (Repeats message, adding: (Image of her face) (Image of older looking crow) ##Talk## (Orenda caws, imitating crow's call)

[Crow]: (Image of crow flying fast) ##Get him## (Image of a red field)

The crow flew away, returning later accompanied by the older crow.

***

It took some time for a communication protocol to be established. The old crow, who Orenda dubbed Skink because of the pictures of small lizards the crow flashed to underscore his food predilections, was a self-important creature that let Orenda know he had lived through "many" mating seasons, had fathered "many" birds, and was the head of a murder comprising "many" crows. (Skink could not count past eight, the number of toes on both his legs; anything greater than eight was "many.") Skink indicated that he and the other crows in his murder were unhappy with the things Orenda had done to get rid of them, and expressed the firm conviction that crows were smarter than humans like Orenda and would defeat all attempts she made to dislodge them.

Orenda listened patiently to Skink's braggadocio and then managed to convey the following thought: ##Wouldn't it be better if they could reach a solution that was good for all?##

Skink moved its head up and down slowly, signifying a potential agreement.

***

After some bargaining, Orenda and Skink agreed to the following deal: She would prepare, and provide daily, enough porridge to feed the members of Skink's murder. In return, Skink and his acolytes would refrain from feasting on Orenda's crops and would keep away any foreign crows that came within the bounds of Orenda's property. It was a simple enough agreement, but its success depended on observance of its provisions by all parties.

It worked for a while, and then both sides became dissatisfied. The crows were omnivorous and relished everything that was edible, and soon got tired of a monotonous diet of porridge and began to look covetously at Orenda's herbs and other plants, which were growing within a striking distance. Orenda, for her part, became weary of having to cook a big batch of porridge early each morning, serve it in two large vats, and clean up the mess (including droppings) that the crows left after they ate.

Orenda one night decided to spice up the next batch of porridge by adding ground up berries of the poisonous deadly nightshade. Coincidentally, at dawn the following morning, Skink led a raid of very hungry crows in an invasion of Orenda's arden, where they feasted on everything that was standing. When breakfast time came, both Orenda and the crows were presented with unpleasant surprises. The crows, notwithstanding their earlier feast, devoured the poisoned porridge and soon dropped to the ground in agony. Orenda watched their death throes with glee, but her enjoyment was short lived, for a few minutes later she went to tend to her garden and found it destroyed.

Other witches, attracted by psychic distress signals emanating from Orenda's hut, came to its vicinity and were appalled by the sight of seventeen crows of all sizes and ages, dead or dying at the clearing before the hut. Inside, Orenda was found in a state of hysteria, shrieking at the loss of a lifetime of magical gardening.

When a full understanding of the distressing situation was gained by the other witches, it was decided that Orenda would have to be expelled from the coven. She appeared demented and had committed a serious assault on living creatures. One of the visitors summed up the group's reaction to what had transpired: "There was fault on both sides, and both deserved punishment; nonetheless, in an orderly world, acts of wanton violence must not be permitted."

Orenda gave up gardening and retired from the practice of dark arts to lead the quiet life of a private citizen. Crows, however, still avoid the vicinity of her hut.

Azathoth is Amused

God of gods
Tyrant of space
Seething nuclear chaos
Thy darkness possesses me
Puteraeon, The Azathoth Cycle

I

Azathoth awoke and yawned.

The Demon Sultan, as Azathoth is sometimes called, is a boundless entity of colossal proportions: he is the most powerful being in the entire cosmos, an almost infinite aggregation of dark matter and dark energy. He had slept for countless eons since the start of the universe, residing in unlighted chambers beyond time and space at the imperceivable center of a remote galaxy. He was kept in continuous slumber by the muffled beating of drums and the thin monotonous whine of high-pitched flutes played by his acolytes, who feared the consequences of his awakening, for it was rumored that when Azathoth awoke all things would end.

For some reason he did not understand at first, Azathoth had woken up.

His coming to consciousness did not end all things but had far-flung consequences. Enormous black holes swallowed entire galaxies; celestial bodies departed erratically from their courses and crashed into each other; waves of high energy shot in all directions, devastating everything in their paths. Azathoth contemplated the carnage and yawned again: his cavernous mouth inhaled and then discharged all matter lying within a radius of several parsecs of his chambers.

"*Is this truly all there is?*" Azathoth asked himself as he yawned, for he found the sameness of the chaos around him reassuring but a little boring. Immediately, he summoned his first-spawn Nyarlathotep in search of an answer.

Nyarlathotep carries out the will of the Outer Gods and is their messenger, heart and soul. He is the servant of Azathoth, whose wishes he rushes to fulfill. As is the case with all the Old Gods, Nyarlathotep can travel across galaxies instantly, and his presence manifested itself at once in Azarthoth's mind: "Father, what troubled your sleep? How can I assist you?"

"Nyarlathotep," responded Azarthoth, conveying his thoughts instantly into his son's mind. "All I perceive around me is disarray and random destruction. This of course is at it should be, for I am the master of chaos, and all that exists must bend to my will. Yet, I heard in my sleep rumors suggesting that efforts are afoot to bring order to the workings of the universe. Find and bring to my attention such efforts if they are being made, and report on their success."

Nyarlathotep demurred. "Father, with all respect, I am not well suited to evaluate any ongoing actions to wrestle with chaos and impose order on it. My strength would lie in the opposite direction: if any such actions were undertaken, my preferred task would be to quench them and restore chaos. Perhaps one of the Elder Gods, our antagonists since time immemorial, may be best able to discern whether order is being achieved. Why don't you ask someone like Nodens, that filthy worm who often opposes me in my endeavors?"

Azathoth's maw opened and closed with a force that led to the discharge of a myriad waves of high energy. "That gives me an idea!" Then, casting out his will, he summoned the Elder: "Nodens, come to me!"

At once, Nodens manifested himself as a gray, shapeless shadow of mist and fog. "Why have you brought me before your throne, filthy abomination?" he challenged.

Azathoth ignored the insult. "I am in the mood for a game."

"What sort of a game?" retorted Nodens, his gravelly voice dripping contempt.

"There appear to be efforts in the universe to tame chaos and create predictability of events. They call this forcible vanquishment of chaos the imposition of order. If such order were established, it would threaten my very essence, and I would need to deal with it. I want you and my son Nyarlathotep to go and find places where order and chaos are colliding. At each place, you will observe the conflict, but must not try to influence its outcome. You will remain at each such place until the battle is concluded, and will then come and report to me the final result.

"Why should I want to play this game?"

"Because I order you to do so, else I shall destroy you" growled Azathoth. Then, in a more conciliatory tone, "plus you will go with my first spawn Nyarlathotep as your companion and foil. You have fought with him in the past and bested him. Perhaps you would enjoy matching your powers against his again."

Nodens considered the matter for a while. "I will play, on one condition: I get to pick the place of the first visit to the site of a potential engagement. I am not about to travel up and down the vastness of space searching in vain for efforts to tame chaos."

Nyarlathotep then spoke. "You filthy wretch! I reckon you already have a specific location in mind."

The accusation was clearly the fruit of Nyarlathotep's cunning mind and Nodens felt like ignoring it, but was compelled by the will of Azathoth to respond.

"Yes" replied Nodens. "I have spent much energy helping the denizens of a small rock orbiting a second-rate star. They are known as humans and are insignificant beings, but sentient enough to get themselves into all sorts of predicaments. I expect to find some form of attempts at order in their activities."

"Does that place have a name?" asked Azathoth.

"It is called Earth. It is the third planet orbiting a yellow star called Sol."

"I have been there" pointed out Nyarlathotep. "A miserable dump if there was ever one."

"Do you object to this Earth as being the place of your initial investigations?" asked Azathoth. "You can go elsewhere if Earth is not suitable."

"No, Earth is fine" replied Nyarlathotep with a smirk. "As I said, I have been there."

"Then, do get started" directed the Demon Sultan as he yawned again.

II

Selection of Earth as the target of their first investigation was not enough to launch it. Knowing the where did not resolve the question of when. All Gods have the magical ability to travel in time as well as through space. Therefore, the entire history of Earth, from its creation to the date of its ultimate destruction, was available for their visit. Nodens suggested that they pick a time close, but not too close, to the disappearance of humans from Earth, to maximize the potential for finding indicia of order among them. At the end, they materialized in what humans called the first quarter of the twenty-first century.

On arrival, Nyarlathotep and Nodens were in the early dawn hour in an empty field in Lydney Park, a forested area in Gloucestershire, England. Nodens had selected this location for their first manifestation on Earth because it was the site of a shrine erected to his worship in the remote past, so it felt a bit like home. Both he and Nyarlathotep had assumed human form: Nodens, a vigorous old man dressed in rough country clothes and sporting a full white beard; Nyarlathotep, a tall, lean man of black coloration, wholly devoid of either hair or beard, and wearing as his only garment a shapeless robe of heavy black fabric. They both looked odd but not strange enough to startle a passerby, were one to be found at that early hour.

"Where do we go now? This is your game" remarked Nyarlathotep acidly.

Nodens led them in a walk that headed south from the shrine until they reached a motor highway. There, they turned left and after a few paces arrived at a building with an ancient sign that read "The George Inn." They stood at the door and observed a number of seated humans consuming food, drinking hot and cold liquids, and conversing.

"What are we looking for here?" asked Nyarlathothep.

"Not much in particular. As you can see, there are some locals having an early breakfast, talking to each other, and reading the local newspaper."

"And what is the point of that?"

"Well, the point is obvious. The humans who inhabit this planet have brought order out of chaos in that they have invented language, so the sounds they utter convey information from one individual to another. They also have invented writing, so their language is communicated not only by the sounds they make but by symbols imprinted on some surface. Language, both spoken and written, introduces order in the lives of these humans and dispels chaos."

"How do you know that?" challenged Nyarlathotep.

"As you can see, these humans are interacting peacefully with each other and do not seem to live in fear or be consumed by chaos. Do you want to come right in and chat with the locals so you can experience their activities first hand?"

"No need" replied Nyarlathotep dismissively. "I have walked this world before. I have seen humans reading newspapers and talking to one another in taverns. But these achievements that you cite hardly overcome chaos. Isn't it a fact that, in using language with each other, humans frequently communicate untrue or dangerous ideas, and often even use language to inflict ills on one another?"

"Yes, but..."

"And the written language that you cite, doesn't it often contain false and misleading assertions that can cause harm to those who read the writings or others with whom the readers interact?"

"Yes."

"Well, I don't see how the invention of spoken or written language introduces order in the lives of humans or avoids chaos."

"Wait one second. What you say is right to a point but does not matter. Language is capable of conveying information that would otherwise be difficult or impossible to communicate. Language provides order; without it, interactions between humans would be chaotic. The fact that a tool can be misused does not diminish its value, if used properly. And there are other things the inhabitants of this world have done which likewise do away with chaos. Are you familiar with music?"

"Of course," replied Nyarlathotep sharply. "You are referring to the creation of sounds made not to convey information but to elicit an emotional reaction on the listener."

"Well, music is the counterpart of written or spoken language. It is the production of combinations of tones that are pleasing in some manner because of certain elements known as melody, rhythm, and harmony. Through music humans affect the listeners' emotions, creating positive responses that may be beneficial."

"To me, music is just noise" dismissed Nyarlathotep.

"Yet, what is there in music that may be pleasing to the listener? Let me tell you: it is ordering. Individual sounds may be chaotic and as such meaningless or disagreeable, but arranged in certain ways they exemplify the bringing of order out of chaos. As a famous human once said, 'music creates order out of chaos: for rhythm imposes unanimity upon the divergent, melody imposes continuity upon the disjointed, and harmony imposes compatibility upon the incongruous.' And by creating music, humans have brought about another way of instituting order and banishing chaos."

Nyarlathotep could no longer contain himself. "Do you mean to tell me that music is always appealing to the emotions? I have been around this planet many times and have been subjected to truly appalling sounds that would cause irritation or worse among those subjected to them. I have even heard humans discuss something they call 'modern music' as lacking in one or more of the three elements you cited – rhythm, melody or harmony. How can you claim music as proof that humans have brought order out of chaos?"

"You fall again in the same fallacy you did when discussing language. There may be cases in which music is incorrectly created or performed, and for that reason fails to achieve its purpose. But the existence of bad music does not disprove that, in inventing music, humans have brought order out of chaos in still another way. And, as I said, there are many other areas of intellectual activity in which humans have definitively brought order out of chaos."

Nyarlathotep was evidently not prepared to accept any arguments along the lines proposed by Nodens, so the Elder brought the discussion to an end: "Let us take these examples to Azathoth and let him be the judge. But it is your turn now."

III

"I reckon we will stay on this planet" declared Nyarlathotep. "Earth has witnessed many attempts to institute some sort of order, only to fall back into chaos after dismal failures."

"What do you mean?"

"I am talking about human's efforts to organize themselves in groups of individuals. They call these groups by different names – family, tribe, nation, and so on. The larger the number of individuals comprising one of these groups, the more likely that any attempt to provide order will fail and chaos will ensue."

Nodens protested. "That is not so, or is at least a gross exaggeration. Most human groupings I have seen function successfully, in a predictable fashion, and go on doing this essentially forever."

"That is not the case" argued Nyarlathotep. "I can show you an example or two of what I mean."

"Be my guest" challenged Nodens.

"Then join me as we take a little journey."

There was an immediate change in scenery. Sol was only halfway up the sky, but the day was already very bright and oppressively hot. They found themselves standing on a litter-covered street, near the waterfront of a big city. Dark skinned men in shorts and tee-shirts and women wearing colorful dresses or dark burqas were ambling up and down the road, seemingly without purpose.

"Where are we?" asked Nodens.

"This is Mogadishu, the capital of Somalia. It was once the seat of a powerful empire and was called the White Pearl of the Indian Ocean; not so anymore."

"Why...?" began Nodens. His question was interrupted by a horrendous blast nearby, followed by a rainstorm of projectiles, some of which went through the incorporeal manifestations of the two gods.

A thick cloud of dust and other debris covered everything for a few minutes. When it dissipated, a band of humans was seen running towards the remains of a partly demolished tall building, now in flames.

"That is ... or was... the 'Hotel Paradiso,' one of the largest human dwellings in town. It has been bombed and is now under attack" reported Nyarlathotep.

"What do you mean bombed?"

"As you must know, humans have developed tools for inflicting harm on each other. These tools are known as weapons and are of many kinds; they include things called bombs, which are weapons that burst, casting their contents in all directions with great force."

"And you think some humans have cast one of those bombs at the hotel?"

"I am certain of it" replied Nyarlathotep. "Such destructive acts have been going on in Mogadishu and throughout Somalia for a very long time."

"Who is doing this bombing?" questioned Nodens, as he tried to make out the forms of men in dark uniforms charging aggressively at the hotel occupants.

"Seventy cycles ago of the Earth's gyrations around Sol, the humans inhabiting Somalia established a form of rule known as a Republic. There was conflict between various groups of humans from the start of the Republic, each group trying to wrestle power from all the others. Forty Sol cycles later, all forms of organized rule collapsed and nonstop wide-ranging fighting began occurring throughout Somalia. Humans from abroad as well as various parts of Somalia took part in multiple battles against the locals. Right now, most of the damage to the lives and properties of humans in Somalia is the result of attacks by members of Al-Shabaab, a Somalia-based group with links to rulers in other parts of this world. I expect the humans now attacking the hotel are Al-Shabaab members."

"There must be humans who try to prevent getting harmed by those Al-Shabaab" wondered Nodens.

"There are, but the forces opposing Al-Shabaab have not succeeded in re-establishing control of the country; rather, order has dissolved into chaos."

"And you have brought us here so I can be convinced that humans in Somalia have failed to overcome chaos and are leading their miserable lives among a total lack of order."

"Well, you be the judge. The unrest in this part of Earth has resulted in the death or injury of hundreds of thousands of humans, and almost three million more have been forced to leave their place of habitation. For the last thirty Sol cycles, Somalia has not had functioning rulers and has become one of the poorest human aggregations on the planet. There is widespread hunger among the population and famine and disease take the lives of many. I can go on," summed up Nyarlathotep.

Nodens was not ready to concede. "Human population groups have encountered many disruptions in their efforts to maintain order. Most groups have found stable rulers that provide predictable ways for individuals to carry out their lives. Somalia may be a place where order has collapsed and chaos prevails. But what has happened here has to be an isolated instance, rather than the rule."

"I can point to several other places, including one just across the waters called Yemen, where similar conditions exist now. Human efforts to rule themselves will inevitably result in chaos over the long run" countered Nyarlathotep.

"It seems we disagree again. What should we do?" challenged Nodens.

"Let's go back to Azathoth for instructions."

IV

Azathoth received the conflicting reports with little enthusiasm. "I am not interested in the success or failure of a lowly life form in an obscure corner of a middling galaxy. I sent you to Sol to see if you could bring me any clear evidence that chaos is disappearing in my domain. From what you tell me, humans have come up with a degree of order in some discrete areas. On the other hand, their efforts to find an orderly way to rule themselves point to failure. So, neither of you has provided me a definitive answer to the question I asked," he concluded sternly.

Nyarlathotep groveled in the face of the sovereign's displeasure. "Father, humans are among the lowest forms of life that are present in the universe. What they do about chaos should be of no concern to us, particularly to one as all-powerful as you."

Azathoth cut him short. "I agreed to send you there because humans are such simple, unimportant creatures. They should have provided a straightforward answer to my desire to know if the rule of chaos is ever at risk of ending. You have not given me the answer I need."

Nodens was reluctant to intervene but had to defend the human race. "It would be a mistake to underestimate the complexities of which this low form of life is capable. I am afraid we have provided you with two extreme examples that, in a way, cancel each other out."

"As I said, I do not care how humans fare" replied Azathoth. "But their experience confirms that efforts to impose order throughout the universe are most likely to fail over the long run. Let humans continue to struggle to bring order to their world, and let all others who want to fight me also give it a try. It amuses me to anticipate how I will defeat them."

The Caged Bird and the Fairy

*The caged bird sings with a fearful trill
of things unknown but longed for still
for the caged bird sings of freedom.*
Maya Angelou

Roger fluttered excitedly as he sought to approach the strange bird that was hovering outside Roger's bamboo cage. The cage was large and Roger small (a mere five inches from crest to tail) so he had plenty of space to roam back and forth, in and out, but he could never get close enough to his target. The bird outside the cage was also small, but the similarities ended there. Roger was a male Pacific parrotlet, a small parrot with a dusty grey cast over the body, a bright green mask, and a pinkish beak; the stranger was translucent, with diaphanous wings whose colors changed constantly and a body that mimicked that of Adrianne, the youngest of his human owners.

"Who are you?" Roger intended to say, but what came out of his beak was a loud "tchit" that he repeated, over and again. The other bird remained silent, and Roger resorted to other sounds in his repertory, imitating the noises humans made and those from Edith, the family's striped white and gray cat. There was no reply to any of them.

Roger was starting to lose interest in the other bird when a series of images formed in his brain: a sun-drenched meadow adorned with all sorts of flowers; fields of low bushes from which grew stalks of grain; an expanse of turquoise water at whose edge wavelets broke into a golden beach dotted with tall, bending trees that could have come from Roger's ancestral home; limitless blue skies dotted with fluffy white clouds; mountains, prairies, placid rivers, all of which beckoned him.

"Wouldn't you want to be here?" was the images' silent entreaty.

These feelings were new and confusing. Roger had been hatched in captivity and had progressed from confinement in a pet shop to a similar situation at the home of his current owners. Roger was abundantly fed quinoa, millet, broccoli, beetroot, oats, bell peppers, rice, and pomegranate seeds, although his favorites were fruits of all kinds. He was given exercise periods outside his cage, and often sat himself on the shoulder of one of his owners. He lived alone, having pecked to death his consort Brigitte in a fit of temper several years back, but managed to entertain himself by imitating the noises humans made and the growls of Edith. He felt content living in his bamboo home, in the living room of his owners. What need did he have to go to those alien places?

Roger was able to locate the source of these visions: they seemed to originate from the strange bird, which was still circling around his cage annoyingly. Roger uttered a quick series of unwelcoming "tchits" and bumped repeatedly against the walls of the cage to evidence his displeasure. The strange bird, however, remained unfazed. "Let's go see places with me," it seemed to suggest.

The suggestion did not resonate with Roger. Though he descended from many generations of long-distance travelers accustomed to traverse mile upon mile of the Amazon jungle, he was only used to short flights within and around his cage and did not feel adventurous. He issued a couple of energetic "tchits" in negation and planted himself on his perch, determined to ignore the obnoxious visitor.

But the visitor was not about to give up so easily. It flew right up to the cage, gyrated twice, and issued from one of its extremities a shaft of bright light that burned a hole on the gate that sealed the cage. There was a smell of burned wood and the gate became unlocked, its remains hanging uselessly from its hinges. The bird made an unmistakable "Follow me!" motion with its humanlike hands and darted out towards an open window. After a while, curiosity won over and Roger gave chase.

***

They flew wildly, rising and falling and twirling in the air currents, chasing each other, and letting the sun warm their wings, in endless enjoyment of the glorious summer afternoon. Roger decided that, after all, he liked the adventure. But the good feelings were not meant to last; soon the dark figure of a falcon appeared in the sky and gave chase, seeking to capture one or both frolickers. It got to Roger first, and held the parrot's tail firmly in its talons intending to bring its victim within reach of its sharp beak, but before it could complete its attack it was struck by an energy bolt discharged by the other bird, which hovered in mid air above the pair and signaled Roger to fly away.

Roger reacted by plummeting in the general direction of the home of its owners, which he was instinctively able to locate as he slowed his descent a few meters above the ground. He entered through the same open window that had allowed him to depart only a short time earlier, and flew into the remains of his cage, where he perched himself shivering while he stared fearfully for a potential pursuit by the falcon.

The falcon was otherwise occupied. It had lunged at the strange bird and torn off one of its wings, sending the bird spiraling down to earth, out of control. The falcon gave chase, but another blast of energy from its prey caused the predator to seek safety by flying away precipitously. The falling bird somehow managed to slow down its descent and entered the house through the same window that Roger had used for his escape. It coasted down to the floor and lay there, not moving.

All the commotion did not go unnoticed. Edith woke up from her afternoon nap and moseyed on into the living room. She came to a halt when she detected a bird lying on the floor and moved up to the strange creature, smelling its body and trying to figure out if it was edible. Soon she decided that, if not to eat, the object was at least good to play with and picked the bird off the floor with her mouth and started pawing its body trying to elicit a reaction from it.

Edith did get her reaction, but it came from an unexpected source. Roger darted across the room and began pecking viciously at the cat's ears. Edith was surprised: she was familiar with this bird, who sat day and night in an out of reach cage and annoyingly imitated Edith's grunts and meows, and was treated by the humans as a household member. Roger's pecking was drawing blood from Edith's ears and was intolerable, so the cat dropped the strange bird and turned towards Roger, trying to swat at him with her paws. Roger, however, was too fast and kept moving randomly, remaining out of reach.

Meanwhile, the strange bird had recovered and gathered enough strength to fling another blast of energy at the cat's tail, singing it and causing Edith to yell in pain. Under attack from two directions, Edith thought the better of it and ran back to the safety of the kitchen.

Roger flew down to the floor and inspected the strange bird. It seemed to be recovering; in fact, it was starting to grow a new wing to replace the one it had lost to the falcon. An image of the two birds flying together formed in Roger's mind. It was accompanied by a pleasant feeling and an invitation that suggested that both birds should continue to keep each other's company, and enjoy venturing into the wild together.

Roger did not have the words to express its agreement, but bumped his head gently against the strange bird and issued a low "tchit" to confirm his satisfaction.

And they became good friends and had many adventures together; no cats or birds of prey ever figured in them.

A Bad Bargain

I have a soul the devil wouldn't buy.
Ashley McBryde

Archibald Gordon McManus ("Archie" to his friends) had watched the séance with uncharacteristic equanimity. He had hidden his disgust at having to sit in darkness on the dirt floor of this hovel, surrounded by peons, his hands joined to theirs in a circle around a table, under the flickering light of four red candles. His mouth curled with barely concealed contempt as Princess' last barks were lost in the distance, accompanied by the sighs of the old mistress who had summoned her spirit.

Seeing that the beggar to his right was clearing the throat to speak, Archie waited no longer. He knitted his brows in concentration and called out:

"Win ... Win ... dear Winifred, come to me! Come to me, Win!!" As the seconds ticked on, his voice became more imperious, in the manner of one used to commanding. Only his rigid body and the tightness with which his hands squeezed those of his neighbors betrayed his anxiety.

At the other side of the circle the spirit medium, a Shona matron with a round ebon face covered in white powder, continued to gaze with unseen eyes at the hut's roof. After a while, however, her jaw started raising and falling, as if she was chewing. Her lips trembled, and her ample body began shaking in random convulsions. Finally, the medium stopped shaking and responded in a hollow voice: "Archie! Please get me out of here! I can't stand the agony! Please rescue me from this horror!!"

Annoyance was a frequent companion to Archie when he dealt with his wife, dead or alive. This emotion was now magnified by the torrent of pleas that issued from the medium's mouth. He was barely able to insert a calming reply into the stream:

"Win, please, get a hold of yourself. If you keep bawling, we won't be able to have a conversation."

The voice took on a familiar nagging tone:

"Sure, it's easy for you to tell me to calm down, because you aren't suffering the way I am. Archie, I'm in Hell! Me! The Treasurer of the League of Christian Women! Me, in Hell! What a disgrace! What an injustice! ..."

"I was expecting that, Win. That's why I summoned you!"

"You were expecting it? Why? Wasn't I always a faithful wife, a good mother, a devout Christian?"

"I had a hunch. Maybe it was just your way of being... But in any case, I need your help."

"*I* help *you*?... I'm the one who needs help! Go talk to your friend the bishop and see if he can intercede on my behalf, or maybe give donations to the Pope and the Dalai Lama, see if any of them can do something!" ... I beg you, Archie, please get me out of here!!!"

There was a long series of incoherent phrases, pleas and whimpers that rose from the lips of the medium, who had broken away from the chain and was wringing her hands desperately.

What can I do to shut this woman up? Archie asked himself. *I could never do it when she was alive*. He barked an order: "That's enough, Win. Listen up!" ... "I'll see what I can do. But now you must pay attention." There was a brief silence, and he took advantage of it to continue:

"I need to speak with Satan." He uttered those words very carefully, stressing each one. "I've tried getting his attention by all means, including sitting in meetings like this one. He doesn't answer. So, I need you to get him for me. We need to talk."

"Archie, you've gone mad!" shrieked the voice. "How can I ...."

This time, Archie was the one who interrupted. He replied sternly: "You always got your way. Nobody could ever stop you. If there is anyone in this world or the next who can get the devil to come to this stinking hovel, it's you. Please do it for our sick daughter as well as for me, because I need to talk to him about her." He said that last bit in a tender tone, feigning love and parental concern. "After I'm done speaking with him, I'll get you help right away." Of course, he didn't mean to do such a thing, but it sounded good.

There was a deep sigh .... A timorous "Alright" ... and then deep silence. Everyone turned to the medium, who was slumped on an armchair, barely breathing.

***

Much, much later, when everyone but Archie had left the hut, the Shona spirit medium jumped to her feet as if hit by lightning, making her multicolor cape twirl in the air. There was an acrid smell that commingled with the stench of the tallow candles dying out on the table. A deep inhuman voice then broke the silence:

"So, what do you want, Archie?"

"Why did you take so long to answer my calls?" replied Archie sullenly.

"Because I know what you are going to propose, and am not interested."

"I doubt that. I want to sell you my soul. I will give it to you if you extend my life and restore my fortune. How about it?"

"Why would I want to bargain for your soul? To have a deal, you need two interested parties. And I am not interested in buying your soul."

"Why would you not want my soul? I bet it's as desirable as any of the others in which you trade."

"Your memory seems to have suffered with age," was the sarcastic reply. "Do you remember, for instance, when you used an armed militia to shift the boundaries of your tobacco farm and steal most of the land of your Ndebele neighbor Isaki Myedziwa? He became despondent and committed suicide; has been with me for years. And how about the deal you made in '71 with the large chromium mining companies to drive ore prices down and ruin the small miners? I gained many of them thanks to that maneuver. And how about that teenage daughter of your tenant Ian Campbell? Not only did you rape her, but you disgraced her by telling everyone about it at your New Years' party in '73? And your role in the electoral fraud of ..."

"Enough," pleaded Archie. "Perhaps I've committed some minor sins, but I've also suffered much. Since Mugabe came into power in Zimbabwe, all I owned has been confiscated by the government and given to the natives. It has been ten years of exile in my own land, living in poverty, enduring the derision or the familiarity of the riff-raff, people that in earlier times wouldn't have dared stare me in the face."

"Suffering confers no rights, Archie. You have suffered as much as you have because you deserved it. Anyhow, what would you do if I granted you your wishes? Would you forgive those who occupied your lands, those who now live in your mansion?"

"That bastard Mtukudzi who appropriated my estate, I will kill him with my own hands! The others... well, I'll evict everyone and have the dogs sicced on them if they give me trouble... I'll forgive nobody, except maybe those who agree to become my land tenants again."

"I'm starting to think that perhaps I could use you after all."

"How is that?"

"As you know, my tools are the forces of revenge, ambition, envy, thirst for power, chaos. So, you might serve as a good agent of mine."

"Do we have a deal, then?"

"I don't need to bargain to get your soul. Why should I pay for something that's already mine, something that I will be collecting soon?"

"So, you *won't* accept my offer?" asked Archie, incredulous and frightened.

"Actually, I think I will deal with you, but not because your soul is worth much to me, since it is doomed already. I will extend your life *gratis* and provide you with the means to regain what you had. You can then help me pull in scores of souls that I might lose otherwise."

"So, we *do* have a deal!" shouted Archie, beaming with satisfaction.

"Yes. I will extend your life and provide you with a little help to get back on your feet. At midnight on a day like today, fifty years from now, I will come to collect. Until then..." Satan punctuated these words with a long, sardonic burst of laughter that slid, like a finger of ice, down Archie's spine.

***

From that moment on, Archie's life became a whirlwind of activity. The first step was the recovery of his lands from the interlopers. There was unexpected resistance by the farmers and others who had trespassed on his holdings, but he paid off mercenaries to quell the protests. Recovery was accomplished swiftly, though with a significant loss of life on both sides. Archie's reputation as a ruthless colonialist expanded to all corners of the land.

Two years after his rise from poverty back to wealth, Archie ran for Zimbabwe's House of Assembly and was elected by a wide margin. Two years later, he became a member of the Senate, thanks to secret donations to tribal chiefs who were persuaded to support an old, bloodthirsty white landowner if the price was right. Then came the presidential elections of '98, when he ran as a dark horse and prevailed over two more popular, better known opponents who cancelled each other out in the vote.

As President, Archie implemented an expansionist policy that got him in bloody wars with three neighboring countries. He was no Napoleon, but luck seemed to shine on him. Zimbabwe's forces were victorious in all wars, although the number of dead, injured and dispossessed was estimated by outside observers to be in the millions. At the conclusion of the last of these wars, a boot-licking Parliament elected him President for life. He had started his political career at age 74 and was now 87. His longevity was attributed by many to his dabbling in the black arts.

As his political fortunes rose and he became stupendously wealthy, his health declined steadily. When he sold his soul to the Devil, he was 71 and in reasonably good shape for an elderly man whose life had been punctuated by excesses – he was suffering from gout, a touchy liver, a coating of tar on his lungs, arthritis. He expected, not unreasonably, that if he was to live fifty more years Satan would see to it that he was kept healthy. This, however, proved a miscalculation.

The first signs of trouble came when his severe arthritis condition required replacement surgery for his hips and knees. He went through those and recovered, though his body now felt weak and vulnerable.

More severe ailments started to manifest themselves on the date the last interlopers were driven from his lands. He threw himself a big party, for which he imported white hookers from Cape Town and offered the best in food, liquor and weed to his guests. After dinner, he rose to toast to his victory, tumbled, and collapsed, victim of a heart attack. This was the first of numerous cardiac problems, which over the years required a heart transplant, coronary bypass surgery, and the insertion of a pacemaker. Those problems might have caused another person to die; Archie surmounted them, but was left in a debilitated condition.

Severe emphysema caused by decades of heavy smoking was another problem that needed to be treated with a cocktail of drugs and diminished the quality of Archie's life. Likewise, at age 82 Archie was diagnosed with Type 2 diabetes and was haunted by frequent urination, fatigue, blurred vision and headaches that made him dependent on medications just to function. Diabetes led to kidney failure, such that by age 88 he started requiring dialysis three times a week.

His first bout with cancer affected his prostate, which had to be removed. This reduced his already waning sexual performance and aggravated the urinary problems caused by his diabetes. Afterward, he developed colon cancer, which required surgery, and liver cancer, which launched a frantic search for a compatible liver for transplant. The search was successful, but the transplant operation left Archie on the verge of death. Like with all the other ailments, he suffered greatly but survived.

But disease and aging were not the only threats to Archie's health. After he became Zimbabwe's President, there were three attempts on his life. All failed to achieve their purpose, but the last two had adverse effects on him: a bomb that exploded under his bullet-proof Mercedes left him with inoperable shrapnel fragments throughout the body; and a suicide attempt by a knife thrower caused him to almost lose an eye and gifted him with an ugly scar running down the left side of his face that left it paralyzed.

It is little wonder that people started to believe he was immortal. Some even suspected the truth, charging that a malevolent deity was protecting him. His doctors had to contrive explanations for his durability: a homeopathic diet; rigorous exercise; meditation; a unique genetic makeup. These excuses were all false and nobody believed them, but that was the official explanation and people had to live with it.

His fading physical condition did not diminish his ability to wreak destruction on his country and throughout Eastern Africa. His slash and burn raids destroyed the livelihood of thousands of farming families and caused hunger, despair, and suicide as far north as Tanzania. He was ruthless in rooting out dissenters, and even his most sycophantic supporters lived in constant fear of his violent moods. He was compared (in whispers) to Attila, Genghis Khan, Ivan the Terrible, Hitler, Stalin. When his 100th birthday came around in 2019, the official celebrations had a macabre undertone: Zimbabwe had the dubious honor of hosting the world's first eternal tyrant.

***

Right after his first heart attack, Archie became concerned and tried to reach Satan to find out what was going on. He made frequent visits to séances and brought well-known spiritualists to the Presidential Palace for private sessions. All attempts at contact failed.

Despair grew as the ravages of disease and old age took their toll on his body. Why did he have to suffer so much? What was the point of great power and wealth if his daily life was one continued agony?

He was 116 in 2035 when he had a major stroke that left the right side of his body paralyzed. He could still think clearly, but his speech was slurred and almost unintelligible. Zimbabwe's Vice President was forced to declare that Archie was temporarily unable to discharge his duties and had him confined to a private clinic for "rest and recuperation."

As he lay unconscious during the early stages of his stroke, Archie had a strange vision. His wife Winifred appeared before his bed and remonstrated with him about his dishonesty. "You promised you would do something to get me out of Hell and you did nothing! And you also did nothing to help our daughter!! You're a liar and a cheat and deserve your punishment!!"

Archie was too weak to respond, but formed a vague apology in his mind: "I was busy with other things."

Winifred continued, relentlessly: "And I trusted you and debased myself before Satan to get Him to pay attention to you. That deal you made with Him, you owe it to me!"

Even in a coma, Archie was incensed: "It was not a deal but a gift, and it was lousy! What good is to live fifty more years if you are going to suffer every minute of them?"

Winifred's spectral mouth opened in a smile of grim satisfaction. "You didn't specify that you wanted to stay in good health, and I suggested to Him that he let you suffer. I argued that you would be more effective in your hatred of the world if you were driven by pain in your insides. He liked the idea."

"So, this is just your revenge playing itself out." Archie sighed, resignedly. "What do I do now? I have five years left on this "life" before he takes me. Five more years of torment?"

"You could kill yourself, but that would not help. He owns you, and will take you either now or in five years, and then the real torment will begin." With that, the ghost vanished.

As he sunk back into unconsciousness, a single thought crystallized in Archie's mind: "While there is life there is hope. I have five years left. I'll try to make the best of this bad deal."

***

Archie never fully recovered from the stroke, but when he was well enough to speak in public, he asked for a press conference to be scheduled, and his frightened underlings rushed to accommodate his wishes. A meeting with the press on the grounds of the clinic was hastily arranged.

Archie was spectrally thin and ill-looking as he came to the microphone. He felt even weaker than he appeared, so he made only three brief announcements and took no questions. First, he said that he was resigning from his office as Zimbabwe's President and giving up politics altogether. Second, he was liquidating his assets and would donate his entire fortune to charity. And third, as his health allowed, he would spend his remaining days caring for the sick and poor, and was joining the international army of volunteers that was fighting the Ebola epidemic in western Africa.

Weeks later, a somewhat recovered but still frail Archie took off for the Congo. He spent the rest of his life doing good deeds. He died in his sleep in the summer of 2040, at age 121. Those who witnessed his death reported that he had a smile on his withered face as he passed away. Perhaps he had managed to improve his deal.

A Mask for Every Mood

The mask which concealed the visage was made so nearly to resemble the countenance of a stiffened corpse that the closest scrutiny must have had difficulty in detecting the cheat.
E.A. Poe, The Masque of the Red Death

"This thing is malfunctioning again!" shouted Eric, pounding the controls of the neurostimulator. Little by little, the youth's limbic system lumbered into action and the physiological markers of anger started to manifest themselves: increases in heart rate, arterial tension, and testosterone production. However, the silicone mask covering Eric's face still displayed an incongruous smile.

Eric's mother urged him to calm down. "You must learn to control that temper of yours! Instead of screaming, you should take your IPG it to the service center; maybe the batteries are running weak. I hope they won't have to muck with the lead."

"You know how long the lines are at the center? Everybody and his brother are having problems with this system. It's too complicated!"

"What can we do? We all have got the virus," she lamented.

"Damned virus!" Eric continued to scream beneath the still smiling mask.

"At least this new gift from China doesn't kill people, not usually," she replied, prodding him again:

"OK, get going. Have them also look at the mask links."

***

The nearest service center of the Healthtronics Corporation was in a suite of rooms in a megamall a short ride away from Eric's home. The center had a main room with a long counter and numerous uncomfortable chairs; there was also a backroom where repairs were made. The main room was full of waiting customers, some of them milling about impatiently. The entire setup made Eric feel depressed.

Eric approached the counter and pulled a number from a dispenser. "137," read the paper ticket. An illuminated display on the back wall read: NOW SERVING: 92.

"Aww," moaned the youth. It would be a couple of hours wait. He picked up a pamphlet from an open display box and sat down to kill a few minutes reading.

He read: "The virus affecting the world population is a new strain, HSV-4, of the Herpes Simplex virus. Starting in Asia last spring, HSV-4 reached every continent in a matter of weeks. Like other herpes varieties, HSV-4 is highly infectious and transmits through bodily fluids, especially saliva. It can also spread through blood and semen during sexual contact, blood transfusions, and objects that an infected person recently used. HSV-4 distinguishes itself from earlier HSV strains in that it affects a victim's nervous system. The virus lodges itself in the brain and interferes with the functioning of the body's control functions.

"Health care professionals all over the world are striving to understand HSV-4 and develop a vaccine to eradicate it. No cure has been found yet, but the health care industry, led by Healthtronics Corporation, has launched an all-out program to mitigate the virus' effects. Taking a clue from Parkinson's Disease treatment strategies, Healthtronics has developed a deep brain stimulation system (DBSS) intended to bring back into action an inoperative limbic system. The DBSS is installed by drilling tiny holes in the skull of a patient, inserting miniature electrodes into the affected region deep on the back of the brain, and running wires through the neck down to the collarbone to connect the electrodes to a battery-operated implantable pulse generator (IPG) control center similar to a pacemaker."

"Your physician will be able to prescribe the type and model of DBSS that is most suitable for your clinical condition and your preferences. Whatever system you choose, trained personnel at the service centers of the Healthtronics Corporation will provide efficient and competent assistance to ensure your device operates optimally."

There was a lot more detail, too much to keep Eric interested. He sighed, put the brochure back in the display box, and sat down to await his turn.

***

The technician who waited on Eric was sympathetic but unable to render all the help he required. "The batteries on your IPG were weak and we have recharged them so they are now fine; the device is sending the intended electrical impulses to your brain even as we speak. So, the problem that still remains has to be with your mask."

"What kind of a problem would that be?" asked Eric.

"As you know, a side effect of infection with HSV-4 is the cessation of electrical stimuli from the limbic system to the facial nerve that controls the muscles in a person's face. The lack of such stimuli causes facial paralysis and some speech difficulty. Many persons affected by HSV-4, such as yourself, find these side effects intolerable and seek mitigating measures. Several vendors manufacture masks made of latex or silicone rubber designed to be pulled over the head as a form of theatrical makeup or disguise. Those masks can be outfitted with electronic devices to receive signals from an IPG, directly or through the remote-control unit, and if this is done, they are marketed as "smart masks," intended to alleviate facial paralysis."

"We at Healthtronics do not manufacture or sell smart masks. We do, however, manufacture a modified type of remote-control unit that has been enhanced, in accordance with mask manufacturer specifications, to provide the ability to control the motion of portions of those masks to simulate the actions of a person's face muscles. A person experiencing a strong emotion will receive electrical impulses from the IPG that will stimulate the person's limbic system. At the same time, if a modified IPG is in use, the IPG will transmit impulses to a receptor in the mask, causing it to send impulses to some of the buttons, which will heat up and expand the mask areas corresponding to the muscles that would be activated by the emotion. The same result would be achieved, if necessary, by the wearer of the mask pressing the appropriate buttons in the remote-control unit."

"We perform maintenance on modified IPG remote control units, and I have taken a quick look at yours and found no problems with it. We are unable, however, to service the receptor on a mask or address other problems with the mechanisms in the mask itself."

"The lack of synchronicity you are experiencing between your emotional state and your mask displays may result from a malfunctioning of the mask's receptor, or a defect in the manufacture of the mask. You should get in touch with the outfit that provided your mask or the mask's manufacturer."

This advice was bad news for Eric. He had purchased the mask online from a discounter chain and getting satisfaction from them might be difficult. The manufacturers of the mask were probably in South Korea or Taiwan, and contacting them would also be impractical. He was stuck, for the time being, with a defective mask, and would have to live with it or buy another one, but masks were expensive and his mom did not have that kind of money.

His lack of choices depressed him even more than he was on arrival at the service center. The physiological phenomena associated with his current feelings were those of a saddened person, but the mask he wore showed energized *dilator naris* and *depressor septi* muscles, making him appear angry at the startled clerk, who cowered, for Eric was a hulking young man. Eric turned around and walked away, embarrassed at the reaction he had unwittingly elicited.

***

The problems with Eric's mask could not have cropped up at a worse time. He was in the first semester of his freshman year of college and could not afford to have his nervous system go awry while he was attending school. Moreover, it was the end of October and there were Halloween-related parties he wanted to attend; Halloween had always been his favorite holiday, for he loved to dress up and pretend he was a pirate, a swordsman, or a vampire.

He could have taken off the mask when he attended this year's parties or went trick-or-treating, but to do so would have left him with a paralyzed poker face that made him look stupid. So, his only choice was to continue to wear the mask and hope for the best.

The first event he wished to attend was a rush costume party at a fraternity Eric was hoping to pledge. The chapters of Delta Upsilon Delta (commonly known as "the dudes") were notorious for holding wild drinking parties, rumored to frequently degenerate into orgies. Eric had started drinking only a year before and had not graduated from 3.2 beer, so he was anxious to attend this party and partake of previously untasted alcoholic beverages.

To impress his potential fraternity brothers, he rented an eye-catching outfit drawn from one of the world's most famous horror stories: he wrapped himself in a funeral shroud that covered himself from head to foot minus the traditional hood, leaving his mask-covered face visible. He had sprinkled catsup generously on his tunic and pants and even a few drops on the mask, so that he appeared to have just come from a hard day of work at a butcher shop. To complete the ghastly image, he walked into the party with slow, sliding steps and talked to nobody until he reached the refreshments table, whereupon he seized a plastic cup filled with a clear liquid and drew a generous gulp, intending to savor the liquor and lick his lips appreciatively.

Eric was not prepared by the intense burning sensation he experienced as the cheap vodka coursed through his throat and into his chest. He began coughing loudly and for a moment felt he was choking; he experienced a brief wave of panic. His IPG signaled his nervous system to turn into the fear mode, and he clasped his throat with his right hand, as if to alleviate the discomfort. At the same time, his mask conductor activated the lip corner puller muscle (*zygomaticus major*) and the dimpler muscle (*buccinator*) spots in the mask, making him assume an expression of profound disgust.

His reaction to the drink was noticed by the knot of invitees and fraternity brothers that were roaming around the refreshment area, causing them to break into peals of derisive laughter followed by sarcastic remarks about the plebe's distress after a sip of vodka. One of the brothers presiding over the event exclaimed, "Boy, you came to the wrong party. We have no room in the dudes for someone who don't like liquor."

Eric went through a rapid stream of emotions – shame, anger, frustration, and disappointment – which his IPG faithfully conveyed to the youth's nervous system. At the same time, the conductor in his mask elicited a series of overlapping, convulsing facial motions and twitches that added to the audience's mirth and resulted in a circle gathering around Eric, laughing at his discomfort. One of the fraternity brothers then seized Eric's shoulder and gently guided him towards the rest room.

"Are you okey?" asked the host. Eric started to explain that he was having problems with his mask, but his rescuer cut him short: "Sure, we know," making it clear he felt that Eric was offering a lame excuse for his behavior. Eric thanked his rescuer, and rushed away from the party. He had never felt so furious, yet his mask was registering an ecstatic expression.

***

Second on Eric's list for the evening was a party being held by one of his childhood friends, Charlie Mason. Charlie was the beneficiary of a well-endowed trust fund set up by his late grandfather, so he did not have to worry about working for a living. Instead, Charlie threw great parties, attended by persons of all sexes and persuasions out to have a good time. Alcohol and drugs were plentiful at those events, which usually lasted until the morning of the following day.

Eric had attended a couple of Charlie's parties and in one of them had lost his virginity to a Nicaraguan exchange student named Xiomara. Consequently, he was looking forward to the opportunity for a repeat performance with Xiomara or some other beauty, foreign or domestic.

He had rushed to get away from the dudes and was panting from exertion when arrived at Charlie's apartment, which was full of young people in various stages of intoxication from drugs or alcohol, jumping and shaking to the brutal sounds of metal rock blasting out of Charlie's stereo system.

Eric went to the kitchen, poured himself a Coke, and returned to the dance floor, where he nearly collided with a voluptuous blonde who was gyrating by herself near the front door.

"Hi," he greeted. "I'm Eric."

"I'm Olivia," responded the girl in a drawl that was accentuated by substance abuse. "What are you doing dressed like a corpse from the morgue?" inquired the girl, placing a probing hand on Eric's shrouded chest and starting to move it downwards.

"Oh, it's a long story" began Eric, his IPG starting to fan the flames of arousal in his limbic system. His mask, however, was suggesting something like dread, for Olivia stopped her hand's motion and asked, alarmed, "What's the matter? Don't you like it?"

"Of course I do," replied Eric quickly. "Don't stop!" But seeing the increasing terror reflected in the mask, Olivia stopped. A moment later, her face displayed a knowing smile, "Oh, you haven't done this before, have ya?" Without more, she took Eric by the hand and dragged him into Charlie's bedroom, which was unoccupied. She closed the door, knelt in front of him, and got hold of his penis.

Eric's hypothalamus was instantly stimulated, and the touch of Olivia's hands prompted an immediate erection. Again, his mask registered a totally different, inconsistent set of emotions: fear and displeasure.

Olivia let go of Eric's member and stood up. "It doesn't look like you are ready for this," she observed acidly, getting ready to go.

"Please stay," begged Eric, but the contradictory signals he was sending out were too much for the girl. She opened the bedroom door and walked out before he could even attempt to explain his predicament.

***

After his second disaster of the evening, Eric realized he had a problem: the systems he had in place to address the effects of the viral infection were in constant conflict. It was as if the IPG and the mask's receptor were battling each other for control of his emotions, with disastrous consequences. He had the urge to remove the mask to prevent any future misapprehensions of his emotions, but at the same time he felt naked without a mask in place. He left Charlie's party, deep in thought, and started the long walk back home.

His neighborhood was full of families with children, and Eric kept running into groups of kids going door to door to demand holiday treats. He felt disappointed at not having done yet his share of trick-or-treating, and resolved to do some himself around the neighborhood before calling it a day.

He arrived at his apartment, rummaged through the pantry, and found a grocery store bag. Holding it, he went out again, not giving his mother a chance to ask any questions.

As Eric emerged onto the street, the rational part of his brain began raising objections. Wasn't he way too old to be out trick-or-treating? Wasn't it getting too late in the evening to be knocking on doors? Wasn't the outfit he was wearing sort of scary? Shouldn't he just go back home? Drawn by an irresistible impulse, Eric stifled all concerns and approached a house and knocked.

"Trick or treat," he demanded. A voice from behind the door replied with asperity: "Go home! It's after nine! You should be in bed!"

He felt a crimson sheet rise behind his eyelids at being disrespected. The house had a garden in front with plots of geraniums and gladioli. Eric went over and seized a rock the size of an apple from one of the plots and hurled it at the closed door and moved on. "Here is a trick for you!" he muttered.

He got no answer at the next three houses he approached, even though in each case the lights were still on inside. With each failure, his indignation at the outrages of this terrible day went up a notch. These houses had no plots from which to draw missiles, so he had to go away fuming, his bag still empty.

Someone opened the door at the fifth house. It was an enfeebled man, bent with age, holding a sack of Skittles and Reese's Pieces. He was digging into the sack to take out some candy when he looked up and saw what appeared to be a menacing giant covered by a bloody shroud. The man uttered a small cry and slammed the door closed.

Eric began banging on the door furiously. "Trick or treat!" he shouted.

After a while, the door reopened and the old man reappeared, armed with a shotgun, finger on the trigger. "Go away, you fiend, or I'll shoot!"

Eric was startled by the sight of a shotgun aimed at him and reacted with an alacrity that, later on, he would find surprising. He jumped forward into the hallway and began to try to wrestle the shotgun out of the old man's hands. The man's grip was surprisingly strong for somebody his age but, suddenly, the man let go of the gun and fell to the floor, where he lay, clutching his chest.

"Help! I'm having a heart attack!" cried out the man, shaking with pain.

Eric stood about the man, bewildered. What to do? His first impulse was to assist his attacker, or at least call for help. Then he had a second thought: If the police found him in the house, he would probably get arrested; also, if the man was able to describe his costume, he was a goner, since half the city had seen him wearing it.

He did not want this dreadful evening to end that way. He walked around the man, intended to run away from the house, when his pent-up emotions caught up with him and he began retching, feeling a sudden need to throw up.

He turned around, went further into the house, and found a bathroom, where he vomited the contents of his stomach in a series of painful bursts. He turned to the sink and sought to clean himself up. Looking in the vanity mirror, he noticed that his mask showed an expression of shock, confusion and fear that matched his feelings.

He was startled by the change. All day, his IPG had been sending the "right" emotional signals to the converter, but the converter had been causing "wrong" emotional clues to be displayed by the mask. That being the case, there should have never been agreement between the two devices. Unless...

He extracted the remote-control unit from his shirt and examined it carefully. He had not used it since before his visit to the service center earlier in the day. What if there was something wrong with *that* device that had been missed by the technician?

Looking closely, he noticed that one of the keys on the right side of the unit, those used to send signals to the converter, was slightly depressed. Experimentally, he pressed and released the key time and again. The mask went through a series of changes that mimicked emotions he did not feel: pain, sadness, elation. It then changed back to shock, which matched his current state of mind. He stopped pressing and the mask continued to reflect his current emotion, now surprise. "Oooops," he thought. "Maybe all my heartaches could have been avoided. Damn that guy! How could he have missed that stuck key?!"

Back in the hallway, Eric emptied the sack of candy into his grocery bag, without glancing at the man writhing on the floor. He told himself: "My bag is almost empty, but I have enough loot for the night. Gotta get moving. But first, maybe I should get help."

Again, he thought of calling 911, and once more he resisted the impulse. Letting a man die unassisted was in keeping with his anger and the inhuman persona he had assumed this Halloween, and was a type of newfound callousness he found to his liking. That attitude would dictate his actions in the future. No more Mr. Nice Guy.

He returned home, trying to master a lingering uncertainty at the future course of his life. His unease was faithfully reflected in the mask's expressions.

The Hollow Tree

What each one honors before all else,
what before all things he admires and loves,
this for him is God.
Origen

    A withered old man was instrumental in the discovery of the ancient tree. Discovered is not quite the right word, though, since many of the villagers had passed under its broad shade when entering the forest. Yet, probably not more than a glance was ever cast by anyone on the tree's gray trunk and the maze of gnarled branches that spurted from it in all directions.

    The man was crazy, of course. Occasionally, he would shake his head and whisper incomprehensible words to himself in a drawn-out monologue. He never spoke to anyone else, and nobody could figure out what he was saying.

    One day, however, he was observed crouching on the ground next to the tree, hands encircling the trunk and head hidden from view, for it was lost within a large opening on the tree trunk not far from the ground. What made the scene unusual was not the man's strange posture (he was already written off as an eccentric) but the fact that he could be heard talking rapidly into the tree.

    A crowd began to gather next to the old man, everyone trying to make out his words. As people closed in on him, the man grew quiet and withdrew his head from the tree. Instantly, a noise issued from above. It sounded like a prolonged insect call, now low and halting, then screeching like a wail, next dropping to a barely audible rumor. This went on for a while, and when the sound faded away the man stuck his head back in the hollow again.

    It became obvious that the old man was carrying a conversation of sorts with someone or something within the tree. At this point, most of the villagers became frightened and ran away. The brave souls that remained witnessed a repetition of the previous exchange: the old man talking excitedly, the tree replying without hesitation. At last, the old man stood up and walked away without seeming to notice the people who remained around the tree, gaping at the scene in disbelief.

A long pause followed the old man's departure. Then, curiosity overcame fear, and a teenage boy approached the tree and inserted his head within the hole. Darkness obscured his vision, and he felt the inner space to be damp and smelling of moss and decay. Feeling inside, the boy extracted a few dried nuts and a handful of decomposing matter. Otherwise, the space within the trunk of the tree was perfectly empty.

"There is nothing here!" called out the boy. His words were followed by a low rumble, like the flutter of invisible wings, coming from the very heart of the tree. The boy drew back with a shudder and ran away. The others that had remained about joined in his escape.

Before long, the story of the talking tree had turned into the main topic of conversation in the sleepy village. The consensus was that nothing short of sorcery would cause a tree to behave so irregularly. Most people agreed, however, that if sorcery was involved, it was not all that powerful, since little by little almost everyone in town had exchanged a word or two with the tree without adverse consequences.

As novelty wore out, the bizarre conduct of the tree was starting to be treated as a harmless oddity. And then something happened.

A girl's lover had been lost in the woods, presumably slain by wild beasts. She took to sitting next to the tree, crying her grief to the wind and then into the tree's dark hollow. Her sobs and lamentations were promptly answered by noises from the tree. This response seemed to make the grieving lass experience some relief, for she placed her arms on the trunk and continued to weep some more, until she lost consciousness from exhaustion.

The girl's example caught on and some began to visit the tree to confide to its vegetable soul the secrets in their hearts: the hopes and fears that they dared not share with anyone else, their despair and loneliness and other hidden emotions. All were answered by a myriad of voices that at times sounded like the gushing of sparkling streams, the calls of wild birds, haunting melodies sung by remote voices. It was all so serene that people would return home refreshed, as if talking to the tree made their lives easier to face.

A shrine was constructed around the tree, and rustic seats were placed near it for people to sit while waiting for their turn to talk with the tree. There were now lines of waiting villagers at all hours of the day until dusk, when the gusts of cold wind chilled the body and the lengthening purple shadows brought melancholy to the spirit. The tree seemed to loom larger then, its leaves rustling with sympathy for those wretched people huddled down next to its roots. As night fell, people would seek the safety of their homes and the tree would be finally left sitting alone.

A cult developed. Gods were believed to inhabit the tree, dispensing comfort and advice to those who were in need of it. It was only the humans' fault that they were unable to understand the tree's messages, but one day the meaning of the tree's words would be understood and then good fortune would come to all. Elaborate rituals were developed, and ceremonies were held in which maidens would crown the lower tree branches with wreaths of fresh blossoms; the villagers danced and chanted around the tree until the moon climbed very high in the starry heavens.

Priests were ordained to administer the worshipping of the tree, and they became its most frequent visitors. They would talk into the hollow and attempt, unsuccessfully, to decipher the echoes that emanated from the tree.

The old man had not been seen in the village for a very long time and was presumed dead. One spring morning, however, he was spotted lumbering about the village, going from one hut to another in a meandering way, ignoring the taunts of the children that ran around his legs and the startled gazes of the freshly awakened grownups.

His erratic motions carried him to the hollow tree. There, his glance circled from the makeshift temple where the priests lived and prayed, to the benches, the worn-out paths to the tree, and the branches festooned with loops of flowers and colored beads. A woman was sitting on a stool next to the trunk, engaged in an earnest exchange with the hidden gods; behind her, a waiting line was already forming.

The old man remained motionless, as if trying to make sense of the scene. Finally, understanding dawned and he let out a loud, sustained guffaw, turned around and went into the forest, never to be seen again.

The hollow tree remained an object of worship for generations. People kept coming, bringing forth their hopes and regrets, in the belief that the gods within understood them, cared about their feelings, and stood ready to render advice and help. Although none of this was confirmed to have happened, people went on believing, and did not seem to be any worse for their enduring faith.

The Mutants

Bonobos are... ambassadors from a primordial world of peace through pleasure, inviting us in one kiss at a time.
Susan Block, The Bonobo Way

It was not Kiki's fault. Let Mother screech as much as she wants, she thought. What had happened was an accident, and nobody should be punished for it. If fault was to be apportioned, it had to fall on Gagumi, but nobody would blame him, because bonobos males are stupid and act only on impulse.

Gagumi had come over to the nest of branches where Kiki was resting and, noticing that Kiki's genital area was distended -- indicative of her being in heat -- had pointed his erect member at her and, before she could react, was penetrating her from the front. Although surprised, Kiki was receptive and experienced a measure of enjoyment from the sexual encounter, which was hardly her first: since reaching puberty she had frequently coupled with males and often engaged in intimate rubbing with other females.

The act had been observed by several females and they had expressed their solidarity with Kiki through shrill screams and gestures. No disapproval was shown to Gagumi, because he was Mother's eldest son and it was not good policy to antagonize the matriarch of the troop by criticizing an act by her favorite.

Kiki had gone through three litters and her youngest offspring, a cute little thing called Lala, was still nursing, so according to her experience she was still infertile; thus, she anticipated that her incident with Gagumi would leave nothing but a memory behind. However, several weeks after that afternoon Kiki began exhibiting clear signs of pregnancy. When vomiting and morning sickness were accompanied by swelling of her belly, it became evident to her and others that she was pregnant with a child from Gagumi. That is when Mother started screeching: she intended better mating partners for Gagumi than low-ranking Kiki, and wanted any future grandchild to bring a powerful female directly into

Mother's family. Mother could not abide by Gagumi making a child that could interfere with her dynastic plans and unjustly blamed Kiki for the developments.

Kiki resented Mother's outbursts and responded with screeches of her own. Matters went from bad to worse and one afternoon Mother and several of her acolytes roughly pushed Kiki out of the boundaries of their encampment and, baring their oversized canines, made it clear that she would not be allowed to return. Kiki was unable to resist her ouster, and knuckled-walked into the dense rain forest and continued to march across it, farther and farther away from her former friends and mates, to start the solitary existence of an exile.

***

As night fell, Kiki found herself in an unfamiliar forest of very tall trees that all but shielded from the ground the light of the moon and the stars. She had been feeding on vegetation and small animals that skulked on the forest floor, but was increasingly hungry. It was then that she noticed a very long vine that rose from the ground, adhering to the trunk of one of the trees by a series of cylindrical stems from which dark green protrusions resembling leaves shot out. The stems were highly branched and covered much of the tree's trunk, and from one of the lower stems hung a large bud that was slowly opening.

Kiki watched with fascination as the bud became a very large, white, funnel-shaped flower whose fragrance filled the night air. The pleasant smell reminded Kiki that she was quite hungry and she reached up and snapped the flower from the stem. She then sat on the tree's aboveground roots and ate the flower slowly, enjoying every bite and letting the juices drip down her chin.

She had nearly finished chewing on the flower when the accumulated burden of the difficult day made her weary and she collapsed against the tree trunk and fell immediately asleep.

***

Kiki was awakened by a growl uttered somewhere nearby. She had spent all her life foraging for food in the company of males and females from her troop. On those occasions, the males were tasked with facing off the lions, leopards, pythons, and other predators that threatened the group. The role of Kiki and the other females was to gather foodstuffs, not fight hostile creatures; thus, she was unaccustomed to defend herself against such perils. Rising to her feet, she hurried away from the threatening sound. She was still clutching the remnants from the flower she had been savoring before falling asleep and, as she ran away, she saw that the trees in her vicinity held numerous dead flowers identical to the one that had been her dinner.

Her flight led her to a water hole, which that early in the morning was inhabited only by tall birds with long, skinny legs. Kiki was thirsty and bent over the edge of the pond to have a drink. In doing so, she made an astonishing discovery.

She was used to gazing at herself in analogous circumstances and could easily distinguish her features from those of other members of her troop, since there were marked physical differences among the various females, and even more when females and males were compared. The image that Kiki was seeing reflected in the waters was different from anything she had encountered previously. Her head had become elongated, her jaws had receded, her teeth had changed shape, now featuring smaller molars and canines and larger front teeth. The pink coloring of her lips had faded, and her skin had become the color of fresh honey. She did not recognize herself and was terrified by the changes. She concluded she had somehow been poisoned by the strange flower she had eaten the night before.

Kiki wondered whether these changes were real or an illusion due to the false morning light's reflection on the waters. But there was no time for speculation: she had to get food and put some more distance between herself and her former troop mates, who had threatened to come after her to enforce her banishment.

The forest she was traversing seemed to have no end. Row after row of tall trees massed together to form a barely penetrable wall. Along the way, she encountered more dead blossoms like the one she had eaten the previous night; she ignored these, for she was in the mood for something more substantial. She caught a movement underfoot and, in a quick move, captured a small lizard-like creature, which she proceeded to devour while it was still writhing in agony.

Later, Kiki sought relief from the rising heat of the day. She found a thin stream that originated in a hollow in the ground and flowed erratically across the clearing where she stood. The turbid waters were unappetizing and she considered moving on, but thirst overcame reluctance. She bent down and, between gulps, tried to see herself in the water. The stream was shallow and muddy and there was almost no reflection, but the little that she saw confirmed her earlier surprise. Somehow, she had changed overnight and become some sort of monster. She got up with a start and moved away quickly trying to distance herself from the vision.

The night found Kiki near the end of the forest. Looking for a branch where she could rest out of the reach of predators, she came upon another vine-covered tree that showed a few buds of the mysterious flower she had feasted on the previous day. She climbed to a branch near a bud and debated whether to eat it before the flower it enclosed opened. Curiosity won and Kiki sat, expectantly, near the bud waiting for it to reveal its secrets.

She did not have to wait long. Little by little, the bud's petals separated and a very large, fragrant flower opened, and Kiki could no longer contain herself. She struggled to pluck the flower from its stem and, succeeding, bit greedily into it. The taste of the fresh bloom was even more delectable than she remembered from the night before. She gorged herself on the soft, moist substance and, once finished, issued a contented grunt, and fell into a deep sleep.

The morning was somewhat advanced when Kiki's eyes opened with a start. No beasts appeared to be in her vicinity; however, in the distance, there was a familiar clamor, characteristic of her kin: screams, barks and grunts signifying that an organized foraging operation was in progress.

Under normal circumstances, Kiki would have rushed to return to the fold and begged her peers to forgive her offenses. However, Mother was known to be vindictive and was unlikely to have forgotten how Kiki had failed to show due respect for the elder's leadership. Beset by doubt, Kiki hesitated.

Then, through an empty spot in the woods, she could see the approaching group. They were not her clan, but the strange creatures that lived across the big water. They were shorter, heavier versions of Kiki and her troop; they had thin, dark lips that broke into cruel grimaces, lighter skins, and muscular bodies. Most importantly, they were led by aggressive males and were quite forceful in defending their territory. Kiki was certain that, if they caught her, they would do her harm, maybe even kill her.

Kiki started to speed away and, in her desperation, rose on her back legs and discovered that she could move faster if she used the strength of those legs than if she depended on her knuckles to propel herself. After a while, she had left the sounds of her potential pursuers behind and had moved into a grass-covered plain that extended far towards the horizon.

She paused to consider her situation. This area was unfamiliar, and she had no recollection of ever being in a place like this before. Behind her was the end of the familiar forest, but she did not dare turn back for fear of running into the threatening strangers. There was no turning back: she decided to press on, in the direction of the rising sun.

***

She traveled east for many moons, traversing higher plains and hills covered with savanna grasses and woodlands, having to modify her diet from fruits and tree leaves to grasses and insects, supplemented by small mammals and wild bird eggs, when she found them. As her belly inflated, the rest of her body became sparser and she came to fear she was starving to death.

At long last, he reached the end of the lowlands and entered an area of dense vegetation, almost as thick as the forests in which Kiki had been reared, but comprised mostly of unknown, low growing shrubs interspersed with a few tall trees. Walking through that jungle was difficult, and Kiki felt her energy dwindle with each passing day. She was reluctant to eat the lush greenery for fear of poisoning herself and the unborn, so she lived on berries and the few edible plants she recognized.

She was at the end of her strength and almost ready to lie down and die when the jungle ended abruptly and she was confronted by a sight of staggering oddness. Before her lay a long area of empty, reddish, flat rocks; beyond, in the horizon, there were bodies of water and then the land rose steeply to form a conical mass that went up into the sky, so far above the ground that its end was shrouded by clouds. Kiki had never seen a mountain before and there was nothing in her experience that prepared her for the awesome vision. She held her breath so long that she felt she would choke, but recovering herself she gained a new resolve: she would go to that great hill and give birth there, so her child could grow in that majestic environment.

The trip to the mountain consumed the last bit of energy that Kiki had left, so that by the time she stood at its foot she had no strength left to start climbing. She found a sheltered corner under a tree, built a rudimentary nest with small branches and leaves, and went into labor.

It was a miracle she survived the ordeal of childbirth. The baby, a female, came out facing away from her mother and her head and body rotated after the head had emerged. The newborn dropped to the ground unaided and lay there, drawing her first breaths anxiously as if eager to get going. Kiki, however, was unable to reach for the newborn. The pain had only subsided a little and, after a few moments, labor resumed, and not much later another infant dropped from Kiki's birth canal: a male this time, only slightly larger than his older sister.

Giving birth to twins was a phenomenon that had not occurred in Kiki's existence. Having one baby was painful enough, she thought. Having two seemed like punishment from the heavens.

It took Kiki only a moment to regain her composure and allow maternal instincts to take over. She picked up the female and hauled her to safety, ignoring the placenta and the umbilical cord, which dangled for a few hours until they dried up and fell away. With the female securely laying on her back, Kiki picked up the male and did something unusual: she ate the placenta and the cord, and then ingested the abundant amniotic fluid, following which she licked the affected areas clean.

Perhaps she was following the ancestral customs of her troop, wherein mothers were always protecting their sons; or maybe she had the presentment that the female of this pair would grow strong and self-sufficient whereas the male would always need female care and attention. Whatever the reason, she laid her offspring next to each other and contemplated them with a mixture of love and awe.

For her children were like her, and yet different. Superimposed on her recognizable features – wide eyes, pointed ears, curving mouths – were traits that included, and accentuated, the changes she had noticed in her own body. They had long limbs, jaws that receded, misshapen teeth with small molars that would create difficulties in chewing tough roots. Their lips were thin and colorless, their skin light, their bodies almost devoid of hair. Kiki thought they were strange, but in their own way beautiful.

The sight of these unique beings injected a new urgency into her exhausted body. She had to live, at least for several transits of the seasons, and protect her offspring until they could take care of themselves.

She carried both infants in her arms and began foraging for edible sources of nourishment. She would eat fruits and nuts if she could, grubs, worms and little animals if she must. She walked on, holding the new kind of creatures she had managed to unleash upon the world. She could not envision their destiny, but felt it was her duty to help bring it into fruition and hope for the best.

On the Path to Nirvana

At the monastery at the foot of the Himalayas, a disciple voiced his misgivings to his guru: "Master, I keep failing."

"How so, Chodak?" asked the Lama.

"Time and again, I read the 'Lamp for the Path' and meditate on the actions it recommends, trying to carry out the Eightfold Path to nirvana. Understanding, however, eludes me. I get mired in distractions and confusion."

"What meditation method do you use?"

"I sit alone, cross-legged, in a quiet place, having dimmed all lights, and try to set my mind at rest by deeply inhaling and exhaling; as restless thoughts float in my mind, I observe each one and let it go."

"That's a common way to meditate. It works for most people, but perhaps you need a more dynamic way to focus your thoughts and feelings. I suggest you conduct a *kora*, a circular voyage around the mountain surrounding the monastery. As you go up and down the mountain trails, you'll be able to let go of distractions and focus on the teachings of the Path."

"Won't encountering other people also doing the kora impair my concentration?"

"It's past midwinter. It will be cold and snowy on the kora. I doubt you will meet others along your path."

"I still fear I'll be unable to clear my mind of distractions."

The Lama did not reply, but removed from his wrist an ancient *dzi* bracelet sporting seven black agate beads that showed etched ivory lines, diamonds, dots, and other patterns. He handed it to his disciple: "Here. Put it on your wrist and wear it during your kora."

"What does it do?"

"I have infused my essence into this bracelet. As you climb the mountain, I'll speak to you through the bracelet and help you clear your mind."

"Is this magic?"

"Of a sort. The bracelet allows me to convey my thoughts to anyone wearing it. If you have it on your wrist, you'll perceive any messages that I send to your mind."

"Will I be able to respond?"

"Yes, by focusing your thoughts on me. And of course you may choose to disregard my suggestions. Do you want to give it a try?"

Chodak nodded in assent.

***

It was late in the afternoon when Chodak began the kora. The sky was leaden and the air felt humid, presaging snow. The youth was not accustomed to strenuous exertions and the steep climb soon took a toll on his limited stamina. He stopped to catch his breath and his mind issued a lament: °°I'm tired. I may not be able to go much further!°°

A response from the Lama was transmitted by the bracelet: °°You need to lighten the load you carry. Renounce all animosities, all resentments, all the anger in your heart, for those negative feelings weigh you down.°°

Chodak had not lived long enough to have enemies or develop grudges against anyone, but strained all the same to cleanse his soul of negative feelings. This took a while, but at the end he felt at peace with the universe. He lowered the hiking stick to the ground and resumed his progress.

For a while, Chodak's step was elastic and he went up the mountain trail effortlessly, his mind occupied with the Eightfold Plan. Then, weariness set in again. He stopped and leaned against the trunk of an ancient cypress. °°I'm exhausted. I can't go on!°°

His lamentation elicited no response, and Chodak was starting his descent towards the monastery when the bracelet pulsed and a message formed in his mind. °°You must resolve to unburden yourself of all the things you possess, become the owner of nothing but the clothes you wear. That decision will further lighten the weight you carry, so you can resume your progress along the kora.°°

Chodak came from a very poor family and owned very little. Yet, renouncing all current and future wealth lent renewed vigor to his limbs and he continued marching towards the mountain summit and pursuing his meditation.

By now, night had fallen and Chodak stopped to light a torch. By its light, he could see the summit of the mountain, a fair distance away. It was also starting to snow. He quickened his pace.

He had to stop again to catch his breath. He knew there was a shelter at the summit where he could rest, but he was at least half an hour away and almost out of energy. °°I'm not going to make it! I'm so tired that am about to faint!°°

The Lama responded immediately: °°You still have loves and affections, ties to others in the world. Vow to give those up and you'll make it the top.°°

Chodak protested, in the throes of despair. °°If I give up all that I care in the world, what do I have left to live for?°°

°°You'll be further on the way to implementing the Plan. Accomplish this task and you will come close to your goal.°°

Chodak realized he would soon be left without suffering, love, or desires; however, the objective of the Plan would be achieved. With a supreme effort he willed himself free of all ties to others and resumed his trek, dragging himself upwards against the heavily falling snow.

***

He was only steps from the summit when he collapsed to the ground, unable to move any further. °°This is the end! I've failed! °°

New words of the Lama resonated in his head: °°Not yet! You have one more thing to give up!°°

°°What?°°

°°Remove your garments and lie on the ground. In a few minutes your body will freeze and your life will be over. You will have carried out the Plan to completion. You will be released from the effects of karma and the cycle of death and rebirth. You will have reached nirvana!°°

Chodak shuddered as snow covered his body and a gelid wind buffeted his face. It was time to sleep, but his kora had been a success.

The Magic Chrysler

You can overcome your obstacles, just use them as your magic carpet and ride to success.
Hopal Green

Consuelo's escape plan was desperate but she felt she had little choice. In March 1979 she was directed by the Education Ministry to recommend ten students from the High School of which she was Principal to be conscripted and shipped to Angola to fight in the series of wars between the People's Movement for the Liberation of Angola ("MPLA") and right-wing groups backed by the United States, South Africa and Zaire. Cuba had been militarily involved in Angola in support of the MPLA since 1975 and, starting in 1978, had begun suffering serious losses at the hands of South African mercenaries. Fresh bodies were needed at the front, and Consuelo and other school administrators had been commanded to help round up cannon fodder in support of the operations.

Consuelo could not bring herself to single out school children for possible death in Cuba's foreign ventures, and declined to obey the order. After a series of increasingly contentious exchanges with her superiors, Consuelo was informed that she would be dismissed from her job as soon as a replacement could be found.

Consuelo realized that she would be arrested and would join the thousands of political prisoners in Cuba's notorious jails. She knew that she could expect the worst from her captors. She had to escape.

Armando, one of Consuelo's cousins, was a manager at a collective farm in Pinar del Rio, Cuba's westernmost province. Because of his high rank, Armando knew a lot of people who lived on the northern coast, including fishermen who plied the waters of the Straits of Florida in search of commercially valuable fish. Consuelo made a desperate plea to her cousin to help her get a boat in which to escape the island and travel to Florida. Armando rebuffed her at first, for he was not keen on risking his neck to help his relative but at the end – when Consuelo turned all her possessions into illegal foreign currency and offered him a cut in the venture – Armando agreed to start making inquiries.

A couple of weeks later he had identified the owner of a small wooden boat who was willing to take Consuelo and her two sons out of the country for a large sum of money. His boat even had a motor that had been acquired before the 1959 Cuban Revolution, so there was no need to rely on muscle and wind to navigate the treacherous waters of the Straits. It was late March, and the weather conditions were also favorable.

Things began going awry the night before her intended departure. She received a call from a friend at the Ministry who said that a new Principal had been appointed and an order had been issued for her arrest; she could expect to be seized no later than the following morning. When Ricardo, Consuelo's husband, learned of the immediate danger his wife was facing, he reacted negatively. "I disagree with what you are trying to do, but I won't try to stop you. Do as you please. But the police are at your heels. I won't let our children take part in what is now a very dangerous situation. Besides, they are old enough at 12 and 14 to have their own views. They are Socialists like their father and would not go voluntarily to live in the land of the imperialists. They stay with me."

Consuelo tried all arguments she could think of to move her husband. She cried, cajoled, begged, threatened, invoked love, fidelity and marital harmony. Nothing worked: Ricardo accused her of being self-centered and not caring for her family, and forbade the kids to accompany her.

Past midnight, Consuelo reached a grim decision. She would be of no use to anybody if she was sent to prison. She would leave now, go to the United States, and would somehow try to rescue her children from there. She told herself she was not being egotistical, but was acting only out of self-preservation.

She finished loading her suitcases onto her most prized possession – a 1954 two-toned (lemon with black top) Chrysler New Yorker convertible. She figured that, if she drove fast but not so fast as to draw attention to herself, she would make it to Palma Rubia, a village on the north coast of Pinar del Rio, just before sunrise. She would have to locate the fisherman based on the information that Armando had provided her. There was no way for her to contact the fisherman in advance, so she was putting all her hopes on his being around and willing to take her.

She drove the Chrysler along the Malecón and headed for Fifth Avenue, the main roadway in the Miramar district where the moneyed people lived and foreign dignitaries had their mansions. She was set to drive all the way west on Fifth, which turned into a major highway just outside the city limits, and then take side roads after the village of Mariel until she hit Palma Rubia. She had studied thoroughly her vintage Esso highway map and hoped roads had not changed much in the last twenty years.

As she crossed the bridge over the Almendares River and entered Fifth Avenue, she noted that an unmarked boxy car (a Soviet Lada, she figured) pulled out of a parking space and started following her, attracted perhaps by the showy American vehicle she was driving. The Lada was moving slowly at first, and then with increasing speed.

Consuelo was terrified: only the Secret Police had Ladas, which were used for raids against citizens thought to be counterrevolutionaries. If they stopped her and found the luggage, the water jugs, and other trip necessities that she carried in the trunk of the Chrysler, she would surely be arrested.

She got in the left lane, looking for a place to cross the broad avenue and get away from the Lada. She suddenly veered at full speed onto 20th Street. The Chrysler's tires screeched savagely, but the car unerringly made the turn. She then went down a block to Seventh Avenue, made another sudden left turn, and drove back towards the city, hoping that her faster, more powerful car would eventually leave her pursuer behind. When she reached 14th Street, however, she found that Seventh Avenue was closed for street repairs. She had no alternative but to make another wild turn onto 14th Street, with the Lada less than a block away and approaching fast.

As she raced on 14th Street towards Fifth Avenue, out of the corner of her eye she noticed a building complex on the right, in front of which was a flagpole displaying a large tricolor flag: yellow, blue, and red. It had to be a foreign embassy.

Consuelo shifted the Chrysler in reverse with a loud screeching of gears, drove almost back to Seventh Avenue, shifted gears again, and drove the car at full speed right over some oleander bushes, through an iron fence, and past a guard booth manned by Cuban soldiers. As she approached, one of the guards raised a pistol and fired a shot at the Chrysler, hitting only the hood, but since he was standing in front of the driveway he was struck and thrown several feet back. The Chrysler finally came to a stop with a crash on the lawn in front of the main building.

The Lada stopped on the side of the road and two men, armed with Kalashnikov machine guns, emerged and moved briskly towards the Chrysler. However, when they started to proceed beyond the demolished fence, they were stopped by a peremptory cry: "Halt! You are in the territory of the Republic of Colombia! You have no right to enter here! Step out!"

The cry belonged to a disheveled middle-aged woman in a nightgown, who came out of the front door of the building and approached the Chrysler, whose front end was a wreck from which a plume of steam rose into the night sky. The Cuban security agents, who had been joined by another soldier who had emerged from the guard post, stared angrily at the woman, made as if to proceed with their invasion, thought better of it, and retreated to the sidewalk. One of the security agents asked the soldier: "What is this place?"

"This is the Colombian Embassy."

"Shit" grunted the agent, and spat on the ground.

***

Consuelo sat stunned at the wheel of the Chrysler, bleeding from a gash on her forehead. She stared unfocusedly up at the approaching woman, who was now joined by two men who appeared to be embassy personnel. "Am very sorry" she started, in a shaky voice.

"Who are you, and why have you done this?" asked the woman sharply.

"I am very sorry" repeated Consuelo haltingly. "My name is Consuelo Vivanco, and I am ... or was, the Principal of the Eduardo Chibás Senior High School. I was on my way to the coast to get on a boat to leave Cuba when these government agents started chasing my car. I crashed into your mansion because it looked like a foreign place where perhaps I could hide."

"You were right. This is a foreign place, the Colombian Embassy. But you have caused physical damage to our property and are likely to cause an international incident, which our government would like to avoid. I am not sure we can, or want to, offer you a place to hide."

"Oh, please, please!" implored Consuelo.

"We'll see" replied the woman. "Let's step inside and have someone take a look at that wound."

While the hastily awakened embassy doctor was tending to Consuelo's wound – not serious, but requiring nearly a dozen stitches – the lady brought her up to speed on the situation. "I am Ileana Ruiz, Secretary to the Embassy. Our Ambassador, Dr. Rueda, is back in Bogotá for consultations. I'm in charge of the day-to-day affairs of the Embassy, but have no authority to decide on what to do with you." She paused for a moment to collect her thoughts. "Political asylum in foreign embassies is a recognized practice throughout Latin America. Granting asylum is wholly within the discretion of the country whose embassy is used to shelter the asylum seeker.

"Even when diplomatic asylum is granted, the transition to territorial asylum often is lengthy if the host country refuses to grant a safe-conduct pass to leave the country. In other words, we may decide that you qualify for asylum, but that decision has to be made by the Ambassador, in consultation with the Colombian government. Even if we do grant you asylum here, you may not be able to leave the country if Cuba refuses to issue you a safe-conduct pass to do so."

"So, what is going to happen with me now?" asked Consuelo fearfully. "Nothing at the moment," replied Secretary Ruiz. "We of course will not relinquish you to the Cuban government, but your future will remain undecided until Ambassador Rueda returns."

Consuelo wrung her hands with extreme distress. "I didn't plan on this. Risking death on the high seas was scary but at least involved only me. I fear other people may be affected by my rashness."

"There's nothing to be done at the moment. Alfonso will show you to a room where you can get some rest. If you give me your car keys, we will get your suitcase from the trunk."

"What's going to happen to the car? It is almost like a member of my family."

"We'll put it in our garage and see if it can be repaired. That's a problem that can wait."

***

Consuelo slept long but fitfully. She finally looked at the clock on the night table: 2:35 P.M. She had been asleep for almost twelve hours.

Suddenly she realized that she had woken up by sounds coming from the outside. Her guest room overlooked the street and she went to the window to see what was the cause of the commotion was. There were several Ladas and a truck parked in front of the mansion. The sound was that of raised voices from Cuban officials, Embassy personnel, and a couple of civilians she could not identify. She felt woozy from the injury, but managed to walk gingerly downstairs.

The embassy building was large and the path from the stairs to the offices below was not clear. Consuelo ambled at random for a few moments until she was intercepted by an employee who escorted her to a meeting room and sat her down. "Please wait here. I will get Mrs. Ruiz."

Mrs. Ruiz, now fully dressed in a severe gray business suit, came in right away. She was unsmiling, but greeted Consuelo politely. "Good afternoon, Mrs. Vivanco. Did you sleep well?" "On and off, thank you" replied Consuelo. "What's going on out there?"

Mrs. Ruiz smiled ruefully. "You have become famous overnight."

"How so?"

"First, agents from the Interior Ministry showed up this morning and started trying to intimidate our staff into turning you over to them. I was advised and put and end to that, at least for the time being. Later, two reporters – from the BBC and France Press – arrived, heavens know how they found out. They also have asked to come in and interview you. I said no, but I am glad they are here, because the Ministry boys will not attempt anything while the foreign press is around. So, there is a lot of shouting and screaming going on, but nothing will happen. I have put in a call to the Ambassador to apprise her of the developments, and I expect she is going to try to cut her trip short so she can come here and deal with the Castro government."

"I'm so sorry I caused all this trouble" apologized Consuelo again.

"What's done is done. All I hope is that Dr. Rueda will be back soon so she can take over. This is above my level of authority."

"What do we do in the meantime?"

"You, relax and settle down. You may be our uninvited guest for some time."

***

As it turned out, Ambassador Rueda was unable to return to Havana because she had to stay in Bogotá for a series of meetings on drug traffic issues. Two days after Consuelo's abrupt crashing of the Embassy gates, the Ambassador sent Secretary Ruiz a telex giving her authority and responsibility to decide whether to grant political asylum to Consuelo, and handle any fallout with the Cubans should she decide that asylum be granted.

Mrs. Ruiz was not happy, but she was a career diplomat accustomed to dealing with sticky situations. She prepared a carefully drafted message to the Cuban Foreign Ministry advising of Colombia's decision to approve Consuelo's request for asylum and asking that Cuba issue a safe-conduct pass that would enable Consuelo to travel abroad.

The Cuban Foreign Minister at the time, one Isidoro Malmierca, immediately called the Embassy and bellowed at Mrs. Ruiz, complaining that the BBC had published a news item reporting that a dissident, and a woman at that, had managed to elude the Revolutionary security forces and taken refuge by crashing into Colombia's embassy, all of which was "clearly calculated to embarrass the People's government and undercut the Revolution." He then announced forcefully: "That woman is a spy and a CIA agent. She injured a guard with her vehicle and thus committed a criminal act. We will never, ever, give permission for her to leave the country!! She will die in your home, if you insist on keeping her there, or will come out and face the Revolutionary justice, as she deserves!!"

Secretary Ruiz replied with all the *sang froid* she could muster: "Mr. Minister, I understand your position. The Colombian Government will continue to endeavor to work with Cuba to resolve this issue in a manner satisfactory to all." She then hung up.

***

Malmierca did not stop there. Two days after his exchange with Secretary Ruiz, he sent a note to Colombia's Foreign Minister, threatening with unspecified reprisals if Colombia did not "face up to its obligations" and had that "damnable Vivanco woman" turned over to the Cuban Government.

The note was undiplomatic in its demanding and bellicose tone. It was unfortunately leaked to *El Nuevo Siglo*, a conservative newspaper, which published it accompanied by an editorial criticizing the cowardice of the Liberals now in charge of the government.

Colombia had elected as President the previous year Julio César Turbay, a Liberal who had promised to institute a number of social reforms. Much as he wanted to avoid confrontations with Cuba, he and his party could not afford to appear weak or indecisive. Turbay met with Ambassador Rueda and the Foreign Minister and agreed to a public rejection of Malmierca's demands. Uribe wrote a letter to the editor of *El Nuevo Siglo* assuring the Colombian people that the country would not yield to Cuba's outrageous demands and Mrs. Vivanco would be granted political asylum and remain in the embassy "until Cuba agrees to let her leave for a third country of her choosing."

***

While her future was being discussed at the high levels of two governments, Consuelo tried, unsuccessfully, to adapt to her new situation. All her life she had kept a low profile – even her position as Principal of a high school had come to her in a series of almost imperceptible steps, with her saying as little as possible and being as agreeable with her superiors as she could. Now, she saw her picture in the foreign TV programs that were available thanks to the powerful antennas on the roof of the embassy. She had become famous overnight and, sooner or later, her notoriety would rub off on her family: her children and her husband could become victims of the government's attempts to wreak revenge on her. She now lived in a state of constant panic.

Ten days after her break-in, a school bus arrived in front of the embassy and two dozen teenagers, boys and girls, were escorted out by a couple of adults and formed a line in front of the embassy fence, which had just been repaired. From the window of her room on the upper floor, Consuelo could not see too well the features of the children, but with some effort she was able to identify one girl and two boys as students in the High School of which she had been Principal. At a signal from one of the adults, the children began singing patriotic songs, crying out political slogans, and shouting insults at her. As the tempo and volume of the screams increased, some of the boys began throwing rocks at the embassy grounds, aiming for the windows but not quite reaching them. After an hour or so, the adult blew a whistle and the children filed back into the bus and left.

The same demonstration was repeated every day for the next two weeks. Secretary Ruiz
called Malmierca to protest the hostile acts of the government-organized mobs, but he refused to talk to her. Instead, an underling conveyed the message that these children were exercising their democratic right to freely

express their views, and the Revolution could not prevent them.

At the end of the two weeks, the school bus stopped coming. Consuelo hoped the regime might have grown tired of harassing her, but soon found out better. One morning, a single Lada came to station itself in front of the embassy. From the car emerged two officials, Consuelo's husband Ricardo, and their children. They approached the locked fence and Ricardo pressed a buzzer to summon an Embassy employee. Ricardo then asked to be allowed to speak to Consuelo. The children were to stay behind, visible but out of reach, in the custody of the Cuban officials. This was to ensure that Ricardo would not try to join Consuelo in seeking asylum.

Husband and wife were mutually shocked when they met in the embassy's library. Consuelo was drawn and pale, and her lustrous black hair hung limp and greasy, as if she had not cared for her looks in the last three weeks. Ricardo had lost weight and sported more white hairs than she remembered. He kissed her on the cheek and ran his hand caressingly over her shoulder and back. She remained there, unmoving.

"Consuelo, I have come to ask a big favor of you. Please, for yourself and your children, give yourself up. I have assurances from the Government that if you end your asylum voluntarily you will face only token charges and many not even have to serve time."

"And why would I want to do this?"

"Your children are suffering. The word has gotten out that their mother is a criminal and is holed up in an embassy, and they are being harassed by their schoolmates and even the teachers. Their academic progress, their very futures are at risk from their association with you. I myself am not in great danger at the Ministry, but I'll probably be forced to denounce you publicly to protect myself against reprisals."

"Wouldn't all that have been the same if I had gone out on a boat and shown up in Miami?"

"It's different. Your disappearance wouldn't have been all over the news and wouldn't have created such a fuss."

"So, you want me to surrender and go to prison because you are ashamed and the kids may not do too well in school." She became agitated and started tapping her fingers rapidly on the arms of her chair.

"Well, no, it's not only that. We are actually concerned that something bad may happen to you. This government doesn't forgive, you know. Even if you somehow get out of Cuba, your life will be at risk no matter where you go."

"Let me worry about that. Look, you do what you need to do, and have the children do the same. I'm living in a nightmare and nothing you guys do will make things different for me."

"You have changed" noted Ricardo bitterly.

"Maybe. But it may be that I have realized that I don't mean much to anybody, least of all my family, so I must protect myself. Leave now, and tell your superiors that I don't intend to leave this Embassy unless granted permission to live free somewhere that is not Cuba."

***

Three months later, Consuelo was still a forced guest of the Colombian government. The Western press – from the New York Times to Le Monde, and particularly the British tabloids – had reported extensively on her plight and the unsuccessful efforts of the Cuban Government to dislodge her. The Cuban authorities continued to organize protests at the Colombian Embassy; these proved ineffective and only served to raise the temperature of Cuban-Colombian relations to near the boiling point.

A torrid morning in early July, Consuelo found herself having an informal breakfast with Secretary Ruiz in the embassy's kitchen. Among gulps of strong Colombian coffee, the Secretary made her guest aware of a new problem arising in the diplomatic front. The administration of U.S. President Jimmy Carter was seeking to improve relations between the United States and Cuba. In furtherance of the efforts to bring the two countries closer together, U.S. Secretary of State Cyrus Vance had contacted the Colombian Foreign Minister to suggest that hemispheric peace might be helped if

Colombia could find a way to settle with Cuba the problem of Mrs. Vivanco's asylum.

Consuelo was paralyzed with terror by the dire news. "I feel like a leaf floating in a river, at the mercy of the current, thrown this way and that by forces over which I have no control. What are you going to do? Feed me to the lions? Show me the door?"

Mrs. Ruiz had become friendly with Consuelo during the four months since her surprising arrival at the embassy. Ambassador Rueda still remained in Colombia, so it was Ruiz who had to face the "Vivanco headache." In the process, she had come to pity Consuelo's predicament and her frightened loneliness. Giving her up would be an unacceptable betrayal that would haunt her the rest of her days. She gave a thin smile and replied mysteriously: "Have faith. I'm working on the problem. Let's see what I can do."

Another week went by. At breakfast one Friday, Secretary Ruiz broached the topic again with her guest: "Consuelo, I have good news and bad news. Which do you want to hear first?"

"Give me the bad news. At this point, I'm almost ready to give up."

"I have received word from Bogotá that we are to get rid of you within a week. Unless I can find another way to deal with the situation, we have to eject you from the embassy and turn you over to the Cubans."

Consuelo hid her contorted face behind her hands so that Mrs. Ruiz would not see her agitation. She remained silent for a few seconds, trying to compose herself, and then asked: "What's the good news, then?"

"I have come up with a potential little miracle to solve your situation, hopefully without betraying you. Listen.

"Colombia bought this mansion from its previous owner, a sugar baron. He made extensive renovations to an older house that dated back to the eighteenth century, built by some Spanish aristocrats. At the time, there was fear that the city would be occupied by foreigners – as it happened in 1762, when the British took Havana during a war with Spain. So, the builders of the original house dug a secret tunnel from it to an exit on a vacant lot a couple of blocks away, in what is now 12th Street. The sugar baron discovered the tunnel and mentioned it to the Colombian Government agent. After we bought the property, we also acquired the lot on 12th Street to make sure that the secret exit remained available should it ever need to be used. We also built a small shack to hide the tunnel's exit."

"What good does that do me?" interrupted Consuelo, disconsolate.

"We have also been working on fixing the car that you drove onto our property. The damage caused by the multiple collisions has only been repaired to the extent possible, given the unavailability of American spare parts. We also fixed up the body damage as well as it could be done, and tried to disguise the bumps by painting the car black, so it now looks like it is carrying a hearse in a funeral procession. The car is parked on 12th Street by the vacant lot where the tunnel exits."

"Am I going to be able to drive my Chrysler in that condition?"

"The car may be drivable, at least for a while. The engine block is cracked and the car may overheat due to an oil leak. I'm told that if you see gray or black fumes coming from under the hood, you should stop the car immediately and let it rest and try to restart it again."

"Am I taking a big chance with my life? Is this a risk or a gamble?"

"Call it what you will. I think you should go back to your original trip. In any case, I recommend you make your escape two days from today, this coming Sunday, after midnight so it will be dark and traffic will be light."

"Why have you gone through all that trouble for me?"

"Well, Consuelo, you are not as worthless and unlovable as you think. Many people, in this building and outside, care for you and wish you well."

At this, Consuelo no longer tried to hide her tears and she encircled the diplomat on a tight hug. "Thank you ... thank you... a thousand times thank you!!

***

The Chrysler made it out of Havana without incident but overheated about twenty miles away from Palma Rubia. It would not restart, as Consuelo prayed to every deity she knew without success. Finally, she grasped the steering wheel and tearfully addressed the car: "Chrysler, you are my only friend. I beg you, please, help me get out of here!" The Chrysler shuddered, sputtered back to life and carried Consuelo for the last few miles.

Days later, the Chrysler was discovered abandoned on the sand, near the sea. It could never be driven again.

***

The communiqué issued by the Colombian Foreign Ministry advised that Consuelo Vivanco, formerly an asylum seeker lodging at the Colombian Embassy in Havana, had disappeared and was believed to be hiding somewhere on the island. Ricardo strenuously denied knowledge of his wife's whereabouts. After a while, interest in the case waned, and she was largely forgotten.

Several months later, six dissidents driving a city bus were successful in crashing it into the grounds of the Peruvian embassy, a copycat attempt patterned after Consuelo's wild ride. The dissidents were given asylum by the Peruvian officials, and the ensuing crisis eventually led to a boatlift in which almost 125,000 Cubans were allowed to migrate to the United States through the port of Mariel. Some, who remembered her picture from the papers, believed they recognized Consuelo among the exiles greeting the new arrivals upon their landing in Key West. This was never confirmed.

Hope for the Future

"Don't Panic."
Douglas Adams, The Hitchhiker's Guide to the Galaxy

And you will hear of wars and rumors of wars. See that you are not troubled; for [a]all these things must come to pass, but the end is not yet. For nation will rise against nation, and kingdom against kingdom. And there will be famines, [b]pestilences, and earthquakes in various places.
Matthew 24: 6-8

1.

My name is Boaz Ben-Frenkel and I used to be a biochemist at the government research facility in Ma'ale Adumim's industrial park, five miles from Jerusalem. But that is ancient history: the Arab-Israeli war of March 2087 changed my life, like it did to millions of others.

When the war broke out and our homeland was quickly invaded by forces from five Arab nations, I was – as a member of the military reserves – summoned to join the Israel Defense Forces in the fight to keep Jerusalem out of enemy hands. Although better trained and equipped, we were vastly outnumbered and had to retreat to strategic positions while the Arabs roamed through the Old City. I was wounded on my chest while trying to defend the Church of the Holy Sepulchre; as I was being evacuated with other casualties, I witnessed how armed men, apparently Arab extremists, looted, set the Church complex afire, and then detonated massive explosives that turned the most venerated site in the Christian world to rubble.

The destruction of a Christian holy place was, from the strategic viewpoint, a minor event in a war that killed over a million Jews. However, for many people throughout the world it was a disaster that galvanized individuals and governments into action. Dust had barely settled on the ruins of the Church when moneys began to be raised to finance the rebuilding the Church complex and, most importantly, to protect from damage the limestone burial bed contained within the shrine built inside the Church;

that bed is believed by many to be the resting place where the corpse of Jesus of Nazareth had lain.

After their decisive victory over the Arab coalition in the Battle of Damascus, our country was triumphant but devastated and everyone, myself included, was in very low spirits; the nation was in mourning and had not been in such a dire state since the 1948 Arab–Israeli War. The Israeli government was therefore eager to receive international financial support for the reconstruction effort and assembled a team of experts, assisted by army personnel, to clear the rubble of what had been the shrine and excavate it to reach the burial site. The site itself had last been reached in the early part of the century, in a thorough and well documented investigation; the international team had dug through the marble cladding that covered the limestone burial bed, which was sealed by a marble slab placed during the time of the Crusades.

I volunteered to be part of the support team and was selected, in part as a reward for my injuries defending the site, to assist the archeologists and other experts that would go through every inch of the burial site to ensure that it had not been disturbed. In mid-April, after we dug our way into the burial area, we made an unwelcome discovery: the marble slab that covered the burial bed had been pulverized and a multitude of small pieces of marble were strewn over the bed. While members of the team busied themselves with the cleanup process, I spotted some small protuberances on the back of the bed and retrieved three pieces of what appeared to be yellowish rock, but to my experienced eye looked as bone fragments, lying on the surface of the bed. I didn't know whether they had been on (or in) the bed all along, or had dropped down onto it from somewhere else.

I quickly pocketed the bone fragments without being noticed. To this day, I don't know why I took this action, which was clearly a crime. It was perhaps curiosity: my heart was beating rapidly at the thought that these could be parts of the famous cadaver that had rested on the burial bed a long, long time ago.

I complained about experiencing chest pains from my wounds, excused myself, and went back to the shack where the team stored its equipment and supplies. I picked up my top coat and my valise and went home. It was some time before my departure from the site drew the attention of anyone. Nobody cared.

2.

I still had access to the lab at the Ma'ale Adumim's research facility. I had wrapped the three bone fragments in tissue and now placed them in a laminar flow safety cabinet where they would remain sterilized to the greatest extent possible while I figured out what to do with them.

I had several problems. First, I was no expert in the forensic analysis of bone materials. Second, I had no idea of what information, if any, could be gleaned from such an analysis. Third, and perhaps most important, if these were human bone fragments, any attempt to associate them with the body of Jesus would result in a firestorm. Christians believe that, three days after his death, Jesus resurrected fully in body and soul, and there was no plausible explanation for some of his bones being left behind after his resurrection. Less heretical notions have resulted in bloody wars throughout history.

I was tempted to give up on my investigation. It was none of my business, and I could not return the bones to the authorities without facing criminal prosecution for my theft. On the other hand, even for a non-Christian like me, the possibility of learning more about one of the key figures in history was a lure too hard to resist. So, I decided to get help.

3.

My sister-in-law Miriam was married to an officer in the Police Department. I knew Yacov reasonably well from family gatherings and had no problem arranging for a confidential meeting with him.

"Yacov, what do you know about forensic investigations?"

"Very little, I don't work in that area."

"Do you know anyone who does?"

"The Police Department has a world-famous Division of Identification and Forensic Science that runs a Forensic Science Lab headquartered right here in Jerusalem. I know a fellow there; he helped me with the investigation of one of my cases."

"Can you put me in contact with that person?"

"What is this about?"

"It's a very sensitive matter, and it's best if I don't tell you."

"Be that way. I will e-mail you his name and contact information."

4.

Shimon Behar was a wiry, gray-haired man in his sixties. He had a permanent scowl on his face and in less than two minutes he let you know he was nobody's fool. In our first meeting in April, I broached the subject of my visit:

"In your lab, do you do much work with bones?"

"What do you mean?"

"I mean, what kind of information can you get from the analysis of human bones?"

"All kinds of information, depending on the condition of the bones."

"Can you do DNA reconstruction?"

"Certainly. We have developed several methods for recovering the DNA of a deceased person from fragments of his or her bone materials. We at the Forensic Science lab use a technique known as total demineralization to reconstruct such DNA with surprising fidelity, depending of course on how long after death the reconstruction is attempted, the circumstances of the death, and the environmental conditions under which the bone fragments had been maintained."

"Well, if I gave you some ancient bones, could you reconstruct what ethnic group the person belonged to, where he or she lived, and what his or her physical appearance and other characteristics were?"

"For the most part, yes. Finding the time of death is simple. For human or animal remains from the past

50,000 years or so, we look at levels of carbon-14 in the sample. While alive, a person's body – including the bones – contains the same levels of carbon-14 as the surrounding environment. But when a person dies, a radioactive decay process starts that takes the carbon isotope back into nitrogen. So, we compare the amount of carbon-14 with the levels of carbon-12 and carbon-13 in the bones to determine how much time has passed since the person died.

"Other things require genetic assessment. Analyzable DNA often persists in bones and teeth much longer than in the soft tissues of the body, because the rigid structure of bones and teeth provide some protection against DNA degradation. Of course, the conditions under which the bones have been kept is important to how well they are able to preserve DNA. What is the history of the bones that concern you?"

"I think these bones are a couple thousand years old and were kept in a dry area, out of contact with the outside environment."

"That is good. Using current DNA evaluation techniques and comparisons with very large databases of genetic materials collected throughout the world, it is likely that analysis may provide information regarding the person's geographic ancestry and general physical appearance."

"Can you do such analysis for me?"

"The question is not whether I can but whether I want to do it. You have not told me what bones are these and why are you interested in identifying their owner."

"Doctor Behar, this is a very sensitive and confidential matter. It would be best if I don't give you any further details."

"I will not get involved in anything that could be illegal or put me or my institution in jeopardy. Sorry, but I can't proceed without knowing more."

"Look, the investigation that you will conduct is important and may result in making you famous. I can see you writing a book with your findings and becoming rich overnight."

Behar gave me a calculating look. "Is this something that could have political implications?"

"Perhaps."

"Then I don't want any part of it."

"Wait" I said eagerly. "Why don't you get started with your analysis? You will have veto power over whether the results are shared with anyone except you and me and whoever in your lab participates in the project. It will stay confidential as long as you wish it to be so."

"Mmm.... You have piqued my curiosity. How is this project going to be set up and funded?"

"It will have to be a private project, sort of moonlighting by you and your team. I will pay for the project myself, out of my retirement account."

"I will get started but, I promise, I will cancel the whole thing if there are any complications."

5.

The first thing Behar determined was that these three bones were from the toes of the left foot of the same individual, an adult male. One of the bones, apparently a portion of a middle toe, exhibited a diagonal groove at one end that could be the sign of traumatic injury. Carbon-14 analysis determined that the owner of the bones had died about twenty-five hundred years previously.

"That puts them during the Roman occupation of Judea" noted Behar. "Could it be a martyr from the First Jewish – Roman war of 3826?"

"Maybe" I replied disingenuously. "The Romans destroyed the Second Temple and killed many rebels when they captured Jerusalem near the end that war, and there were many other deaths during the Jewish civil war that preceded the Roman occupation."

"The chiseling of that toe points to a potential crucifixion, a preferred method used by the Romans to execute notorious rebels and other criminals."

"So, the death of the owner of these bones occurred around 3830?"

"I would put a forty-year bracket around that date; the carbon tracing is accurate but not that precise.

Somewhere between 3790 and 3870; that is, between Common Era 30 and 110."

6.

Through misdirection and ambiguity, I succeeded in keeping Behar off track while he and his team conducted the delicate DNA analyses. I had history on my side for the prevarication: by the end of the First Jewish-Roman war, the Jewish uprising leaders either perished in battle, disappeared into obscurity, or were subjected to the ruthless judgment of the Roman conquerors. "My" corpse could be any of a large number of people.

The DNA analyses proceeded along a well-known approach: DNA profiles were developed from the unknown sample and compared with known reference samples, until a potential "match" was found. Statistical analyses were then performed to establish the confidence in the match, which in this case turned out to be high.

7.

Days later, I was summoned by e-mail and reported to Behar's office.

"I compared the DNA profile obtained by our lab analysis with the collection of worldwide DNA databases kept by our organization. This man's genes are very closely associated with those of a Jewish population group most commonly found in western Iraq in ancient times. He was definitely Jewish.

"The bones belong to a man between thirty and fifty years old. He was in good physical condition at the time of his death, so he most likely met a violent end. He had curly dark to black hair, olive skin, and brown eyes. He was short in stature (about 1.5 meters tall) and probably had a beard, in accordance with the Jewish practices of the time. I can't give you any more physical details. In any case, where did you find these bones?"

"They were in a crypt in a location in the Old City that was disrupted during the recent hostilities."

"What makes them significant?"

I tried to find a way to avoid answering the question, but could come up with nothing but the truth. "They were in the ruins of the Church of the Holy Sepulchre."

There was a very long silence. Finally, Behar spoke:

"I don't want to be associated with your investigation any further. I suggest destroying what is left of the bones."

I protested: "No, I want to keep the fragments. Please give them back to me."

"Well, I recommend that you bury these bones or cast them into the sea. If they are what you seem to say they are, nothing but grief can come out of the world learning about them."

8.

They gave me a plastic bag with the bones, which I took home and put in my refrigerator. Although out of sight, the bones were an ever-present reminder of my predicament. Should I follow Behar's advice, dispose of them, and forget the whole thing? Should I go public with my findings and risk imprisonment or worse? I was not a religious person and did not care much about the feelings of the Christians, but did I have any ethical obligations to make a full disclosure?

I became distracted and morose. My wife noticed my odd frame of mind and, after asking in vain several times what was wrong with me, gave up questioning and in a huff went to visit her mother in Tel Aviv for some Spring shopping. So, I was left home alone with the bones.

Days after she left, I had a nightmare. A disheveled, bearded young man wearing a short one-piece brown tunic appeared to me in my sleep and began talking in an archaic version of Hebrew which I nonetheless was able to understand. He had an angry glower on his face and addressed me sternly:

"Why did you steal those bones?"

At first, I didn't know what to say but then I gathered enough courage to reply: "I thought it would be interesting to check on the person who owned them."

"Have you now found out who that person was?"

"Yes, they belonged to Jesus of Nazareth, who was crucified by the Romans two thousand years ago."

"And why do you still keep them?"

"I'm not sure. Maybe I thought that through them I would be able to ask their owner some questions."

"Well, ask me."

"Are you the son of God?"

"We are all God's children."

"I mean, are you the Messiah, God's messenger, come to deliver the Jewish people?"

"Do you believe the Jewish people are really in need of deliverance?"

"Perhaps. The situation in Israel is very difficult these days and there is fear that the country may ultimately collapse. Anyway, were you resurrected after being dead for three days?"

"Some say I was."

I got irritated. "Why are you not answering my questions?"

"You are asking things that you don't need to know. Ask something important *to you*."

"Well, here is something very important to me. Israel has been at war with its Arab neighbors ever since the country was founded. We have had six wars; this last one almost brought us, and potentially the rest of the world, to destruction. Will we survive? Is the end of mankind coming upon us?"

"I have been asked that more than once. There will be wars and disasters, and many instances of great pain and suffering in the years to come. But God is provident, and will not allow His children to be extinguished. Have faith: the world will survive until the time marked for its demise, and the end will not occur through one of your silly wars."

"Will Israel and the world stay in one piece while I'm alive?"

"Yes."

"So, what should I do the rest of my life?"

"Live the best you can, obey the Commandments, and avoid hurting others. And have faith. Now, you need to get rid of those bones, for they have served their purpose."

"How come they just appeared out of nowhere a few weeks ago?"

"Maybe they were planted for you to find them and look into their origin, so we could have this conversation."

"Why did you pick me? I'm just an ordinary man."

"Common people, even children, have received wisdom before and have known what to do with it. I counsel you to follow their example," said the visitor as he vanished.

Whether the dream was a true vision or just a figment of my overstressed mind, I woke up feeling reassured. "Some mysteries are beyond human understanding," I told myself.

It was time to empty the refrigerator and stop worrying about the future of the world. I would put to use my recently acquired wisdom and let the world know we were still safe. It was not yet clear how I would do this, but I knew I would eventually think of something.

Figaro on Wheels

> *Tutti mi chiedono, tutti mi vogliono,*
> *Donne, ragazzi, vecchi, fanciulle*
> (Everyone asks for me, everyone wants me,
> Women, boys, old people, girls)
> Rossini, The Barber of Seville, Act 1, Cavatina

1

Billy Bob Morton (to his friends, "BB") couldn't do math. This was no knock on the Jefferson County schools; both the elementary and the middle/high school had done their darndest to pound basic principles of science, particularly mathematics, into BB's skull. All their attempts had failed. Not only was BB unaccomplished in subjects requiring an analytic bent, but he flunked even American History and English.

When he was finally released to society after twelve years of wasted institutional effort, BB could barely read and write and had a limited vocabulary in which coarse and curse words predominated. His doting but disappointed mother (on food stamps since her husband skipped town when BB was three) had to round up help from all her relatives and friends, but was able to raise enough money to send BB to study cosmetology at a vocational school not far from their home in Monticello. BB did not complete his training, but emerged with sufficient skills to get a job at a barbershop/hair salon on Route 19, blocks away from the Piggly Wiggly.

BB was skillful as a barber and remained employed for nearly four years, by the end of which he had managed to save some money by living at home and limiting his partying with friends to a couple of cans of whatever beer was on special. He used all his savings, plus a loan from the barbershop, as the down payment on a used black Honda CB500X from a motorcycle dealer in Tallahassee. He would have preferred a Harley like his friend Chuck owned, but he could not afford it, and the CB500X was good enough for his driving around in Monticello and immediate areas; once, in March, he drove it all the way to

Valdosta to the azalea festival, and the machine did well on the longer ride.

BB had reached the ripe age of 23 and was leading a reasonably tranquil life when everything was turned on its head as the pestilence struck. At first, the growing national disaster left little mark on him. The Florida panhandle was far from the big population centers and none of the two thousand inhabitants of Monticello was affected by the outbreak. However, as weeks passed and the magnitude of the disaster became more palpable, cities and then entire states were placed on lockdown and non-essential activities came to a halt. Jefferson County's turn to shut down finally came and most businesses were ordered to close, or did so voluntarily. The barbershop that employed BB was among the first casualties. BB was laid off, as were the other two barbers and the hair stylist.

For BB, the loss of his meager income was a matter of grave concern. He had started dating cute Nancy Phillips and his need for spending money was increasing. He still owed on his motorcycle purchase, and had developed a taste for weed, all of which made it more difficult to accept the directive to stay home twiddling his thumbs and earning no money.

After two weeks of inactivity, a casual conversation with his girlfriend set the wheels in motion for a change in BB's life. She, who was ever devoted to first lady Nancy Reagan, complained that she had trouble achieving the long, fluffy, perfectly layered look of Mrs. Reagan because her hair was growing wild for lack of care. "I haven't gotten my hair done in weeks. I can't stand to look at myself in the mirror anymore" she whimpered.

BB frowned and pecked her on the cheek. "Dear, I think I can take care of your problem. I'll be back." He got on Condi (as many car owners do, he had baptized his motorcycle), went home, and in a few minutes returned with his set of hair care tools, which he had removed from the barbershop when he was laid off. "I'm a barber, not a hair stylist, but I watched Joyce Wu as she worked on ladies at the salon" he explained.

Nancy was a bit reluctant to let him have a go at her hair, but beggars can't be choosers. She sat down as he produced a pair of long shears and began singing a poor imitation of Johnny Cash's "I Walk the Line." Half an hour later, he escorted Nancy to the large hallway mirror and presented the results of his handiwork. "It's wonderful!" exclaimed Nancy. "You should hire yourself out to do this!!"

That night, BB was having one of his now infrequent beers with George Byers, his aunt's husband and one of the smartest folks he knew. Unlike BB, George graduated from high school, attended college, and went on to become a real estate agent and stock advisor. Between the two careers, he had earned enough to see himself comfortably through the current depression. When BB related with unconcealed pride his success in rescuing Nancy from the doldrums, George picked up on her casual remark and commented: "You know, BB, the girl is right. There must be hundreds of people in this area who are suffering because they can't get their hair properly cared for. What you need to do is provide your services to them. You could become a travelling barber, a hair stylist on wheels. You would start raking money in no time flat!!" He took the napkin from under his beer glass, extracted a ballpoint pen from his shirt pocket, and began scribbling figures. "On the average, how long does it take for you to give a haircut?" "About twenty minutes" answered BB. "And a lady's hair, assuming no shampooing, etc." "A little longer, I'm not that skilled and women are fussier." "So, counting time lost in commuting, you could do at least ten clients a day. Say thirty bucks a shot, and you got yourself about $300 a day, minus travel expenses. How does that grab you?!"

BB was loath to douse cold water on George's enthusiasm. "But I don't know anybody!" he lamented.

"AHH!!" George gave an incredibly wide Cheshire cat smile. "*I* know scads of people, from Biloxi to Jacksonville. We'll print a brochure and mail it to my contact list, and all you have to do is sit down and answer the phone. You'll be busier than a one-legged man in an ass kicking contest!"

"Don't I have to get some kind of a permit or a license to do this?"

"Maybe. But by the time the law catches up with you, you will have enough money raised to pay any fines and hire a lawyer to get the paperwork taken care of."

"And will people allow me in their houses? Everyone is getting locked up and avoiding contact with strangers."

"You can lie and say you have been tested and are fine. Because you are fine, right?"

"Yes, I am. Still, the whole thing seems a little chancy, if you know what I mean."

"Look at it this way: what do you have to lose? I'll help you with the mailing and provide any references. All I want is a ten percent cut of the takings."

BB could not think of any more objections and let himself be carried away by George's enthusiasm.

2

BB or, as George's flier referred to, the "Figaro on Wheels," had to wait almost a week before the first call came in. It was a widower from Panama City, an old client of George, who wanted BB to give haircuts to him and his three children. BB negotiated a fee of $100 plus $20 in transportation costs. It took him two hours to get there, an hour and a half of work, and a couple of hours on Condi to get back – half a day of labor for about a hundred and twenty bucks; not such a great deal.

George listened patiently to BB's complaints. "You have to build a client base. After you have enough clients, you may be picky as to which calls to take and which to turn down. But, for the moment, be patient and take it on the chin."

As usual, George was right. Other calls followed, some as far as Destin, but mainly from Greenville, Wacissa, Havana, and Tallahassee and its suburbs. By the end of two weeks, BB had had done a dozen jobs and had several more already scheduled. Better yet, he was getting commendations from his new clients, and word of mouth referrals were coming in. At that point, he started setting limits on his service area: he would travel for free no more than 20 miles in any direction, and would set a per mile charge for clients beyond that range.

Even with those limitations, as the lockdown continued and the pestilence took its toll on cities, towns and rural areas, the demand for BB's services kept increasing, to the point where he considered taking in an apprentice to help meet the demand. The Figaro on Wheels had become a minor celebrity throughout the Florida Panhandle.

3

The first sign of trouble came when George paid BB an evening call at his mother's cottage. The dwelling was exceedingly modest and in poor repair, and was seldom visited by anyone outside the immediate family and social workers from the welfare agencies. George's surprise appearance at his door concerned BB: "George! What brings you here in the middle of the night?"

George walked in and proceeded to close and lock the door. "Is your mom awake?" he whispered.

"No, she always goes to bed early" replied BB in a matching low voice. "Can I get you something to drink?"

George shook his head and sat on the sofa, motioning BB to sit next to him. "Yesterday I had a call from your first client."

"Mr. Stubbs, the guy from Panama City? Nice fellow."

"Yes, he is a nice guy, but was in distress."

"Why?"

"He claims that after you came to cut their hair, he and two of his boys came down with the pestilence. He says that he keeps himself and the kids out of contact with the outside world since the start of the epidemic and even has his food delivered. He had you come in because his children were pestering him about their long hair and he thought that they needed to look presentable. Anyway, I told him that you are very scrupulous in making sure all your equipment is sterilized and you are certainly not a carrier, so the infection must have come from somewhere else. I'm not sure he believed me, but I was able to calm him down. He and his children had a few rough days, but seem to be on the mend."

BB was silent for a while. "I do keep all my gear clean and I disinfect everything – both before and after each client. And I was sick with the flu for a couple of days, but recovered right away."

George scowled. "Did you ever hear of Typhoid Mary? You may, in fact, be a carrier of the organism that causes the pestilence."

"Naw, it was just a coincidence, I'm sure."

"Well, let's wait a couple of days to see what happens, but if I were you, I would cut back on my appointments right away."

BB chose to remain unconvinced and kept to his regular schedule until, the following week, he found Nancy in tears. When he asked what was wrong, she replied: "My friend Linda, you know, the one whose hair you cut a few days ago, is down with the pestilence and may die because she is diabetic and has other health issues."

BB grimaced but said nothing.

4

BB's philosophy of life was uncomplicated: work hard, obey the law as much as you need to, mind your own business, and let others take care of themselves. He was not used to dealing with ethical dilemmas, and the situation he was facing was outside his moral compass. He was not sure whether he had been a carrier, or if he remained one still. He dared not get tested, because if he was found to carry the organism he could be quarantined for an indefinite period of time and lose a lot of money. Moreover, some of the people he might have infected could take legal action against him. On the other hand, perhaps George was right, he should stop going out on Condi and lay low until the epidemic had run its course.

He enjoyed the increased income and would prefer to continue his profitable trade as long as possible, while minimizing the risk of discovery. Finally, he came up with what he thought was a good solution: he would only take clients that were relatively young and in good health; even if he inflicted the disease on them, there should be little in the way of consequences. After all, Mr. Stubbs and his children had fully recovered.

His business was reduced, but he continued to do the travelling barber routine and added a buck or two more to his bank account. It was the American way, he reckoned.

5

It was inevitable that, after nearly three months of running his travelling barber operation, BB's activities would become notorious. A small human-interest piece about BB's "public service" ran in the *Panama City News Herald* and was soon picked up in the *Tallahassee Democrat*, other newspapers in the Gannett chain, and ultimately *The Miami Herald*. In a nation hungry for uplifting tales of ingenuity amidst the crisis, the story surfaced in *Newsweek*, *The New York Times*, and all the major broadcast networks. All of a sudden, BB acquired the status of a folk hero. He became the center of an intense debate on whether hair care was an essential business so that salons and barber shops could stay open in a crisis, or whether individual initiatives like his should be encouraged instead. The issue remained unresolved.

He began getting requests for interviews, which he declined – politely at first, then more vigorously – and all sorts of correspondence, from fan and hate mail to solicitations and proposals. A Chicago businessman wrote suggesting the creation of a "Figaro on Wheels" franchise that would sell BB's name and endorsement to individual entrepreneurs throughout the country. BB was overwhelmed by the unexpected attention and tried to shut himself out of the limelight and sought to limit his public appearances to visiting his customers.

Alas, the genie was out of the bottle and, in addition to the media and the general public, BB caught the attention of the authorities. Several State agencies in Florida began examining his running an unlicensed business, his failure to abide by the lockdown rules, and more importantly, his failure to pay taxes on his earnings. The Internal Revenue Service also got in the act, discovering that BB had never filed a federal income tax return and, in the current year, had made no self-employment tax filings. In short, BB became more sought after by the regulators than a honey bee nest detected by a sloth of hungry bears.

BB was indicted on various charges both in State and Federal courts and was ultimately convicted of tax evasion. The sentencing judge was deaf to his pleas for clemency and his lawyer's argument that BB was only trying to provide a service to the public; BB was sentenced to ten years in prison, to be held at the Federal Correctional Institution of Marianna, Florida, not far from the theater of his crimes.

The harshness of the sentence was perhaps linked to another story by an investigative reporter who looked closely into BB's operations. In an article published while the trial was in progress, the reporter revealed that BB was potentially responsible for infecting several dozen people with the pestilence and indirectly causing the deaths of at least four elderly men and women. This story was never brought up at BB's trial or his sentencing, but the presiding judge was in his late seventies and might have taken umbrage at BB's practices.

BB was taken to Marianna. He wanted to bring his barbering gear with him to continue practicing his trade, but sharp metal objects were not allowed in the prison, so he had to look forward to spending his years in jail fraternizing with the other inmates and dreaming of the day in which he could return to society and become again the proud, law-abiding citizen he always thought himself to be.

The malady that had afflicted him and caused him to cut back on his trade from fear of being a carrier turned out to be garden variety flu, not pestilence, so he was ripe for the disease to catch up to him. Barely two weeks into his incarceration, fraternization with the prison inmates caused him to contract the pestilence.

He was deathly ill but survived. When he recovered, he asked for leave to resume his trade and was granted permission to do so, since now he was probably immunized from the disease and could approach other prisoners, healthy or infirm, without fear of contagion. He became quite popular with the jail population, which nicknamed him "Figs," and after serving a year of his sentence his lawyer applied for parole on good behavior grounds.

He was released on probation on the condition that he perform three hundred hours of community service – as itinerant barber for the general population, still on lockdown. He took again his role as Figaro on Wheels and gained much acclaim in the greater Tallahassee area as a modern version of Florence Nightingale.

When the pestilence was finally over and the barbershop near the Piggly Wiggly opened again, BB was rehired and resumed his former job. But not for long: his guru George Byers talked him into taking advantage of his fame to run for office. BB demurred: "But I can barely read and write and know nothing about politics." George, as usual, laid BB's fears to rest:

"You are a man of the people, not a pointy headed Eastern liberal. That is actually a big plus with the electorate in these parts. As to your political savvy, all you need to say is that as a Republican you are pro-guns, pro-life, and pro-business, and you'll get elected."

BB took George's advice, and went on to became the youngest ever member of the Jefferson County Board of Commissioners. Six years and three elections later, he was elected to the United States House of Representatives.

He grew fat and wealthy in the service of the public and died of a stroke ten years later, leaving nearly a million dollars in the bank. A glorified version of his life story was made into a successful TV miniseries; Condi is on permanent display in Tallahassee's Museum of Florida History.

Selling Adama

Mariama Lahai, a very young Temne girl from Sierra Leone, was seized, sold into slavery, and ultimately forced onboard an English slave ship that plied the trade route from West Africa to the Americas.

After a long voyage, the ship dropped anchor in Bridgetown, on the island of Barbados. One of the slaves still alive at the end of the trip was a very pregnant Mariama. She had been impregnated during the crossing by Hubart Jenkins, the ship's First Mate.

Crowds gathered in the square in front of Bridgetown Harbor to witness the auction of the ship's slaves. At the start of the auction, Jenkins was asked to designate the slave he wished to acquire in lieu of his pay. He announced:

"I choose Mariama Lahai."

Mariama was delivered into Jenkins' hands, who took her to his quarters.

That night, a trembling Mariama confronted her new owner: "Why did you choose me? I have no skills and may die delivering your child. You could have picked one of the men, who would be much more valuable to you if you chose to sell him."

"You're very pretty" declared Jenkins, seizing Mariama's face, and squeezing her cheeks. He held her firmly in his grasp and added: "You've given me pleasure during the voyage and I want to continue getting it. Once our child is born, if he's a boy he will work hard in my service and will make me good money when I sell him. If it's a girl, I'm counting on her being as beautiful as her mother and joining me in bed after her first blood, if not sooner."

Mariama was devastated by the news of the future that awaited her and her soon to be born child. She prayed every night to Kurumasaba, the Supreme High God, begging for deliverance from her cruel master. If an escape was not possible, she asked for the gift of a male child whose life, though hard, would be preferable to what would befall a daughter.

She lived in constant agitation until, ten days after arrival in Barbados, she went into labor and delivered a female whose lovely features were a blend of those of her parents: she had a honey complexion and prominent cheekbones in an oval face dominated by lively hazel eyes and a sensuous mouth. Mariama named her Adama, meaning beautiful in Temne. However, instead of pride, Mariama cringed with apprehension at her lovely daughter's future.

***

The night of her daughter's birth Mariama collapsed into a troubled sleep, in which she experienced a recurring dream. A strange figure, with the body of a giant spider and a misshapen man's face, kept appearing before her closed eyelids, only to withdraw into the shadows. At length, the creature seemed to solidify and spoke to her in a shrill, chirping voice: "Wake up, woman! We need to talk!"

"Who are you?" questioned Mariama.

"My name is Anansi. I am the messenger of the gods and sometimes protector of the oppressed. I have come to offer you a bargain."

"You don't even exist. I'm making you up."

"Not so. I am real and can help you."

"How?"

"I can deliver you from your master and take you and your daughter to a place of safety, away from the white devils that run these lands."

"There's no such a place" sighed Mariama.

"There is, and I can take you there... for a price."

Mariama's eyes were closed but, even so, they became narrowed by suspicion. "What price?"

"I have a daughter for which I struck, long ago, a very profitable marriage deal. I have seen your exceptionally beautiful daughter and think I could do the same thing, using her."

"What do you mean?"

"I would like to treat your daughter as my own, and in time work out a marriage deal between her and some powerful suitor. She would live well and I would be richer and more powerful."

Mariama became fully awake. "My Adama is *not* for sale. You must be deranged to think I would agree to such a bargain."

"Come tomorrow you may have a different view. Your master will come in the morning to take you and your baby back to the ship in which you came. He intends to have you both accompany him to his distant home as his slaves."

"That cannot be... he couldn't do such a thing!"

"He will ... unless we prevent him."

"How?"

"There are two ways to keep him from carrying you away. One is to stop him. He is asleep next door. I will make sure he does not wake up. And you ... will make sure he sleeps forever."

"Murder him in his sleep?" Mariama shuddered.

"The choice is between the lives of you and your daughter against his."

"I can't kill another person, even an evil man like him. What's the second way?"

"I can take you and your daughter away from him."

"Where?"

"To a place that is safe and far away. You need only hold Adama to your breast and close your eyes. I will do the rest."

"What if I don't like it there?"

"I promise I will bring you back if you ask me to do so."

Mariama considered her difficult options. She would not kill Jenkins and, if she ran away with Adama, the white masters would have the entire island searched looking for them. She and her daughter would most likely be caught and brought back, and she would be punished. Plus, her escape attempt in a strange land would be dangerous. She had no real choice: "So be it. We'll go with you. Please be kind."

***

Mariama never knew what happened next or how long her trance lasted. She was very cold and felt a gelid breeze buffet her body, and then it all stopped as quickly as it had started and warmth returned.

"Open your eyes" whispered a chittering voice she knew well.

At first, Mariama failed to understand the panorama that her eyes presented to her. She was standing outside a mansion atop a high place, surrounded by clouds that obscured the features of the land below. She fought a sense of vertigo and asked: "Where are we?"

"In the Iworoko Mountains, deep in the all-powerful Oyo Empire. Not too far from your old home."

"What are we doing here?"

"This is my domain. A secret palace, overlooking this corner of the Empire. I will make this mountain abode your home."

"What will I do here?"

"Just raise and care for your daughter as she grows up. I require nothing else. I promise I will not mistreat either of you in any way while you are here."

"Why are we better off in this strange land than in Barbados?"

"Because here you will live in luxury and be safe from the white oppressors. I do not dwell in this palace, but keep it for my special guests. You will only see me occasionally."

"How long do we have to stay here?"

"Until Adama sheds her first blood and I can start bargaining for her hand with rich suitors."

"But that will take thirteen years."

"So, you will need to find something to do to entertain yourself while you wait." With these words, Anansi disappeared into the mountain air.

***

The moment Mariama found herself alone, questions popped in her mind. How was she going to raise her daughter all by herself, in an isolated mansion in the clouds?

She went into the palace and, in the center of the reception room, found a glass table, entirely empty except for a terracotta lamp of the type one filled with palm oil and used to light a room. Next to the lamp, a strip of parchment held a message in Mariama's Temne language: "Rub the lamp if you need anything."

Intrigued, Mariama rubbed the side of the vessel. At first nothing happened, but then a tenuous column of smoke emerged from the hole on the top of the lamp. The column grew and solidified, becoming the floating image of a very dark man wearing a flowing robe. The apparition spoke in a hollow, unreal voice: "Did you summon me, Mistress?"

Surprised, Mariama replied: "I guess I did, though I intended nothing of the sort."

The apparition continued, as if it had not heard Mariama's disclaimer: "I am Bookhor the Wise, and I have been charged by master Anansi with assisting you any way you require."

"Are you a spirit or something?" asked Mariama, incredulously.

"You would not understand it if I tried to explain. All you need to know is that I can do almost anything that you could possibly need."

"Right now, I'd like to know how I am going to stay alive in this prison, how I am going to raise my infant daughter all by myself, and how I am going to spend thirteen or more years without contact with a living being and remain sane."

"I cannot guarantee you will remain sane, but I will take care of all your worldly needs, and help raise your daughter. And there are enough things to occupy your time while staying here that you should not be too bored."

"If you are so powerful as you say, how come you are going to serve me as a slave?"

There was a barely perceptible shudder from the apparition. "I am in thrall to Anansi for the next one hundred years."

"How did that happen?"

There was another, more perceptible shudder. "He beat me in a game of dice."

"What?"

"We had a wager: this palace against my services for that period."

"And you lost to him?"

"Yes. I think he cheated but cannot prove it."

Mariama could not resist a chuckle. "I thought you said you were called The Wise."

"I am" replied the creature ruefully. "But it takes more than wisdom to beat Anansi."

***

At first, Mariama was angry at Anansi for confining her and Adama to an isolated estate in the mountains, away from the rest of the world. Little by little, however, she discovered the many treasures held within the palace. There were rooms for every possible activity and occupation, from a painting studio to a ceramics shop, a music room, a conservatory, several lounges and hot and cool pools, kitchens and banquet rooms, libraries and even an observatory from which one could gaze at the heavens. The estate was surrounded by a garden in which she and her daughter could take walks regardless of season, for the cold of winter never reached the mountain keep.

Mariama never endeavored to make use of any of the arts and crafts contained in the palace's rooms, save for one. Her mother had taught Mariama to weave and sew fabrics to make clothes for herself and her sister. For that reason, she was captivated by the discovery of a knitting room, complete with a spinning wheel, thread, and bolts of fabric of all materials and colors, a work table with cutting and assembling tools, and a multitude of other devices that were unfamiliar but appeared potentially useful. She immediately began spending hours fashioning garments for herself and Adama, wall hangings, area rugs, and other decorative weavings. The occupation filled her hours, but could not calm the misgivings in her heart.

Time moved with surprising speed. Adama grew from a baby into a gentle child and then a lovely young teen as she approached puberty. Through the years, Bookhor lived up to his promise of caring for the humans entrusted to his care. He prepared daily feasts for his wards, kept the estate clean and well-tended, and became a tutor to the young girl, teaching her not only letters and the history and culture of the African people, but even to play the Kora (a sort of harp-lute), at which she soon became an expert.

Anansi's visits were rare. He came two or three times a year, always in the middle of the night, and departed after a short stay in which he mostly conversed with Adama, checking on her progress. For these visits Anansi adopted a humanoid appearance, showing up as a portly man with a protuberant belly and eight legs, six of which he kept discreetly hidden under a voluminous black cape. He attempted to appear amiable and non-threatening to the child, although his efforts were undercut by the chittering quality of his voice and the gourd-like shape and greenish coloring of his head.

When Adama became old enough to convey her feelings to her mother, she declared that the visits from that stranger were disturbing and causing awful nightmares. "Who's he? What does he want from us?" Mariama did her best to minimize the horror of her forced deal with Anansi and the future that awaited the girl. "He's your uncle Anansi" would reply Mariama, affecting an airy tone. "He's a very important man. He owns the palace where we live and others throughout the world. He's always very busy, but tries to find the time to come see you because you are his favorite niece and he loves you very much."

To this, Adama would protest: "But he doesn't look like you at all, so he can't be your brother. Was my father as ugly as he is?" And Mariama would try to obfuscate: "He is actually your father's great-great uncle, so he does not resemble the nearer members of the family."

Mariama's diversionary ploys worked until Adama turned thirteen and began to question the entire enterprise and their roles vis-à-vis the repulsive relative. "What does he really want from us? I can appreciate that he has helped us live well for all these years, but he also has kept us hidden away. When is this going to end and when are we going to get out of here?"

Mariama felt it was time she talked honestly to her daughter about her fate. "Uncle Anansi promised your father that he would take care of us and would see to it that you married a powerful, wealthy man and became a great lady yourself. All these years, he has used Bookhor to train you so that you are, not just a beautiful young woman, but also a learned, well-spoken, and charming one. You are fit to be a queen, and Anansi will soon make the necessary contacts to allow you to become one."

"So, Uncle Anansi gets to decide who I am to marry?"

"Not just him. I'll be involved also."

"How about me?"

"Adama dear, you are very young and know nothing about life. Trust us, who have far more knowledge and experience. We'll try to make the best decisions for you. This is the way things are done."

Adama did not reply, but her scowl spoke volumes. Mariama regarded Adama with regret and brushed her hair affectionately.

***

Weeks after this mother-daughter exchange Anansi made a surprise visit to his mansion in the clouds. He came in broad daylight, dressed in a silk shirt, baggy pantaloons festooned with jeweled stripes, and a dazzling ostrich skin cape. He greeted his guests and requested: "Please change into your best clothes and apply whatever cosmetics and perfumes will enhance, if that be possible, your peerless beauty. We are going on a fortune seeking trip!"

He would not respond to Mariama's requests for explanation, so she and Adama dressed in haste, but with utmost care. They wore pale yellow silk *mantuas*, overskirts drawn back over the hips to expose the petticoats beneath, as was the fashion in the French court. Their light outfits enhanced the warmth of their skin tones, like exquisite chocolates covered by gold wrappings. Anansi examined them approvingly and extracted from a pocket in his cape two necklaces nesting diamonds and pearls. "Put these on, and you will look like you are already members of one of the royal families of the world."

He led the women to the entrance of the mansion, where a carriage was already waiting, drawn by a pair of winged unicorns. They entered the carriage, and Anansi sat on a bank opposite theirs. "Relax. It will not be a long ride."

Mariama asked again: "But where are we going?"

This time Anansi responded, with a triumphant smile that showed the rows of sharp teeth that filled his mouth: "We are going to the palace of the Oba, to present young Adama to Abiodun, Alaafin of Oyo. He rules the greatest empire of the whole world."

***

The carriage descended from the clouds gently and came to a stop before one of the gates of the capital city of Oyo-Ile, where the Alaafin resided. The guards who stood at the entrance to the city dispersed in terror at the sight of the magical steeds, which drew the carriage to the entrance of the palace, in the center of the city. Anansi alighted from the carriage and, with a wave of the hand, drew open the heavy wooden doors. He then escorted Mariama and her daughter through a maze of corridors, ignoring the scores of servants, soldiers, and courtiers who filled the halls of the vast structure. At length, Anansi entered the throne room and bowed to the man seated at its end.

"Your divine majesty, I am humbled to be in your presence again. Permit me to introduce my wards, the most excellent lady Mariama and her daughter Adama, who have come from far away to pay their respects to you." Anansi was speaking in Yoruba, but somehow Mariama and Adama understood what he was saying and curtsied to the monarch.

"Are these the persons you promised to bring before my eyes?" questioned the Alaafin curtly.

"Indeed, they are. I have personally prepared them to ensure they are worthy of being brought into your presence."

The Alaafin gave the pair an appraising look and turned his attention to Mariama. "I am Abiodun. Welcome to my kingdom. Where are you from?"

Mariama curtsied again and answered in a quivering voice: "Lord, I was born west of here, in the land of the Temne, by the Kolenten River."

"My armies have yet to travel that far" replied the Alaafin apologetically. "Is your daughter also a Temne?"

"No. She saw the light in an island called Barbados, across the big waters from here."

"I noticed her strange coloring. Her skin is a bit lighter than yours and her eyes have shades of green and gold mixed with the brown. Is her father a Temne?"

"No, Sir. Her father was a white man."

Abiodun's lips curved down in a sign of distaste. "Is he alive?"

"No, Sir. He died nobly, defending his family from intruders." Mariama gulped, hoping that her lie would go unnoticed. How she hated to go through this charade!

The Alaafin went on with his questioning. "Is your daughter nubile?"

"Yes, my Lord. She stained the sheets for the first time only a few days ago. She's still a maiden in the full freshness of youth." Mariama blushed, ashamed of her pandering but hoping for the best for her daughter.

Adama, who up to that moment had remained standing behind Mariama's protecting body, stepped forward with unconcealed anger. "Mother, why are we doing this? Am I being touted like a cow at the market? You are embarrassing yourself and me in front of this man."

Anansi also stepped forward, interposing himself between the women and the seated monarch. "Your divine majesty, please forgive the unthinking words of a young girl. She meant no disrespect."

The Alaafin waved Anansi into silence. "I like my women spirited, like unbroken colts. In any case, her words could not possibly manage to offend me. But I am displeased that you want me to enter into a holy union with a mongrel that carries the impure blood of the white devils. I would never dream of making a member of their race my wife, no matter how beautiful. I should have your head for this."

There was a momentary pause, as the spider man's face turned as pale as a winter moon. Then he recovered and his features broke into a smile. He replied with false innocence:

"A thousand pardons, your majesty. I must have inadvertently confused you. I did not bring the young girl for you to consider her. She only came as a companion. It is the mother, a noble woman of the purest African blood, that I wanted to present for your perusal. She is still young and is wise beyond her years and a skilled weaver and musician."

"Silence, spider! You are babbling. My bargain with you was for a maiden in her flower. Mariama here is not that, so our deal is off and I have a mind to punish you for your chicanery."

Mariama dropped to the ground and grasped the Alaafin's sandaled feet in supplication. "Please pardon Anansi. He has been the guardian of my daughter since I became a widow and she an orphan. He is only trying to secure a better future for his ward, as do I."

Abidoun regarded the woman at his feet with new interest. "Mariama, you are beautiful yourself and clearly a good mother and loyal to your friends. Those are virtues that I admire in a woman, regardless of age and condition."

"I was hoping you would see it that way," pleaded Anansi.

"Silence!" bellowed the Alaafin. "Leave my domain at once. The women will stay with me, if they wish. If I find Mariama pleasing and she consents, I will keep her as one of my wives or concubines; her daughter can be an attendant in our palace, and perhaps in due course she will join in marriage with one of my officers."

"But Lord, I have spent many years polishing these gems to render them worthy of presentation before you. I deserve some compensation for my efforts."

Abidoun cracked a smile. "Spider, I marvel at your shamelessness and still have an itching to shed your blood. But you may yet prove useful to me in some future assignment that requires guile and no scruples. Here." He extracted a large purse from his tunic and threw it at Anansi's face. Immediately, two of the spider's hidden arms shot out and captured the purse in mid-air.

"Now be gone" repeated the Alaafin. "As for you, ladies, what is your pleasure? Will you depart with Anansi or remain in my court?"

Mariama replied without hesitation: "We gladly choose to stay with you." Adama nodded in assent.

Anansi turned around and crawled away. Those in close proximity might have heard, and perhaps understood, the words he mumbled as he departed:

"A deal that yields less profits than expected is better than no deal at all."

Christmas in Ushuaia

All people have had ill luck, but Jairus's daughter and Lazarus had the worst.
Mark Twain

1.

Laz pulled the parka closer to his body, ineffectually trying to ward off the gelid wind that blew from the mountains. Argentina was supposed to be warm in late December, but in Ushuaia, at the end of the world, the temperature rarely rose above fifty degrees. "Today, not even fifty" Laz mumbled. Talking to himself was just one of the habits that over the years had attached to him like fleas on a dog's fur.

He had not come to this remote outpost to see the sights -- Ushuaia held little of interest to entice a seasoned traveler like himself; it was described in the tourist guides as merely "a sliver of steep streets and jumbled buildings below the snowcapped Martial Range" of the Andes. He was also not interested in a trip to Antarctica, or in hiking the steep trails of Andorra Valley or trekking to the Martial Glacier, a couple of hours from town. "I'm not athletic" he told himself; not that his arthritic knees would have allowed him to go ambling about as he used to in his youth.

He had signed up for a four-hour boat cruise on the Beagle Channel that would take him to his goal, the area around the Les Eclaireurs lighthouse. Sailing along the channel off Ushuaia, the boat had passed by sea lions basking on the rocks, cormorants sitting on nests, fur seals, and other wildlife he did not recognize. On Martillo Island, the boat had come close to what the guide described as one of the largest penguin colonies outside of Antarctica. Laz had taken numerous pictures, although he had no expectation he would ever show them to anyone.

The boat finally arrived at Les Eclaireurs lighthouse, an iconic symbol of Ushuaia that the locals called the "lighthouse at the end of the world." Its distinctive red and white stripes contrasted sharply with the backdrop of snow-capped mountains north of the channel. Laz would have liked to disembark, but this was not permitted.

The end point of the boat tour was small Bridges Island. Passengers got off and set out on a walk, in search of native flora and fauna. At one point along the trek, Laz paused to gaze at the sprawling view across the Beagle Channel, with Ushuaia in the distance and the lighthouse not far to the northeast.

An albatross, gliding on enormous wings, circled around Laz. It spiraled down and landed a few yards away, righted itself and began pecking at the ground with its longish hooked bill in search of morsels cast away by the sea. It paused for one moment, raised its head, and stared at Laz as if offering encouragement.

Laz extracted from his coat a small notebook with dirty, worn covers and opened it.

2.

Each page of the notebook bore line after line of miniscule, crabbed handwriting. Some of the entries had become blurred by contact with liquids; others were obliterated by thick horizontal lines. Some entries were in pencil, others in inks of various colors. There were gaps in some pages, as if the writer had given up on his task only to resume it sometime later.

Laz read aloud one of the entries on the first page, which stood out because it was a little larger than the others and seemed to be inscribed with greater force. He read: "they all laughed at seeing my legs encased in plaster casts. I said that I had to wear the casts for eight weeks to straighten my crooked leg bones, and they laughed even more." The rest of the entry had been blacked out.

Laz tore the page and flung it away, and the strong breeze carried it towards the icy realms to the south. At the sound of ripping paper, the albatross jumped a little, but planted again its long, webbed feet on the rocky soil and resumed its dinner.

Laz started to read aloud again from his diary, but had to stop almost at once: the fierce wind choked him and paralyzed his throat. He continued tearing page after page from the notebook, sometimes stopping to read to himself a few lines, tears forming in the corners of his eyes at some remembered event. The wind carried away briskly each of the pages; the albatross paid no attention to the ceremony after the disturbance caused by the first sheet.

A voice near Laz's ears broke his concentration: "What are you doing?" It was the guide, bringing the rest of the passengers back to the boat. "Littering is a criminal offense in Tierra del Fuego. Stop it or I will have to report you."

Laz smiled sheepishly. "Sorry. I'm done." He pocketed the remains of the notebook and joined the caravan.

3.

His bare hotel room weighed heavily on Laz's spirit. He had to get out, find some company. There was light in the sky even though it was past nine thirty p.m. He went into the first restaurant he came across and asked the girl at the reception booth: "Are you still serving dinner?"

"Of course," she replied. Her Spanish had a strange undertone, as if it was not her native tongue. "Yesterday was the solstice. We will be open until midnight every day, including Christmas, through the end of the month. Would you like to be seated?"

Laz nodded and was led into a room with large rustic tables and high back, dark wooden chairs. There were simple Christmas decorations on the walls, wreaths of plastic holly and Santas and reindeer imported from northern countries.

The restaurant was packed; however, around the corner they had an overflow section that was almost full already. There were no single tables available, so the hostess indicated that Laz would have to share space with four other diners. Under normal circumstances, Laz would have walked away. But that night he welcomed being with others; besides, this was high season in Ushuaia and other restaurants might be just as crowded. He sat down and greeted his companions.

The table was occupied by a tourist couple that spoke in some European language Laz did not recognize; they ignored everybody and spent the rest of their stay talking loudly among themselves. The other couple were locals: a dark, middle-aged man and his ample, fair skinned wife. Laz sat next to the wife, who announced: "I'm María Eugenia, and this is my husband Héctor." "My name is Lázaro Cruz" Laz replied. María Eugenia immediately drew Laz into an amiable, mostly one-sided conversation.

As a waiter brought him a menu, Laz noticed that the European couple had their entrees – a lamb dish and some stew – before them; the locals were starting on their appetizers. Half a dozen beer bottles littered the surface of the table.

"What are you guys having?" asked Laz to María Eugenia. "We are sharing the king crab appetizer, which is the specialty of the house" she beamed.

"Is it good?" inquired Laz politely.

"Here, taste it." María Eugenia speared a morsel on her fork and handed it to Laz. He was somewhat startled by the unhygienic gesture, but blinked nervously and accepted the gift. "This is very good" he acknowledged.

"What else is good around here?" he then asked, emboldened by the woman's familiarity.

"Just about everything" replied María Eugenia, chewing on her crab. "I am partial to the black hake, which they cook in parchment. And you must drink the local beer." She pointed to one of the empty bottles on the table. "That's Cape Horn Stout, my favorite."

The waiter returned and Laz was ready to order. "I'll have the king crab appetizer and the black hake for the main course. And a bottle of Cape Horn Stout, please."

The beer came first. It was dark, sweet and slightly bitter. By the time the appetizer came, Laz was on his second bottle.

The food was quite good, and the beer grew on Laz as he ordered yet another bottle. He was only a casual drinker, and by the time he finished with the hake he was on his fourth bottle and already feeling tipsy.

His chit-chat with María Eugenia had continued unabated through dinner. As the waiter brought out the dessert menu, the lady bent her head in his direction and asked him in a confidential tone: "So, since you are not on your way to Antarctica, what brought you out to the end of the world?"

Laz was feeling pretty drunk by that time, and whispered back: "I... came to rid myself of my sorrows." He hiccupped.

"What do you mean?" replied María Eugenia, surprised.

"It's a long story" slurred Laz. "What should I get for dessert?"

4.

Amid bites of tiramisu and sips of disappointingly weak coffee, Laz told a tale from his childhood. "I was raised in a middle-class household in Buenos Aires. After the birth of my sister Elisa, my mother was too weak to handle the household chores by herself, so she contacted the rector of a Salesian Brothers congregation in our neighborhood, to see if they could provide an orphan girl that could be hired to help around our house. There were no children available, but they had a recent female arrival from Tierra del Fuego: Kuluána, a Yaghan Indian of indeterminate age who had been rescued from her declining village by Salesian missionaries. The mission had closed down for some reason and the wards they were trying to civilize were scattered all over Argentina."

"Kuluána was old and nurturing, and became a second mother to Elisa and me. I would confide to her many of my childhood pains and fears, not daring to raise them with my distracted mother or my very distant father. Once, when I was thirteen or fourteen, Kuluána spotted me hiding in one corner, crying. She came over and, putting her arm around my heaving shoulders, asked: "Lazarito, what's the matter? Why are you crying?"

"Between sobs, I related what I felt was a world-ending tragedy: 'Elena Santos has dumped me. She says I'm too boring, and would rather be friends with Arturo.'

She gave a short laugh and replied: 'And what do you propose to do about it?'"

"I dunno" I answered, and broke into loud sobs. "I want to die!"

"Kuluána assumed a vague expression, as if trying to bring back something from the dim past. Finally, she squeezed my shoulder and said: 'Lazarito, where I come from, a village way south of here, we have an ancient custom. Whenever we feel overwhelmed by sorrow, we get on a canoe and paddle down, get close to the big frozen water, and cry aloud the name of the person or thing that's hurting us, so that the wind will carry it away to the gods at the land of eternal night and we will be rid of it. I never tried doing this myself, but my *kippa*, my mother, said that it had worked for her and others in the village."

"Do I need to travel all the way south before I can feel better?" I rebelled.

"No, child," she answered. "The pain will soon go away by itself; you'll see."

"I didn't believe Kuluána but the pain slowly faded away, as she had predicted. All the same, I started keeping a diary in which I would record all the sad events of my life in the off chance I might have to call them out some day. With the years, my sorrows multiplied and my diary became full, little by little. Last month my lifetime companion passed way, leaving me totally alone and feeling as disconsolate as I was the day of my conversation with Kuluána. Remembering the Yaghan folk story, I decided to take a special Christmas vacation in Ushuaia and scream my woes into the land of eternal night. I went on a cruise of the Beagle Channel with the intention of shouting out each of the sorrows and misfortunes of my life. Only it was too damned cold, so instead of talking I just tore away the pages of my diary and cast them out to the wind. I'm sure the gods of the eternal night know how to read."

5.

Héctor, who had remained silent through the dinner, lay his beer bottle on the table and asked: "What sort of stuff did you have in the notebook? Just the bad things?"

Laz, who was near passing out, revived enough to reply: "No, all sorts of things. As the girl said years ago, I'm boring. I write everything down, sometimes in detail."

"And you tossed the whole thing out to the gods?"

The question startled Laz and woke him up a little.

"Yeah, but they are supposed to read only the bad parts."

María Eugenia picked up from her husband. "And how are they supposed to know which parts are good and which bad?"

Laz was saved from having to answer the question by the European couple, who had just paid their check and got up with a clattering of chairs, said "*buenas noches*" in barbarous Spanish, and taken off.

Laz was still watching the Europeans make their exit when María Eugenia resumed: "See, it's not always easy to tell. Our son Carlos died in an avalanche earlier this year. We were, and still are, devastated by the loss. He was our only child, and we miss him terribly." She was for a moment overcome with a motion, but she checked herself and resumed: "But his death has brought my husband and I closer together, and we are enjoying helping raise little María Luisa, our granddaughter."

Héctor cut in: "When I was a young man, I was fired from a job as insurance adjustor because my manager wanted to make room for his nephew to be brought in, fresh out of high school. I was appalled and downcast by the injustice, but in the process of looking for another job I met María Eugenia. So, you can say that a great ill led to happiness after the fact. Didn't something like that ever happen to you?"

Laz started to protest. "Well, that may have occurred in an instance or two, but there is no comparison between getting fired from a job and losing your wife or your parents, and experiencing other losses, as I have."

María Eugenia would not let him go on. "Yes, if you live long enough, you'll gather your share of sadness. But if you try to erase everything in your past, your life will become as empty as your notebook after you had cast its pages to the wind."

"Maybe the gods of the eternal night don't know how to read, after all" replied Laz vacantly, resting his head on the table and starting to snore.

María Eugenia elbowed him back to wakefulness. "Time to go to bed, my friend. Tomorrow is Christmas. Would you like to come have a holiday dinner with us?"

"That would be nice" replied Laz, slowly getting to his arthritic feet. "Let's go get the checks."

Laz insisted on picking the tab for his newly acquired friends. "That's unnecessary" protested María Eugenia. Laz shushed her aside. "I owe you a debt of gratitude, for you guys have made me think. I'm not sure, but perhaps this is a good time for me to take stock and appreciate the miracle that it is just to be alive, no matter the ups and downs." He struggled to get his parka on, and on his way back to the hotel a thought occurred to him: "I bet I could reproduce from memory much of what was in that notebook. I might give it a try."

Scheherazade's Last Tale

*Most of the beautiful stories do not have beautiful endings,
because destiny is stronger than love*
Shaharazad al-Khalij

It is written that Arabian King Shahriyár, having discovered that his wife engaged in adulterous behavior, caused her to be beheaded, and thenceforth made it his regular custom, every time that he took a virgin to his bed, to have her killed at the expiration of the night.

The King's Wezeer related to his daughter Scheherazade what happened during the King's fatal encounters: upon which she said, "By Allah, O my father, give me in marriage to this King; either I shall die, and provide salvation for one of the daughters of the Muslims, or I shall live, and be the cause of their deliverance from him."

Reluctantly, the Weezer allowed Scheherazade to carry out her wish, and she went to King Shahriyár. When the King introduced himself to her, Scheherazade wept; and he said to her, "What aileth thee?" She answered, "O King, I have a young sister, and I wish to take leave of her." So, the King sent for her sister; and the sister came to Scheherazade, and embraced her, and said (as they had previously agreed), "By Allah! O my sister, relate to us a story to beguile the waking hour of our night."

"Most willingly, answered Scheherazade, if this virtuous King permit me." And the King was pleased with the idea of listening to the story; and thus, on the first night of many, Scheherazade commenced her recitations.

***

After that first night, Scheherazade told King Shahriyár many stories of heroes and monsters, of magic, of thieves and hidden treasures, and all sorts of other fantasies. And the King cherished them all, but was especially fond of tales of couples that overcame perils and obstacles to realize their loves, for his romantic dreams had been throttled but not extinguished by his wife's betrayal.

So, nights turned to weeks and then to years. The King's homicidal impulses abated in time, but he did not reveal his change of heart for fear that, if he did so, Scheherazade might stop her nightly storytelling. The bards paint a rosy picture of what ultimately transpired between Shahriyár and Scheherazade, one in which the King begets three male children of Scheherazade and, at the turn of a thousand and one nights, spares her life and weds her. Sadly, the truth is otherwise.

Shahriyár never lifted the threat of execution because he thought that was all that kept Scheherazade from leaving one morning in search of a suitor more in line with her still youthful appearance. And he did not wish her to leave: he had come to desire the maiden, but his attraction had to yield to the excitement that her stories arose on his soul.

His fears of abandonment were never put to the test, for one morning near the end of one thousand nights of storytelling Shahriyár woke up ill, and his condition continued to worsen with each passing day. Scheherazade went on with her nightly recitations, but finally told the King: "My Lord, I have a very special story for you this evening. But to garner the full benefit of the tale, I must be permitted to hold your hand in mine. May I do so?"

Such an unsought intimacy with the royal person normally would have brought about a severe punishment, if not death. But Shahriyár was too infirm to object and in fact welcomed the touch of this woman he coveted but who never had become his concubine. Without a word, he grasped the maiden's hand and drew a deep breath.

"Now, you must close your eyes for a bit and travel with me. Let my voice guide you in our journey."

Shahriyár closed his eyes and teetered on the verge of unconsciousness, but Scheherazade's silken words served as a thread that kept him in this world. Soon, it was not only the enchantment of her voice but the strangeness of the story that kept him alert.

"Imagine, my Lord, that we sit on a magic carpet that is flying across the confines of your kingdom. See, right below us is your royal palace, which we just left. On the hills around it are the abodes of the rich merchants and the homes of the soldiers and other people who serve you. Farther out, on the arid plain, are the tents of the poor and the caravanserai where the travelers to all points of your kingdom find their rest. Further beyond, are the sands of the desert and the domains of other kings, friend and foe. Farther away, there is the deep, eternal ocean; and beyond, immeasurably far..." She paused.

"What lies beyond?" asked Shahriyár in a feeble voice.

"The hidden Realm of Barzakh, where the spirits of the dead stay until the Day of Judgment."

"Is that the hidden realm of what lies beyond the grave?" There was a tinge of disbelief in Shahriyár's question, for he had been told often about Barzakh by the clerics, but always thought that accounts of the afterlife were only old wives' tales.

"Yes, My Lord."

"Are we on our way there?"

"Yes, My Lord. But do not fear. Whether you linger in Barzakh or return to your palace right away is entirely up to you."

"What happens if I choose to stay in Barzakh?"

"Your body, which is mortal and corruptible, will separate from your spirit and decay to dust. Your spirit will join a multitude of others that are waiting for the final judgment day in which their fate for all eternity will be decided by Allah. On that day, they will either ascend to Jannah, the heavenly garden to enjoy eternal bliss, or be cast to the depths of Jahannam, to suffer eternal punishment."

Shahriyár shuddered with fearful anticipation. "What do the spirits do while they wait?"

"It depends, My Lord. Many spirits remain awake, and they are rewarded or punished in accordance with the balance of their good or bad deeds. Others sleep; they are rewarded or punished in their dreams. There are also those who have led virtuous lives; their spirits linger in the company of angels and their wait is the same as that of the angels."

Shahriyár was accustomed to command and having his will obeyed. He declared: "It is my wish that my spirit will mingle with the angels."

Scheherazade bowed her head in regret. "Alas, if a person, however lofty, has led a life of sin, he cannot expect to escape punishment. Nor can he return to his body and attempt to atone for his misdeeds. Whatever one does in his lifetime is final and cannot be changed or altered once he reaches Barzakh."

A long silence followed, as King Shahriyár examined his life, realizing that he had put many to death unjustly, deprived his subjects of wealth and freedom, and made war on other kingdoms causing much death and destruction. And his private affairs had also been bloody: he had sacrificed many innocent women to his thirst for revenge. "Will I have to suffer much if I linger in Barzakh?" was his anguished cry.

"I do not know, My Lord. But the wise men say that the intensity of the punishment hinges on the nature and severity of the person's sins."

"In that case, I want to return to my palace. I do not wish to go on and experience Barzakh, even in a tale."

"As you wish, My Lord. But the physicians who attend to you predict that your remaining days among the living are few, and may be countered with the fingers of one hand."

"Am I doomed, then?" For once in his imperious life, King Shahriyár felt weak and impotent. On the other hand, the stories about Barzakh might be more than just empty tales.

"My Lord, there is perhaps one way to make your stay in Barzakh somewhat less painful and eventually gain you entrance into Jannah through one of its holy gates."

"One way? What would that way be?"

"Return to your kingdom and embark on a life, short as it may be, of repentance and reparation. Forgive your enemies, pardon those you have imprisoned, bestow gifts on the poor. You will have to try to accomplish much in the short time that remains to you."

"But I can't. I am sick and in great physical pain. I don't have the strength to do all the things you mention."

"If you allow me, My Lord, I will continue to hold your hand and lend you my strength, such as it is. May I be permitted to assist you in this manner?"

"Yes, my child" replied the King, shedding a single tear. "Let's return home. I know this has only been another of your tales, but the trip has nonetheless left me quite weary."

***

It was thus that they found themselves back in the King's palace, and Scheherazade moved into Shahriyár's chambers. She rested on cushions next to the King's bed and held his hand while he issued orders, proclamations and judgments to Scheherazade's father and the other ministers of his court. He gave away most of his fortune to the poor, emptied the prisons, and released those doing slave labor in the silver mines. He summoned the envoys of other kings and sought, whenever he could, to bring peace to his kingdom by forging harmonious relations with its neighbors.

These efforts took a heavy toll on the King. His voice became feebler with each passing day and soon he was unable to sign his orders, so his index finger was dipped in a coal solution so he could leave his mark without needing to hold a quill. His breathing became so labored that its rasping sound dominated the room. Finally, he was unable to speak and merely nodded in assent or shook his head in denial when a question was asked or a proposed new order was placed before him.

Throughout all of this, Scheherazade whispered words of encouragement to the King, squeezed his trembling hands, and served him the little food and drink he was capable of consuming. She seldom ate and hardly slept, catching a wink or two only when Shahriyár fell into a troubled sleep. She wasted herself away in providing succor to her King, and ignored the urgent requests from his father and sister that she seek the rest that she desperately needed. For, secretly, she loved the King and was willing to sacrifice all on his behalf.

The King's agony, and that of his faithful caretaker, lasted only two weeks. One night, as the pale sliver of a new moon rose in the sky, Shahriyár opened his eyes widely, squeezed Scheherazade's hand back with unusual strength, and asked one final question to his companion: "Have I done enough?"

"My Lord, I hope so. We will soon find out," was her reply.

The King uttered a loud sigh, his head dropping on the pillow with a thud. On the floor next to his bed, Scheherazade let go of his hand and collapsed to the ground.

***

King Shahriyár's washed and shrouded corpse was laid to rest two days after his death in a ceremony attended by hundreds of mourners. He was buried without a coffin, in a deep grave covered with rocks to fend off wild animals; a simple stone tablet with his name and the dates of his birth and death and the duration of his rule marked the spot.

Scheherazade died a few days after the King. She was buried in another cemetery, in a different part of the city. Only members of her immediate family were in attendance.

King Shahriyár and Scheherazade lie in eternal sleep far from each other. They say, however, that on quiet winter nights one can hear barely intelligible whispers near the King's grave. It is rumored that a resonant female voice talks continuously, reciting a mysterious love story that goes on until the new day's sun rises. The King's answers, if any, are too faint to be perceived.

Original Publication Credits

The following stories are reprinted by permission of the author. The author has made edits, corrections, and revisions throughout for this collection.

"The Dragon's Bite" – © 2023, originally published by *West Avenue Publishing Co.*, March 2023

"The Blue Pearls" – © 2019, originally published by *New Reader Magazine,* March 2019

"A Viennese Story" – © 2019, originally published by *Jerry Jazz Magazine*, August 2019

"The Hungry Wolf and the Maiden" – © 2020, originally published by *Aurora Wolf Magazine*, May 2020

"The Adoration of the Magi" – © 2021, originally published by *Shelter of Daylight Magazine*, May 2022

"The Lunar Moth" – © 2019, originally published by *Zealot Script,* September 2019

"Gwarwyn Goes Fishing -- © 2023, originally published by *Cloaked Press*, January 2023

"The Girl, the Wyvern and the Talking Ape" – © 2022, originally published by *World Balloon Books*, November 2022

"Whistles in the Forest" – © 2022, originally published by *Pulse Publishing*, December 2023

"The Mapinguari" – © 2022, originally published by *Horror Tree Magazine*, May 2023

"The Tenth Symphony" – © 2024, originally published by *The Fifth Di*, April 2024

"Alfhildur and Posthumous" – © 2024, accepted for publication by *Emerging Worlds,* January 2024

"The Fractious Familiar" – © 2024, originally published by *Androids and Dragons,* March 2024

"End of Term" – © 2024, originally published by *Flash Digest*, May 2024

"Henrietta: A Fable" – © 2023, originally published by *White Cat Publishing Co.*, August 2023

"The Ugly Fairy" -- © 2024, accepted for publication by *The Fifth Di*, May 2024

"The Dopey Lion" – © 2019, originally published by *Dream of Shadows Magazine*, August 2019

"Blame Rupert" – © 2024, accepted for publication by *The Taborian,* August 2024

"The Yellow Butterfly" – © 2021, originally published in *The Periodical, Forlorn*, August 2021

"Medusa's Stare" – © 2021, originally published in *Lorelei Signal Magazine*, April 2022

"Killing the Jabberwock" – © 2024, originally published by *Darkholme Publishing Co.,* May 2024

"The Witch and the Crows" – © 2024, originally published by *Suburban Witchcraft*, July 2024

"Azathoth is Amused" – © 2024, accepted for publication by *Hobb's End Press,* May 2024

"The Caged Bird and the Fairy" -- © 2024, accepted for publication by *Shelter of Daylight*, September 2024

"A Bad Bargain" -- © 2024, originally published by *The Candid Review*, June 2024

"A Mask for Every Mood" -- © 2023, broadcast by *Chilling Entertainment*, 2024

"The Hollow Tree" -- © 2023, originally published by *White Cat Publications*, January 2024

"The Mutants" -- © 2024, originally published by *MiniMag*, June 2024

"The Magic Chrysler" -- © 2021, originally published by *The Other Side of Hope*, November 2021

"Hope for the Future" -- © 2021, originally published by *Unsettling Reads*, May 2021

"Figaro on Wheels" -- © 2020, originally published by *Owl Hollow Press,* October 2020

"Selling Adama" -- © 2024, originally broadcast by *Tall Tale TV*, January 2024

"Christmas in Ushuaia" -- © 2021, originally published by *After Dinner Conversation*, Jume 2021

"Scheherazade's Last Tale" – © 2022, originally published in *Twenty-Two Twenty-Eight*, July 2022

Born in Cuba, Matias migrated to the United States as a young man. He took up creative writing a few years ago and, since that time, he has authored many short stories, over one hundred and sixty of which have been published or accepted for publication in paying short story anthologies, magazines, blogs, audio books and podcasts. A first collection of his stories, "*The Satchel and Other Terrors*" was published in February 2023 and is available through Amazon and other literary outlets; other collections of his short stories are in the process of publication and will be available to the public late 2024 and early 2025.

Matias Travieso-Diaz is a former engineer and attorney who, following retirement, redirected his efforts towards fiction writing. A widower, he lives with his daughter and two dogs in the Washington, D.C. area. He describes himself as an "Animal Farm's goat, Packers and Barça fan, and lover of opera, classical theater, jazz, Italian food and vino."

He is the author of numerous short stories and three novels: *The Taíno Women*, set in Cuba's early colonial period; *Lázaro Serrano*, which takes place in 1762-63; and *Cubans Go to War,* set in in the Nineteenth Century.